TEASER

Also by Jan Brogan

Yesterday's Fatal

A Confidential Source

Final Copy

TEASER

Jan Brogan

St. Martin's Minotaur

New York

TEASER. Copyright © 2008 by Jan Brogan. All rights reserved. Printed in the United States of America. For information, address St. Martin's Press, 175 Fifth Avenue, New York, N.Y. 10010.

www.minotaurbooks.com

Library of Congress Cataloging-in-Publication Data

Brogan, Jan.
    Teaser / Jan Brogan.—1st ed.
        p. cm.
    ISBN-13: 978-0-312-35998-0
    ISBN-10: 0-312-35998-5
    1. Ahern, Hallie (Fictitious character)—Fiction. 2. Women journalists—Fiction.
3. Investigative reporting—Fiction. 4. Computer crimes—Fiction. 5. Rhode Island—
Fiction. I. Title.

PS3602.R64 T43 2008
813'.6—dc22
                                                                    2008028964

First Edition: December 2008

10   9   8   7   6   5   4   3   2   1

To Clare Mocek, my favorite aunt,
for reading all those grade school book reports

ACKNOWLEDGMENTS

First of all, a huge thanks to my writers group, Barbara Shapiro, Floyd Kemske, and Hallie Ephron, who crack the whip and put up with my messy manuscripts. To my agent, Dan Mandel at Sanford J. Greenburger and Associates, for his support and excellent advice. And to my editor, Kelley Ragland, for her enthusiasm.

I also want to thank Matt Dawson, assistant attorney general of Rhode Island and chief of the narcotics and organized crime unit, for his great ideas, vast knowledge, and many insights. I couldn't have written this book without him.

Thanks also to the following people who gave so generously of their time and knowledge (any mistakes are mine alone): Felicia Donovan and Detective Kristyn Rogers-Bernier of the Portsmouth, NH, Police Department, for showing me the dark side of cyberspace. Providence Police officers Lt. James Desmarias, Major Stephen M. Campell, and Lt. Thomas Verdi, and former Providence Police detective Steven Casbarro, who gave me the benefit of their knowledge and experience. Emily Homonoff, who patiently steered me through the teenage world of social networking; Thomasine Berg at *The Boston Globe;* Boston.com editor in chief, David Beard, and news editor Mark Micheli, who helped update me on the online journalism world; *Providence Journal* reporters Paul Parker, Laura Meade Kirk, and M. Charles Bakst, who help keep me current on investigative and newsroom politics.

I also want to thank my firearms experts, Carol Ferrari, Ken Gerbetz, and Iggy Muravyov, who took me to the firing range and did their best to teach me how to shoot a gun. To Bob Brogan and Joe Cloyd for Web-tracking background, and Tom Brogan for his networking assistance on legal resources. Also a big thanks to Patty Comella for her local knowledge and help with site research.

I'd like to credit, as background research, the *New York Times* series "Through His Webcam, a Boy Joins a Sordid Online World" by Kurt Eichenwald, which provided the inspiration for this novel.

I'd like to thank early readers, Laura Mocek, Robin Kall, Emily Homonoff, and especially Naomi Rand, for their timely feedback and support. Also a special thanks to Beth Kirsch, who so generously edits my final galleys, and to Kira Mascho, for catching online etiquette errors.

As always, I'd like to thank my husband, Bill Santo, who not only helps brainstorm all my plots, but on this book gave me his nautical and navigational expertise. I could never find my way out of a Newport storm without him.

ACKNOWLEDGMENTS

Although this work is totally fictitious, nearly all locations in Rhode Island are real. The exceptions are West Kent, the Centre Mall, and Best Price—I have made these up so as not to imply serious crimes in real places.

TEASER

This is what I've learned so far about Rhode Island chat rooms.

Not everyone is from Rhode Island.

Correct spelling and complete sentences are the signs of a newcomer.

And no matter what the supposed topic of the chat room, two-thirds of the conversations are always about sex.

You might ask what I was doing sitting in the dark in my bedroom, cruising these chat rooms. Especially since I already had a boyfriend and was not looking for sex. I could tell you that I was doing background research on a story for the paper. But that would not be completely honest. That story idea only occurred to me tonight, and I'd been glued to my laptop for nearly a month.

It started one night when Matt was away at a political fundraiser for his boss. I was home alone doing research for work, and I wound up at an online poker site with realistic casino sounds and a flashing welcome urging me to Play Now! Play Now! I've had issues with gambling in the past, so to divert myself from temptation, I clicked onto Rhode Island Buzz, a social networking site. From my very first visit to a chat room, I found the sheer deviance of my online friends riveting.

Right now, for example, Eternalwoman, who usually resided in the "love and relationships" chat room, had moved into "video culture," where she was, once again, advertising herself as a bisexual woman interested in "mostly women" but possible threesomes if "certain conditions are met."

RoarMP3, who might be a bot—one of those automated robots pretending to chat but really just advertising some porno site—replied: "Ck out SEASIDE Ride @ the RI cam directory. Dizzywon stars. Gt ur rocksoff."

Dizzywon starring? This threw me because I knew Dizzywon. I talked to her frequently in the video room. Her spelling was bad, even for the Internet, but she had a good sense of humor, especially when she went into her riff about stalking Adam Sandler. And she agreed with me about the sorry state of most new sci-fi movies.

I immediately clicked the link and was on the homepage of the Rhode Island webcam directory. On it, I saw "Seaside Rides," which had a still shot of the waves breaking over a beach, and several other listings that looked equally scenic in nature. One was of the waves hitting a jetty outside the lighthouse in Point Judith, which advertised an inn there. Another was of downtown Providence, with a view of the Independent Man atop the statehouse dome. And my favorite, a webcam that observed the highway from the heights of the Big Blue

Bug, a nine-foot-tall fiberglass termite perched on the exterminator's commercial building.

After I clicked on Seaside Ride, I decided that RoarMP3 might be a human after all, and that he was playing to an even raunchier side of Eternalwoman. This video wasn't just waves breaking on the beach. There were two girls lying next to each other, facedown, on a big blanket. They both had small, thin bodies that did not look particularly tan, and they wore bikinis. Pink on the left, and lime green on the right.

Could one of these fifteen-year-olds really be Dizzywon? I had never checked her profile page, but by her knowledge of foreign films alone, I'd figured she was in her midtwenties.

It was dusk, or maybe just a poor-quality camera, but I could make out a sweatshirt under one of the girls' heads and a stack of magazines strewn on the blanket.

The girl nearest the camera, in the lime green, reached her hand back and fiddled with the elastic of her bathing suit bottom, trying to get the sand out. There was apparently a lot of sand, because she began to shift from thigh to thigh, trying to rid herself of the irritant. She became increasingly frustrated, until her friend, in the pink, sat up. Pink had her short legs crossed in front of her, and I could see what looked like a tattoo on one of her ankles. She looked into the webcam and smiled thoughtfully. She had a small heart-shaped face, oddly spaced front teeth, and short dark hair. Very short, almost a boy's cut.

It started innocently enough, with Pink merely lifting a corner of Lime Green's elastic, but then she slipped her entire hand under the girl's bathing suit bottom and brushed gently back and forth across her butt. The frustration of Lime Green immediately dissipated. She settled into the blanket and turned her head to the camera, and for the first time, we saw her face, which was Irish-looking, fair and freckled, with a snub nose and almost no chin. She shifted her butt upward, into her friend's hand, and sighed.

The video went dark, but there were giggles just before the clip ended.

Was this kiddie porn? Right here in the open? Next to Chamber of Commerce advertising?

My heart began to beat rapidly. This was partly Catholic guilt, and I switched on the nightstand lamp as if this would wash away whatever venial sin I'd committed in simply viewing this clip. But it was more personal than that. I really liked Dizzywon. Felt a connection. And although you never really knew anyone on the Internet, I was still disturbed to realize I'd bonded with what? A fifteen-year-old? And not just any fifteen-year-old, but some kind of soft porn star.

I took a minute to regroup. I clicked onto Dizzywon's profile page, which said she was from Providence, loved "television, movies, music, and making friends." It said she was "single," into "men," and that Joss Stone was her favorite singer. She offered no formal name for herself but boasted of a cool tattoo on her ankle, so I guessed she was the girl with the short dark hair. There was no photo. Instead, there was a cartoon of Betty Rubble from *The Flintstones.*

Of course, there was no photo on my profile page either. I'm decent enough in real life, but I don't photograph well. I always appear startled by the camera, as if this image-taking business was *such* a shock. So I went the "bare bones" approach and identified myself only as "Hallie," a female from Providence. But am I so immature at thirty-six years old that Dizzywon figured I was a teenager, too?

I hated to admit to myself that this was a distinct possibility.

This might have made me feel just slightly pathetic. Especially since I knew I'd been wasting too much time on the Internet. But by now the reporter in me had begun to sense a story.

I heard a tapping sound and realized my fingers were drumming on the edge of the keyboard. They had skipped past the horror of young girls sexualizing themselves for whatever reason, and were twitching over the fact that since it was a beach shot on a Rhode Island social network, there was a good chance that both these young girls were local.

I played the clip a second time, studying the beach to see if I recognized anything about it. But the pan was too narrow. It could be any beach anywhere from Florida to Maine. I played the clip a third time to more carefully determine the girls' ages. By their skinny little bodies and new breasts, they looked about fifteen. But studying Pink's face more carefully, I decided she could be older, maybe sixteen. Since we saw Lime Green's face for only a moment, she was tougher to tell. But those freckles looked pretty fresh. She could still be in middle school.

I downloaded the clip into my research file on the laptop, quit the directory, and stared at my screen saver. It was a company laptop, and the *Chronicle* logo scrolled past in its official Roman font, reminding me that I really should get a digital camera and upload garden photos to personalize my workspace.

The phone on the nightstand rang. It was Matt calling to say he was on his way home, and giving me the choice between pizza and Chinese food. I quickly decided on mushroom pizza to avoid the many choices a Chinese menu would entail. Because now I'd realized that if I could get Dizzywon to talk to me, tell me why and how they made this clip, I could sell this story to my editor as an exposé about what all this computer literacy was really doing for today's youth. What kids today were doing with their high-priced computers.

Returning to my laptop, I signed on to the teenage chat room and searched for Dizzywon's screen name.

She was there, in the midst of a conversation with someone named ChaCha about the new Justin Timberlake CD.

I decided to hang out a minute and ran my cursor over the list of screen names on the right-hand side of the page. This revealed that most of the names were female, but I could tell that only three of these were likely to be real people. The rest were working girls or businessmen-pretending-they-were-girls trying to promote their porno Web sites. The instant-message screen popped up, and someone named Wiseguy09 asked me if I'd like to chat with him privately.

I put the cursor over his name, which said he was male and twenty-five. He probably thought I was a teenager, too, the loser. I clicked him off my screen.

I sent Dizzywon a private instant message and told her that I loved her clip on the beach.

She replied: "LOL"

Laugh Out Loud. This was the standard noncommittal response. What you say when you really are just stalling.

I decided to be bold. "Mst be good way to meet boyz," I typed with every misspelling I could muster.

"Where u go to school"

I had to think for a minute to figure out exactly where I'd be going to school at fourteen or fifteen. Would I still be in middle school? I racked my brain for the name of one of Providence's high schools. I chose one of the private schools where one of the reporters sent her kids: St. Ann's.

"Cool," Dizzywon wrote.

But suddenly, I realized that I'd screwed up. St. Ann's, a parochial school, might be kindergarten through eighth grade. The oldest I could be would be what? Twelve, thirteen? Would Dizzywon abandon our budding friendship because I was too young?

But it didn't seem to faze her. "U hav cute boys at ur school"—she did not seem to know about question marks. Maybe she wasn't familiar with St. Ann's. Maybe I lucked out. "No way," I typed back.

We chatted back and forth about how all the cute boys go out with the stupid girls. Then she asked: "U got a webcam"

Do all thirteen-year-olds? But if I had one, she could ask me to send a picture of myself, and I didn't want to do that. "No."

"Boys like to see what u look like"

No kidding. Especially old guys on the Internet. I hesitated, unsure how to reply.

"R u cute," she now probed.

The one thing I remembered clearly from high school was that no teenage girl ever liked the way she looked. "Ugh."

"U r prob beautful"

Dizzywon couldn't spell or punctuate, but she was awfully committed to boosting my self-esteem.

"At least I've got boobs." This was the biggest lie ever, but hey, it was all pretense, and I had the sneaking suspicion that boobs would make me more photogenic if I actually did have a webcam. Plus, now I was curious about what Dizzywon really wanted from me.

"U can sometimes get 1 for free," she wrote.

She was talking about the webcam. "How?"

She didn't answer directly. Instead: "U play with any of the guys in the rooms"—still no use of question marks.

"R guys nice there?" I asked.

"Some giv u presents."

Presents? I was on to something bigger than a teenage girl's mere foolishness. And now, I was sure that Dizzywon definitely had an agenda. I didn't want to sound too eager for information, too much like a reporter, so I tried to play it cool. "Yeah?"

"Nice stuff," she replied.

There was a long pause in which I typed, erased, retyped, erased again. What kind of stuff? What kind of guys? What kind of gig was this? But instead, I just waited.

Finally, she asked, "U really like the beach clip"

"It's cool." After a second, I decided to be a bit bolder. "SEXY." All capitals. As if this excited me.

"Boys like it ALOT," she typed back.

"LOL," I replied.

Here, another instant message opened up on my screen. It was someone named BBalls09 asking me if I wanted to talk for a while. His profile said he was thirty-six. My age and hanging around the teenage chat room. I clicked him away.

"I can gt a free cam?" I asked Dizzywon.

"EZ," she typed back.

"How?"

"Can u get to the best price in warwick"

The Best Price was one of those warehouse stores, full of electronics. I was pretty sure it was on Universal Boulevard. And that a teenager could get a bus there from Providence. "I think so."

"Theres a guy jimmy. he's there 2mrw. tell him ur my friend"

But I didn't want to meet Jimmy, who was probably stealing the stuff from Best Price and too smart to talk to me when he saw that I was no teenager. I wanted to meet Dizzywon to see if I could convince her that talking to me would be her fifteen minutes of fame. Off the record, of course, so she wouldn't get in trouble with her parents.

"Nother time," I typed back.

There was a long pause. Then: "U scared"

I figured a teenager would never admit this, so I said: "No way."

"Then go see jimmy"

I waited, pretending that I was thinking about it. I finally typed back, "The bus is a pain."

"From prov not so bad, i do it alot"

Dizzywon was really pushing this meeting with Jimmy tomorrow. I needed a good excuse. What could get in the way? "I hav lacrosse practice aftr school."

"So u can't cut school, either"

"Big game Friday." I typed back, hoping like hell they even had lacrosse teams at elementary schools.

There was another long pause in which neither of us typed anything. Finally, she wrote: "Saturday then"

Were we still talking about me meeting Jimmy? "I don't no."

"What if i meet u there"

I paused again, so as not to be too eager. "Would u do that?"

She told me her name was Lexie, and I gave her my real name, Hallie, which she could easily get from my profile and which sounded teenaged enough. Then, we agreed to meet in the digital camera aisle, Saturday at noon.

"Leav me a messag if u cant make it," she added.

"I can make it," I typed back. I waited a minute to see if she'd write anything else. But after a minute, the instant-message box just disappeared from my screen.

2

"How old are they, you think? Ten? Twelve?" Dorothy Sacks, the city editor, and I were huddled around my laptop in the Fishbowl, the glass-walled conference room in the newsroom. I'd just played the video for her.

Dorothy was herself in her midforties, unmarried and child-less. She always seemed uncomfortable whenever anyone brought a baby or toddler into the newsroom, and clearly, she did not have a handle on teenagers.

These girls in bikinis had breasts, for God's sake. "Lexie is fifteen," I said, pointing to the girl in the pink. "I think this is the one I'm meeting on Saturday."

I expected her to be impressed. What a coup. Getting a teenage porn star to agree to meet with me. And a video clip, parts of which might even be usable online. Instead, Dorothy said, "I can't approve any weekend overtime."

Dorothy was not really like this. In her heart, Dorothy was

a true journalist, a leftover hippie who wore baggy clothes and had socialist leanings. But the new owners of the *Chronicle* were big on cutting "middle management," and Dorothy was big on keeping her job.

"I'm not asking for overtime. I just want to meet this girl and check it out. It's been a while since the team has done anything even remotely investigative. . . ."

"The Siebert resignation," she argued.

This was a defensive reflex, a reference to a state senator who'd been forced to resign because he'd been taking campaign checks from a pharmacy chain.

"That was six months ago," I said.

The truth was that since the last round of layoffs, there was a manpower shortage. All five reporters on the investigative team were needed to cover daily stories and the round-the-clock filing of news to keep the *Chronicle* Web site current. Although the investigative team still met once a month as if nothing had changed, most of our project ideas now had to be approved by Dorothy *and* the new publisher. This meant they were put on indefinite hold.

"This catch-a-predator thing has been done to death," Dorothy was saying. "And technically, I'm not sure this is even child pornography. I mean, it might not even be illegal."

"That's not the point."

"Then what is the point?"

I tried not to stare at her. Dorothy was not this dense. This had to be a manpower issue.

"The point is to get inside these girls' heads and figure out why they do this suggestive stuff. What they hope to get out of it. How the weirdos on the Web have responded to it. Don't you think all those parents out there who buy their teenagers computers and webcams in the name of technological advancement need some sort of wake-up call?"

She shrugged. Emotionally divorced from marriage and parenting, Dorothy clearly had a blind spot when it came to child-related concerns.

I wanted to shake her. Instead, I chose another tack. "Think about it. It'll be the most e-mailed story on the *Chronicle* Web site."

This last assertion gave her pause. In its battle for online advertising revenue, there was nothing the new publisher valued more than drawing traffic to the *Chronicle* Web site.

Dorothy's gaze shifted beyond the glass wall of the Fishbowl. Behind me, the new Online News department, a bevy of eight cubicles with individual televisions and radios blaring, had displaced Sports and Financial, which had been sent upstairs. The paper had hired a new twenty-eight-year-old editor, Corey Weist, who wore short skirts, long earrings, and who sent text messages back and forth to the publisher all day long.

"What makes you think this girl will spill her guts to a reporter?" Dorothy asked.

I was banking on the fact that teenagers generally had an even dimmer idea than adults about the risks of talking to the press and a greater desire for the spotlight it shone on their lives. "Given her video debut, I'm going to guess that Lexie likes attention," I said. "And she might not be the kind of girl who actually thinks through the consequences of her actions."

Dorothy cocked her head. For the first time, humor glimmered in her eye. "Oh, really?"

This was a jab. I've gotten a bad rap in the newsroom for being impulsive. But I didn't care, because I could tell that I was finally making progress with Dorothy.

She turned back to the laptop and replayed the clip, this time pausing at the opening beach scene.

"Any idea what beach they're on?" she asked. Newspaper editors were nothing if not parochial.

I leaned toward the screen, taking in the little bit of sand and utter lack of identifying landscape. "Can't tell," I started to say, but stopped, staring at the rumpled sweatshirt underneath the girl in the lime green bikini. I could make out the crest on the sweatshirt. And the letter *O*.

"That's from St. Olivia's," I said. St. Olivia's was an exclusive all-girls' Catholic high school in Providence. My friend Carolyn's daughter went there on a scholarship, which was why I was familiar with the sweatshirt. And I'd noticed that the girl in the pink was wearing a tiny gold cross around her neck.

Now Dorothy's whole demeanor changed. She sat up and jotted something on the assignment sheet on her clipboard. "We just ran a story about St. O's—the headmaster had some big education program to warn students about the dangers of the Internet."

"I guess it didn't work."

"Geez, those Catholic girls," Dorothy said. She was Jewish.

"So will you go to bat for me on this with Ian?" Ian Clew was the publisher, a thirty-something exported to Providence from corporate headquarters in California.

"Let's see what you come up with first," Dorothy said. And then: "Make sure you find out where the other girl is from. And take your digital recorder, so you can bring back lots of ambient sound."

In the new, altered geography of the newsroom, my desk has been relocated dead center in what is an open floor plan of desks, computers, televisions, and constantly ringing telephones.

It's not a bad newsroom, as far as newsrooms go. The architecture of the building provides floor-to-ceiling Palladian windows on three sides of the room, so there's always plenty of natural light to offset the cynicism of the daily grind. The little bit of wall is decorated with framed pictures of historic front pages—hurricanes, fires, mob arrests—a reminder of the greater glory of the pre-Internet *Chronicle* gone by.

But my desk, sandwiched in the middle of a bank of eight desks, is midway between City in front, and the Online department in back. This means that when either Dorothy and Corey, the online editor, were casting about for a reporter to update the medical condition of last night's hit-and-run victim, or the financial damages of this morning's warehouse fire, they tended to fix their gaze on me.

Dorothy was bad enough, but Corey, called "the Chick" behind her back, was impossible. She had what all the reporters agreed was an acquired attention deficit disorder and tended to react to every minor news development with a reflexive assignment command—sometimes forgetting she'd assigned someone else to another aspect of the same story just hours before.

To avoid Corey, I often took my laptop into the news library to work. And I was sitting at a table, among the flats of East Coast newspapers, when I logged on to RI Buzz to check my message board.

There was nothing new on my board, but immediately an instant-message window opened on my screen: "Where ru"

It was from Lexie. I actually looked over my shoulder, as if maybe she could see me through the laptop, a reporter in the news library.

I checked the wall clock. It was 3 P.M. Should I still be at school at that hour? Lacrosse practice? I scrambled to remember our last conversation. Hadn't I told her that Friday was the big game?

Before I could come up with a good lie, she wrote back. "May b u shouldn't cum 2mrw"

Shit. She was backing out. Had she figured out I was a reporter?

"Why?" I messaged.

"Ur kind of young"

Ah. Someone must have told her St. Ann's was a grammar school. "I am old for my grade," I replied.

"They can get u in trouble"

She was talking about webcams. But why was she warning me? "I want one. Then we can chat w video."

There was a long pause, and I wanted to kick myself again for my mistake. Why hadn't I said the Wheeler School or Moses Brown?

"U need to b careful," she finally wrote back.

"Why?"

"Most guys r real nice but sum u should not stream with. BBalls09. kindof pain wont leav u alone"

Vaguely, I remembered BBalls09 messaging me. His profile had said he was thirty-six. I scrambled to grab a pen out of my backpack and wrote the screen name on the first piece of paper I could find, last week's grocery list. "I promise I'll b careful. I want a webcam bad. I'm going to Best Price. Meet me?"

There was another pause. Then Lexie messaged back. "Ok earlier 11 ok"

"Okay."

"Wear something pink so I know hu ur," she typed back. "Dont talk to Rurik before or tell him ur cuming"

"Who?"

"RoarMP3"

I'd thought he was a bot, an automated message that advertised the beach clip now saved on my laptop. "He told me about ur clip," I typed back.

"Yeah i no be careful"

One of the nice things about having moved into Matt's condo, which is on the third floor of a renovated Victorian house, is that we have a backyard. It's a small fenced-in yard, dominated by two massive oak trees, and shared by the two other condo owners. But in a sunny spot, near the bulkhead to the basement, I got the association okay to plant an eight-by-eight-foot-square vegetable garden. The soil is surprisingly rich, and I lingered in the dirt too long the next morning, harvesting three heads of nearly perfect red leaf lettuce.

Big mistake. Because I hit an accident on 95, and found myself backed up in traffic all the way to Warwick. I got to the Best Price fifteen minutes late.

The good thing about my small stature and never-stay-out-in-the-sun skin tone is it makes me look a lot younger. Up until I was thirty, I still got carded at bars and the package store. But I still couldn't pass for a teenager, so I had not worn pink.

I was hoping to appear as just another consumer on a Saturday, in a collared T-shirt and blue jeans—albeit with a small digital recorder in my pocket. I'd planned to hang around in the aisles nonchalantly until Lexie realized that no almost-fourteen-year-old in pink was going to show. Then I'd follow her to the parking lot and tell her I was a reporter doing a story on teenagers and webcams.

But now I was worried that I might have missed her entirely. The store was a brightly colored place, with every sort of electronic product displayed on clean, orderly shelves under lights that were slightly overwhelming. I'd printed out a still shot from the beach video and consulted the grainy shot of the two girls in their bikinis. Although there were hordes of teenagers clogging the entrance to the store, all the girls I saw were too old, too blond, or too tall.

I ran through the MP3 section toward the back of the store, and into a cramped corner between tall shelves filled with computer keyboards and wireless mice. I nearly tripped over a man kneeling on the floor, examining one of the wireless keyboards.

"I'm sorry," I said, veering around him.

He looked up, irritated, as if maybe I'd mistaken him for a stock boy. He must have been forty years old, but he was wearing a *South Park* T-shirt and baggy-looking blue jeans. His hair was bleached a ridiculous color blond.

The webcams were at the farthest end, stocked on floor-to-ceiling shelves. Inside the clear packaging, they looked like eyeballs, either mounted on a stand or inside a tube. Some were small little eyeballs and others were big monster eyeballs, but all promised to "keep you connected."

I positioned myself at the very end of the aisle, in front of an end-cap display of printer ink cartridges. I picked up a box, as if reading the back of it intently.

After maybe five minutes, three teenage girls turned into

the aisle. They all looked at least sixteen, with very full figures in very tight clothes. Two of them had shoulder-length brown hair, and I searched hard for signs of freckles, but no go. The third had curly black hair. The guy in the *South Park* T-shirt looked up from his position on the floor to check them out.

Behind the girls came a Best Price sales guy. He was Asian, barrel-chested, and had an air of worn patience. He immediately recommended something that he called a quick cam. He pronounced it high quality for under a hundred dollars.

One of the brunettes, who wore about a half inch of lip gloss, said she didn't want to spend a hundred. The salesman pointed to another model, on the bottom shelf, and made a face. "You can buy this one for forty-nine fifty if you don't care about quality."

The girl with the lip gloss said she was pretty sure she could get a webcam cheaper on the Internet and walked off with her friends.

The salesman shot me a look of frustration. "Can I help you?"

I said I was "just looking."

Then, I noticed the guy in the *South Park* T-shirt had gotten up off the floor. He seemed to be following the three girls as they headed up a black-and-white tile path that was like the Munchkins' yellow-brick road cutting through the width of the store.

There was something about his pace and the way he kept a couple strides behind them that struck me as suspicious. He was a skeevy-looking dude, with arms and legs that looked too long for his torso, and jeans that slid off his rear end as if he thought he was a teenager. The dark roots that were showing made his hair look dirty. Metal studs pierced his lower lip and his eyebrow.

As the three girls began to head toward the front of the store, the guy in the *South Park* T-shirt pivoted on his heel and wound his way around the digital camera counters, so he could go in the same direction.

It was now past eleven thirty and still no sign of Lexie; I decided to follow them, keeping a good distance behind.

Up front, I stopped in front of a rack of sports radios, where I could watch as the girls walked through the music section. The guy in the T-shirt walked up the same aisle, but halted maybe ten feet away and began sorting through the jazz CDs.

I checked the front entrance, looking for Lexie, but there was still no sign of her. I told myself teenagers were always late, weren't they?

Somebody somewhere was playing one of the electronic keyboards. A couple of screechy high notes. The volume on high. A few tentative bars of what was it? "Heart and Soul." Abruptly, someone—maybe a salesperson—hit the OFF button.

One of the girls picked up a CD, and the three of them got in line at the far register. The guy with the *South Park* T-shirt immediately followed.

I grabbed a sports radio and got into line at the next register. I was behind a man carrying one of those small portable TVs that you put in a minivan.

"This is an awesome model," he told me. "My brother-in-law got one. They get reception everywhere." I smiled coolly to discourage conversation and moved toward a display of batteries between the two register lines, pretending to sort through them.

"I saw you looking at the webcams," I heard the guy in the *South Park* T-shirt say to one of the girls.

"So?" the girl said.

"So I know a lot about webcams." He had a slight accent that sounded Eastern European.

The girl looked at her friends for advice. Trained correctly by their mothers, they shot her back a look of warning. Weirdo. Pervert. Creep.

The guy in front of me with the portable television had apparently not taken my hint. "You need triple-A batteries," he said helpfully.

"Thanks," I said, trying to inch closer to the battery display.

The *South Park* guy said something else to the girls, but I couldn't hear it. The guy in front of me paid for his portable television, and the store clerk, a boy with two zircon earrings, scanned my sports radio and gestured for me to slide my credit card through the card reader.

At the next register, the three girls concluded their CD purchase. The guy in the *South Park* T-shirt dropped his CD on the counter and followed the girls outside the store. I could see them through the glass front window, standing just outside the entrance. Their faces were now turned to him, listening attentively.

"Slide it again," the clerk said, gesturing to my credit card.

I did. Nothing happened.

"Damn machine is going down again." The clerk waved his hands at one of the managers standing near the entrance.

"Forget it," I said. "I'll come back another time and buy it." I put my credit card back in my wallet and started to leave.

"No, no!" the clerk said. "The transaction is in process."

The manager, a young woman in her midtwenties, was blocking my exit. "It'll be just a minute." She moved the clerk away from the register and pushed several buttons.

"Sign, please." She pointed to the electronic signature taker. I signed it, grabbed my radio, and hurried out the exit, vaguely aware of the clerk and manager watching me, as if the shoplifting alarms would go off as I went through the door. But I didn't care. I ran like a thief anyway.

Too late. The girls and the *South Park* guy were gone. I stood there a couple of minutes, scanning the parking lot in every direction, but there was no sign of them. I took a quick run through the lot, praying to God those girls had not gotten into a car with that guy. I did not know exactly what I would do if I found them. But I had no luck anyway.

It was almost noon now. I headed back inside the store and found the Asian sales guy still hanging around the webcam display. He must have thought I was coming back to buy one because he seemed to brighten as I approached. "Can I help you?" he asked.

"Did you see a teenaged girl, about fifteen or sixteen, hanging around as if she was waiting for someone?"

"I've seen about a hundred teenage girls today," he said.

"Your name isn't Jimmy, is it?"

He shook his head. "Wayne. Why?"

I handed him the grainy printout from the video. "Any girl who looked like either one of these two?"

He took the printout, squinted at it, and shrugged. "Hard to tell from this. But I don't think so."

"Does anyone named Jimmy work here?"

He folded his arms across his chest and studied me intently. Who the hell was I, the FBI?

I scanned the aisle, one last look for Lexie, and then identified myself as a *Chronicle* reporter. I explained that I was doing a story about teenagers and webcam use, but did not whip out my digital recorder, which would have reminded him that he needed approval from a PR director before he talked to me.

"I've worked here for almost six months," he said. "No Jimmy."

"You know anything about that guy in the *South Park* T-shirt who was here earlier, looking at the keyboards?" I asked.

He grimaced. "The guy with the bleach job?"

I nodded.

"He sometimes shows up on Saturdays. Usually later in the day. Security followed him for a while. But couldn't catch him shoplifting. Just one of those electronics geeks, I guess. Is this going to be in the paper?"

"Not right away. I'm just doing some background research." He looked disappointed, so I took down the spelling of his first and last names, and handed him one of my reporter cards so he could call me if he wanted. "You don't, by any chance, know the guy's name?"

He shook his head. "All I know is that he sounds like he's foreign. Russian or Polish maybe."

The accent. Jimmy didn't sound like a foreign name. Suddenly, it struck me: Rurik—the guy Lexie had warned me away from. That sounded foreign.

3

In the year that we've been living together, Matt has come to understand that I've got a compulsive personality. He knows that after my brother Sean died years ago, I developed a problem with insomnia and sleeping pills and had to go to Substance Abuse meetings for many years. But I still haven't told him about the more recent problem with gambling, the two-thousand-dollar debt I only recently repaid, or how hard I work to keep myself off the online poker sites. Still, he's developed whole new sensors about the time I spend on the Web. I was on my laptop only ten minutes when he called from the kitchen, "Are you on the Net again?"

"It's work," I called back. I'd learned to shut off the audio so Matt couldn't hear my laptop dinging. How did he know?

The bedroom door opened. It was Sunday morning, and Matt stood with a dish towel over his shoulder and a hand on his hip. A long, lean man, he had run a lot of miles and played a lot of basketball. His Boston College sweatshirt, which had the sleeves cut off, and boxer shorts revealed all the sinewy muscle that went along with that. A definite distraction.

"It's always work," he said.

That wasn't true. But that's what I always told him. This left me with absolutely no defense now.

He sat down on the edge of the bed, his thigh against mine, and leaned forward to see my screen. I immediately snapped shut the laptop.

"New investigation?" he asked.

I nodded.

"Not going well?"

I nodded again.

Matt was half Irish and half Italian. His eyes were his Italian half—big, brown, and full of commiseration. That was the thing about Matt. As a prosecutor with the attorney general's office, he could understand the frustrations of an investigation. Gently, he picked my laptop up and put it on the nightstand. "You work too hard." His arm went around my waist.

"I know. I know." But I'd messaged Lexie last night with no response. And all I could think was that I'd blown it yesterday, and that I wouldn't have any peace until I'd heard from her and rescheduled.

"You worked yesterday, for God's sake. Let's do something together today."

I knew that I should be grateful that Matt was in such a playful mood. Ever since he transferred to Newport from the Providence office, he's been frustrated at work and miserable at home. It's a small office, with only two prosecutors working in it. Even though Matt is senior, he still must spend a lot of time dealing with the small, piddling crimes like drunk driving and disorderly conduct charges. On the rare occasions that he gets a major crime to prosecute, he never has enough resources.

"Let me check my messages one last time," I asked.

Now, he took my hand, pulled me off the bed, and walked me over to the window. It was one of those sharp, sunny days, with puffy white clouds and a steady breeze rustling the leaves of the two oak trees.

"Kevin said we could use the boat," he said.

Kevin was his older brother. He'd bought a mint twenty-eight-foot Bristol sailboat that he kept on Narragansett Bay. I'd grown up sailing a little sloop my father kept on Green Pond on the Cape. For weeks, I'd been after Matt to ask his brother if he could take us sailing.

"Use the boat? By ourselves?" Although I felt pretty confident about my sailing skills, I doubted that Kevin did.

"He trusts me," Matt said.

Or more likely, Kevin, who was also a lawyer, felt that his brother needed some serious cheering up.

Somewhere in my brain, I knew that watched pots never boil and that clicking in and out of chat rooms wasn't necessarily going to get me anywhere. So I left my laptop on the nightstand and went to the kitchen to pack us a lunch.

We spent the afternoon taking turns at the helm, sailing an easy beat to Jamestown, where we anchored in the harbor and made love in the V-berth.

I almost forgot all about Lexie, but she reentered my head the moment we got back to the condo at ten o'clock that night. We'd had a perfect day, and luckily Matt was too relaxed to be irritated. But he rolled his eyes when I ran straight into the bedroom, first thing, to check my laptop for messages.

There were none, of course.

"**Ian loved the** idea," Dorothy said, meeting me at the reception desk when I got off the elevator the next morning.

It was eight fifteen, and except for the receptionist and a couple of copy editors scattered about, the newsroom was empty. I was used to peace in the early morning, an hour or two of relative solitude to slowly work myself into the chaos of the typical news day.

She had practically skidded across the carpeting in her sandals and now stood before me, dressed up more than usual in one of those awful broomstick skirts and a knit top that was askew. Her eyes were gleaming in a weird way. As if she'd had too much coffee when I knew for a fact that Dorothy drank only chamomile tea.

"*When* did you even talk to Ian?"

"This morning—we had one of those United Way breakfast meetings. On the way back, he was complaining that our ad revenue was down again and that Rhode Island Buzz has been stealing all our classified advertising."

"Circulation?"

"Down again, too. And Jason Keriotis is going to grace the cover of this month's *Rhode Island Monthly,*" she said. Jason Keriotis was a local thirty-five-year-old wonder boy, a real estate magnate who had diversified, pumping a fortune into RI Buzz, which was now one of the first successful regional social-networking sites.

"When I mentioned your story, and how you'd found that kiddie beach clip posted on the Buzz, Ian got all excited. He says the story has juice."

Juice was some sort of California saying—Ian Clew's highest praise. He wanted us to believe he used it to mean "power" or "pizzazz," but what he cared about was the story's appeal to the online nation. Especially its ability to draw those between the ages of eighteen and forty-five to the *Chronicle* Web page. He had personally nixed the last three stories proposed by the investigative team because they lacked "juice."

"We went online to that directory, and I played the clip for him," Dorothy was saying. "He went evangelical. Wants to run a teaser promoting the series: 'Online Dangers: Your Teenager Is Prey.' That's a direct quote, by the way. How'd your interview go?"

To buy time, I leaned over the reception desk to pick up a copy of the day's paper from the stacks. "Another warehouse fire in Pawtucket?" I said, peering at the lead headline.

"Oh my God, she didn't show up, did she?" Dorothy said.

Here, I had to meet her eye.

Disappointment fell hard over her solid, even features. The gleam in her eye died, which was actually a bit of a relief. And she sucked in the bottom corner of her chapped lips and bit too hard.

I did not tell her that I'd blown it by arriving late. Instead, I tried to interest her in the *South Park* guy, the weird stalker who'd followed the teenage girls out of Best Price when he realized they wanted to buy a webcam. "The salesman said the guy is there all the time, lurking," I said. "And it might be the guy Lexie tried to warn me about."

Dorothy mulled this over. She told me to have Bennett Castiglia, my buddy and our investigative team's data guy, do a search through court records on all Ruriks, and see if he could come up with anything. But the focus of the story had to be the teenagers. "You've got to go find that girl, what was her name?"

"Lexie." I decided not to tell her that I'd messaged Lexie all weekend without a response. Or that I'd just come from St. Olivia's, where I'd hung out on the street until the school day had started and not seen anyone who looked like Lexie.

In the news business, you had to be optimistic. At the coffee shop across the street from the school, the woman at the counter had told me all the girls hung out there after class. I could stake it out this afternoon. "Don't worry," I assured Dorothy. "I know where I can find her."

4

St. Olivia's inhabited a beautiful old Greek revival mansion not far from the Brown University campus on College Hill. The mansion had once been the home of one of the city's wealthiest merchants. After losing his only daughter to the flu epidemic of 1918, he had tried to buy her way into heaven by bequeathing the residence to the Catholic Church.

Some sort of private order turned it into an exclusive school with a good endowment. Over the years, it had acquired several nearby lots, where they had built both a gym and a performance center. There was even a building that housed a chapel and dormitory rooms, although most of the students were day students.

On the opposite side of the street, Minnie's Coffee Shop offered an excellent view of the portico entrance to the school. The restaurant was long and narrow, with a couple of tables clustered in front near the window and booths lining the long wall, opposite the service counter. Loopy writing in colored chalk advertised on a blackboard at least fifteen different kinds of coffee and today's special, a "vanilla cookie coffee," sugar-free with no-fat froth. A woman behind the counter, who looked like a college student, put down an *OK!* magazine to take my order. She looked relieved that I only wanted a muffin and a regular cup of coffee.

At this hour, all the tables were empty. I grabbed one nearest the window and sat down with the day's *Chronicle* spread out before me. But my gaze was out the window across the street.

At 2:10, the buses began pulling into the school parking lot. Five minutes later, girls began funneling out the school's front door and gathering on the sidewalk. At first glance, they looked like Girl Scouts, but in maroon. They wore plaid kilt skirts, which I hoped weren't wool, and short-sleeved white-collared shirts. Despite, or maybe because of, the uniform, they seemed determined to express their individuality in their footwear, which ran the gamut from sneakers to clogs to high-heeled slingbacks.

I'd changed into sneakers, in the event I had to chase Lexie onto a bus. But I didn't see any sign of her. Or any teenage girl with short dark hair. Or even chin-length dark hair, just in case it had grown since her webcam production.

A new crowd of girls walked out of the school entrance and started crossing the street toward the store. I peered out the window, inventorying hair color and studying faces, and occasionally shoes. But what were the odds Lexie would talk to me now, when she'd ignored all my messages?

Still, I had no other strategy, so when five of the girls walked into the coffee shop together, I told them I was a *Chronicle* reporter and asked if they knew a girl named Lexie.

"*Chronicle*? Is that the paper?" one of them asked. She was petite, with shoulder-length blond hair, sophisticated-looking high heels, and a cell phone in her hand.

I nodded.

"Not TV?" another girl asked. She was wearing flat, sensible shoes, but had the waistband of her plaid skirt folded over so it would sit low on her hips. These girls looked older than Lexie. Seniors, maybe.

I did not acknowledge their obvious disappointment in my career choice. Instead, I repeated my question about Lexie.

"Did she get arrested for something?" the high-heeled girl asked. She sounded hopeful.

I shook my head. "You know her?"

"What grade is she?"

"Ninth or tenth, I think. She's fifteen or sixteen, with short dark hair. Really short, like a boy's cut."

They all looked at each other, as if trying to see if any one of them could visualize this. None could. The girl who had her skirt folded over said, "I think you've got the wrong school. No one at St. O's would ever cut her hair that short. Everyone would call her a dyke."

They giggled, and then breezed by me to line up at the counter. I turned back to the window. The sidewalk was full of girls leaving the school. Troops of blondes, quite a few redheads, and brunettes with hair past their shoulders toward their waist. Maybe the fear-of-looking-like-a-dyke thing was true. Maybe no teenage girl at St. Olivia's had short hair.

I thought about that haircut, which did seem unusually bold for a fifteen-year-old. Didn't they all try to look like each other at that age? Was she trying to establish herself as a lesbian?

I was pondering this as another group of girls walked into the coffee shop. Still no sign of Lexie. The counter help had multiplied accordingly, and a man appeared out of nowhere to operate the espresso machine.

The newly arrived students all had varying shades of brown hair, from auburn to chestnut to skunklike highlights, all up in messy-looking ponytails. The girl with auburn hair had her back toward me. The other two looked about fifteen.

A couple of high-school-aged boys walked in with a confident air. All the girls seemed to sit up straight at once. The boys scanned briefly and then strode over to the first group of girls, who were now at a booth, and sat down. One of the boys put his arm around the high-heeled blonde.

Another group of girls in kilts arrived. These girls looked young, maybe twelve or thirteen. Too young probably to even know Lexie. I let them pass.

The girl with the auburn hair had turned toward the counter to order, so she was now in profile. That's when I recognized her. The pale freckles splashed across a sharp-looking nose. The girl in the lime green bikini.

As if sensing my gaze, she glanced over her shoulder. They must have used a lot of makeup and lighting techniques on the webcam video, because in real life, she was no beauty. She looked anemic, with pale rimless eyes and poor posture, as if she were caving in on herself. As if she'd rather be anywhere else than where she was. But it was definitely her. Lime Green Bikini. The girl with the sand problem.

She ordered one of those enormous coffees that should last an entire week and then made the counter girl take it back and remove the mound of whipped cream.

How to approach her? She and her two friends took a table near the window, right next to me. But I had to be careful not to stare at her and scare her away.

More girls had walked in from school, and the restaurant was suddenly loud with female voices and the scraping of chairs. Someone's cell phone rang the theme song for *Sex and the City*.

I took a sip of my coffee and pulled my digital recorder out of my pocket, capturing just enough of the *Sex and the City* ringtone and young teenage-girl chatter to make Dorothy and Corey, the online editor, happy—assuming this story ever panned out. Then, I put the recorder away and began to strategize. If I were going to approach Lime Green Bikini through our mutual acquaintance, I should know her name. As if Lexie had given it to me.

So I sat staring down at the newspaper and listened closely to their conversation. After about ten minutes, I realized that teenagers don't use each other's names in conversation. What they do is interrupt each other, swear a lot, and lower their voices unaccountably in the middle of sentences. I sipped from my coffee cup as if there were still some left, trying to look as if I had a good reason to be hanging out at this table when now there was only standing room left in the restaurant.

The girls talked about some boy from La Salle Academy who had two friends, one of them "very horny." Then they talked about a teacher who they were pretty sure was pregnant. And they talked about some girl they didn't like who everyone knew was bulimic. Then they lowered their voices so low that I couldn't hear anything at all.

Standing at the doorway, two girls who carried themselves with the authority of seniors kept looking at my table, coveting it. One of them carried car keys that she jangled impatiently, making a lot of noise. I pretended not to hear it. I took another fake sip of my coffee and flipped to the middle of my newspaper.

Then Lime Green Bikini stood up to go back to the counter. The others shouted their orders to her from the table. Some water. Latte. Four packets of Splenda. All without mentioning her name. She nodded, as if resigned to the burden, and inched up in line.

"Are you going to be long?" the senior with the key ring called to me from the door.

"A little while," I said without taking my eyes off the paper. As if I completely missed the looks they were sending me. There were only crumbs left of my muffin. I picked one up and put it in my mouth.

Lime Green Bikini returned to the table with the order. Instead of popping up to help her with the tray, one of her friends complained. "Not with cinnamon, Whitney. You know I hate cinnamon."

Whitney. Thank God for bitchy teenagers.

From the booth, the high-heeled blonde was pointing me out to her boyfriend: the reporter. But not from TV.

It was do-or-die time. I leaned toward Lime Green Bikini and introduced myself. I told her that I was here trying to find a friend of hers.

She'd been sitting with her back toward me, but now she scraped back her chair, looking at me as if seeing me at the table for the first time.

"Lexie," I continued. Then, in case that was a fake name, "Her screen name is Dizzywon." I saw a flicker of something in her eyes and pressed on. "She was supposed to meet me Saturday at Best Price." And just the teeniest lie. "I told her I wanted to do a story about teenagers and the Internet, and she said she had a lot to tell me, but I got there late and I missed her."

36

"A story?" She sounded confused, apparently missing the part about me being a reporter.

"I work for the *Chronicle,*" I repeated.

She looked me over, as if trying to match my appearance with whatever her notion of a reporter was. Her expression grew apprehensive. She said nothing.

"I met Lexie online," I pressed on. "We talked a lot on the Buzz."

"And she *knew* you were a reporter?"

I hesitated here. The way she had phrased the question made me think Lexie either mentioned our meeting at Best Price or had some reason to avoid reporters. "I wasn't going to use her real name in the paper."

She thought about that for a minute. "You can do that?"

"We hardly ever use the full name of minors in stories."

"The paper used my name in a story," the girl with the chestnut-colored ponytail said. "I play lacrosse." She must have been a big deal in lacrosse. "I'm in the paper a lot."

"We have permission from the school for those kinds of stories," I said. "But we could get in trouble otherwise."

"Who is this Lexie person anyway?" the lacrosse player asked Whitney.

"I met her online," Whitney replied.

I was beginning to realize that the sweatshirt must have been Whitney's. "Lexie doesn't go to St. Olivia's, then?"

Whitney shook her head. Then another thought occurred to her. "How did you know that I was Lexie's friend?"

I either had to tell her about figuring it out from the video clip or I had to lie again. I went with the lie. "I asked Lexie about making friends online, and she told me about you. She said you might want to talk to me, too." I watched her expression closely. "As long as I promised not to use anyone's real name."

"What else did she say about me?" She was probing, trying to figure out if I knew about the webcam production.

I racked my brain. Why was Whitney such a good source for a story on the Internet? The answer here could turn the whole interview. Pull Whitney toward me or push her away.

I searched her eyes and saw something besides the apprehension and fatigue. Something that looked like sadness. A young girl unhappy with herself. "She said you knew a lot of things that might help other kids."

Whitney and her friends exchanged a look, as if I'd hit on something significant. As if Whitney had lessons to teach. "Lexie must trust you," she finally said.

"I thought so."

She had pale eyebrows, too, plucked to an arch. The arch said: *You* thought *so?*

"Well, either she didn't wait for me very long or she didn't show up," I reminded her.

Whitney thought about this a minute. "That might not be her fault."

"Does she have strict parents?" I asked.

She sniffed, as if this was ridiculous, but didn't elaborate.

"A guy named Rurik showed up. Do you know him?"

At the mention of Rurik, the pale eyes began to blink. "Did he know she was meeting you?"

"I don't think so." Given that Lexie herself didn't actually know she was meeting a reporter.

She didn't look particularly relieved. Her eyes darted as if she was trying to piece things together. "This was Saturday?" she asked.

I nodded.

"You sure it was Rurik?"

Given her response, I was surer now than I had been before I got here. "He's a skinny guy with pierced lip and an accent, right?"

She began to shake her head, but not as an answer to me. It was as if to shake off whatever scenario she was seeing in her head.

"Are you all right?" the girl next to her asked. When she didn't answer, the friend glared at me. "What do you want from her?"

"If Lexie is in some sort of trouble, you should tell someone about it," I said quietly.

The girl put her arm around Whitney, consolingly, but Whitney pulled away. The fatigue was completely gone from her face, and the pale eyes looked wildly electric. "Can we talk somewhere else?" she asked me. "In private?"

"Reporters can do things to help people, right?" Whitney asked. We'd left her friends at Minnie's Coffee Shop and were sitting in the front seat of my car, a Honda Element that I was now leasing.

"We try," I said.

It was still before rush hour, and Waterman, a one-way street, had minimal traffic. We were parked at least two blocks away from the school, but Whitney's eyes kept darting to the sidewalk as if afraid that one of her friends would walk by. "And you won't put my name in the paper, right?" she asked.

"No."

"Or tell my mother."

"The whole thing with reporters is that we protect the identity of our sources. Reporters go to jail rather than give up their sources," I said.

She nodded, even though I suspected that she hadn't exactly followed the whole Valerie Plame controversy. An older woman, nicely dressed, walked by with a greyhound on a leash.

Whitney reached into the outer pocket of what looked like a designer laptop bag and pulled out a pack of Benson & Hedges cigarettes. "Mind if I smoke in your car?"

I did, but I was going to have to suffer through it. She'd talk longer and hopefully freer if she got her own way. I pulled out a notebook and pen from my own bag, but decided against the recorder, which I was afraid would scare her. Then I opened my window and flipped open the ashtray on the console. "There's a lighter." I pointed.

But she had her own lighter. It looked like a lipstick, but she twisted it up and snapped a flame. She lit her cigarette, inhaling deeply as she cranked open her window. She held the smoke in her lungs an extra moment as if it soothed her, then exhaled into the street. Not her first pack.

She turned back to me. "Remember you asked if Lexie had strict parents?"

I nodded.

"She doesn't have *any* parents."

"What do you mean?"

Her gaze dropped to my notebook. "Don't even write my name in there, okay?"

"Just your words," I promised.

This settled her. "She lives with Rurik."

"She lives with him?" But she had warned me to stay away

from him. I got a sick feeling in my stomach. "Is Rurik her boyfriend?"

Whitney cringed, but not with the normal revulsion a girl her age should display. "No. But she's been living with him for a real long time."

This was matter-of-fact. An acceptance of just another unconventional family unit.

"Like a foster parent?"

"Sort of."

Fifteen-year-old girls didn't just live with old guys. "Is he some sort of relative or something?"

"She *told* me that he was her uncle. But he doesn't act like an uncle. And when they are together, she never called him 'uncle.' So I think he was like a friend or something. At least he used to be a friend."

"Wait a minute." I was still trying to piece the relationship together. "Is Lexie a runaway?"

"I don't know, but it's weird. She told me sometimes they live in Providence, but sometimes because of Rurik's job, they live in Massachusetts somewhere."

"What does he do for work, do you know?"

"She says he's a mover."

"Like a furniture mover?" I asked.

She shrugged. Clearly Rurik's profession had never been of interest to her.

But my mind was whirling now. Drugs, stolen goods, child prostitutes? There were a lot of bad things Rurik could move. "Do you know where Lexie is from . . . originally?"

"She acts like she's lived here her whole life, but . . ."

"But what?"

"She wears one of those funny gold crosses."

"What's funny about a gold cross?"

"You know, it's kind of stubby. With, like, a clover on the ends," she explained. "Lexie told me she got it when she was born. That it was the only thing she had from her mother."

"An Orthodox cross?"

"Yeah. Maybe. And sometimes, she had a weird way of talking. Not like Rurik, but just a couple of words that are funny."

An accent. As I wrote this into my notebook, Whitney dug into her laptop bag, pulled out her cell phone, and began punching keys. She put it to her ear and kept hitting keys until she found what she wanted. Then she held the phone toward me and a young girl's voice filled the car.

"Hey, Whit. Got your message. I'll meet you, yes, at Andreas, and we'll get something to eat. Six o'clock is good."

It was a soft scratchy voice that sounded as if she had laryngitis. In this small fragment, I couldn't exactly hear the Eastern European lilt, but the way she threw in the yes was clearly not indigenous to Rhode Island.

Then I thought of Lexie's extremely short hair. Somehow that seemed foreign, too. And my mind went back to something else Whitney had said that was disturbing. "What did you mean that Rurik *used* to be her friend?"

Whitney snapped her cell phone shut and threw it in her laptop bag. "Can you drive me home? I hate walking on the street."

"I'll drive you home, but first, tell me, what kind of trouble is Lexie in?"

Whitney took another long drag of her cigarette, diminishing it by half, and exhaled slowly. "She was supposed to meet me Saturday night at the mall, and she didn't show up. I called her all night and on Sunday, too, and she didn't answer her cell phone. Now I can't find her online. And she's always online."

So it wasn't just my messages that Lexie wasn't answering.

"And Rurik going to Best Price without her, that's real weird."

"Maybe she changed her mind about meeting me. Got cold feet."

"Maybe," Whitney said, but she didn't sound convinced. "It's just . . ." The sentence drifted off.

"It's just what?"

"It's just that I think she finally decided to get away from him. I think that's the only reason she would have agreed to meet with you. A reporter. She was going to ask for help."

I couldn't point out the truth, that Lexie had no idea I was a reporter. Instead, I asked, "Why do you think she wanted to get away from him?"

She didn't answer or even look at me. Instead, she flicked her cigarette out the window and watched the stub land on the street.

"Whitney. I can't help Lexie if I don't know what was really going on. What did he do to her that she wanted to get away?"

"Stuff," she said.

"Sexual stuff?"

She was silent again, studying her hands, uncomfortable without the cigarette as a prop. Finally she said, "He bought her things sometimes, you know, so she didn't mind so much at first. But lately, he was a real asshole. He started to complain that she was looking so old—"

"Old? But she's only fifteen—"

"That's what she says, but I think she's really older than that. She can drive a car and shit. And, like, pretty good."

"So why does she pretend to be younger?"

"Because of Rurik. He always makes her go online and make friends—but now he wants her to get them from middle school. And that really was starting to bother Lexie. She didn't want to do it anymore. That's why Lexie was getting so pissed off. That's why she wanted to get away."

So Lexie's job was to recruit new talent. This explained her willingness to meet with a thirteen-year-old and help her pick out a webcam. But then she must have had a change of heart. She'd tried to back out of it, and when I'd insisted . . . maybe standing me up was an act of conscience. "So did she ever talk about running away from Rurik?"

"Lots of times."

"Maybe she just finally did it."

"No way. If she ran away from him, she would have called me. I'm her only real friend, and she would have needed help. And there's another thing."

"What?"

"They had a fight Friday because she forgot to shut down her laptop and he found her messages still on it. She was trying to talk one of her new friends out of getting a webcam. He went all psychotic."

Friday, that's when she had tried to warn *me* about Rurik.

"Did he threaten her?"

"He beat the shit out of her. Then he told her if she ever tried to leave him, that he'd hunt her down and kill her. That she'd never get away."

5

"This is the kid you think is in trouble?" Jonathan Frizell sat at the conference table in front of my laptop, pointing to the wrong girl on the beach blanket.

The two of us were in the Fishbowl, insulated from the buzz of the late-afternoon newsroom by the walls of glass, as we waited for the three other members of the investigative team and Dorothy to arrive. I had been pacing the small room, thinning the carpeted floor, but now stopped directly behind his chair.

"This is the girl who is in trouble," I said, leaning over to shift Frizell's finger from Whitney to Lexie. "The other one is my source."

"But she's not willing to go to police herself?"

I nodded.

Jonathan Frizell, who was in his late thirties, tended to dress like an academic, with corduroy pants and a tweedy sports jacket.

Now, he took off his pretentious-looking reading glasses and folded them. This was a sign that he was ready to impart his wisdom. "If someone is in the lake drowning and you've got a camera, your obligation is to take the picture, not save the victim."

This was why colleges, especially Ivy League colleges, should not be allowed to offer master's degrees in journalism. Because graduates like Jonathan Frizell actually spout this stuff at meetings.

"Good point," I said with enough sarcasm so that he could correctly interpret this as *spare me.*

He shrugged, as if to say *suit yourself,* and turned to the door, where Bennett Castiglia, our database expert, and Ryan Skenderian arrived together, each with his own laptop in tow. They both looked so young that you couldn't believe they were out of high school, but Ryan, who was now in his early thirties, was probably the most highly respected reporter on the staff.

"Hallie thinks this is more than just another Internet porn story," Frizell said in greeting.

He replayed the beach video for them while we waited for Ellen Felty, the fifth member of our team, and Dorothy, who were making their way from the City Desk through the crowded newsroom. Dorothy couldn't advance two feet before some reporter or copy editor flagged her down in the aisle. Ellen, who was in her forties and a longtime friend of Dorothy's, finally grabbed her forearm and pulled her away from the education writer. She didn't let go until they made it into the Fishbowl. They took seats at the table nearest the door.

I gave them no time to settle before I launched into the whole story, my Internet meeting with Lexie, her failure to show up at Best Price, and Whitney's fears about her disappearance.

Ellen interrupted me. "And this is the story Ian Clew already approved?"

Dorothy, who had been taking notes, looked up from her legal pad to confirm this. "He wants a series that exposes the dangers of the Internet. I think the teaser was something like . . . What was it again, Hallie?"

" 'Your Teenager Is Prey.' " It seemed horrifically apt now.

"Anyway," Dorothy continued, "Ian says Hallie's angle on this has *juice.*"

All the other reporters exchanged looks over the "juice" comment. Ellen flipped open her notebook to a fresh page. "So the first girl bagged out, but we've got the other one, right? She's going to tell us about the operation?"

"She's begging us to try to help Lexie," I said. "She says this Rurik beats her."

Bennett and Ryan exchanged a questioning look. I explained again who Rurik was, and how he'd been the one at Best Price looking for fresh young teenagers interested in webcams.

"Scum," Bennett said. He was only about twenty-five years old, pale from too much time spent in front of the computer, but he had an air of authority about his judgments. "You did tell this girl that we can't get involved in *saving* anyone? That this isn't our role as reporters?"

Everyone else was nodding in agreement. I didn't answer.

"Hallie would have us jeopardize this story by going to police," Frizell informed them.

Bennett was usually my ally, but now I could feel his disapproval cross the table. On the other end, Dorothy and Ellen were both shaking their heads.

"She's a kid, for God's sake—and her life could be on the line," I said.

"Unless the other one, what's her name, is messing with you," Ryan said.

"Her name is Whitney, and she is *not* messing with me," I said. "She was really worried."

"But not worried enough that she'd go to the police herself," Jonathan pointed out. "Or even to her parents."

"She's scared of getting into trouble."

"Which is why she posts these little sex videos of herself on the Web?" Dorothy asked.

"She's a teenager, for God's sake. They don't think things through."

Bennett helped out here, explaining to Dorothy that kids are drawn to the Web because of the false sense of anonymity. "You wouldn't believe the pictures these teenagers post of themselves on MySpace and the Buzz," he said. "They're half-naked, smoking bongs."

"The point is that there's a kid out there in trouble. Abused by this Rurik guy who is doing God knows what to her. Someone should go to police. Or DCYF." The state's Division of Children, Youth and Families had a hotline to report child abuse.

"Not you," Dorothy said. "It's not your job to bring information to authorities."

The finality in her tone left silence in the air. Her message was clear. Violating this order could be grounds for dismissal.

Dorothy asked, "Did this Whitney give you a way to try to contact Lexie? Where she lives? A cell phone number?"

"According to Whitney, Lexie never gave her an address. And she was afraid to give me the cell phone number. She says this Rurik guy monitors the incoming calls."

Ellen Felty had a hard blond exterior and ice blue eyes that could be dismissive. But now her expression was sympathetic as she attempted to soften Dorothy's stance. "You can't really report it to DCYF anyway, because we don't even know for sure this girl lives in Rhode Island."

"According to Whitney, she lives in Providence most of the time, but I don't know where."

It sounded bad, even to me. Ryan and Bennett exchanged an amused look over the "most of the time." I expected Frizell to roll his eyes. Instead, he was actually the one who helped calm me down.

"Going to police might not be the best way to help this kid anyway," he said. "You said this Lexie person didn't have a legal guardian, and she didn't appear to be enrolled in high school anywhere, right?"

I nodded.

"So there isn't even anyone to file a missing-persons report. And the cops aren't going to do squat without a missing-persons report."

In most cases, I hated to acknowledge when Frizell was right. But here it offered comfort. There was no point violating the tenets of journalism for no purpose.

"The best way to help this kid is to investigate the story ourselves," he said. "Get as much evidence as we can about this whole recruiting operation that's supposedly going on. Find other teenagers who are lured into this. We get a big series on this splashed across the front page, police will have no choice but to go after this Rurik guy. And if we do our jobs right, they'll have enough information to put him away and shut down this teen-porn thing."

"No wonder everyone hates the media," Walter said.

I'd come from my morning run on the Boulevard to meet him at Rufful's for breakfast. We were among the first customers there. I'd managed to devour my BLT on rye while complaining nonstop about the heartlessness of my investigative team.

Walter, who had been driving people back and forth to the airport since 4 A.M., was taking a break from his cab shift. He held his fork backwards as he made listless stabs at his western omelet.

I'd met Walter at a Substance Abuse meeting years ago in Boston when I was first dealing with my sleeping pill addiction. He'd helped me through tough times, and bailed me out again when I'd gotten into trouble gambling. But now, he was the one who needed the shoulder. Five months ago, his fiancée, Geralyn, a reporter friend of mine from the Boston *News-Tribune,* broke off their engagement and asked him to move out. He'd just learned that she was going out with a coworker, the newly hired, just-out-of-college police reporter.

That happened in the newspaper business. Especially on the night shift, where everyone in the newsroom went out for drinks after deadline to dilute the adrenaline. But this information didn't help Walter much. It just fueled his new hatred for the media.

"So I think you should ignore your editor and report this Rurik asshole to the cops," he said, pushing away his half-eaten omelet. "Stop this pervert from hanging around Best Price and stalking little girls."

I explained again about how I could get fired if I did that. But I also mentioned something Matt had told me: Warwick police weren't going to do anything unless I gave them proof that Rurik was doing something illegal. "Hanging around a store and buying young girls webcams isn't against the law."

"But if he sells any of those videos, it is. Even transmitting them on the Internet," Walter said.

"Right, we just have to catch him at it." My tone underscored how unlikely that was.

We were in a booth in the very front of the restaurant, which is in a strip of stores in my neighborhood. It's a family place with an efficient counter, snug booths, and a bulletin board with photos of customers' kids and last year's Christmas cards.

The front window looked out on Wayland Avenue. Walter's gaze shifted to his cab, which was parked right outside. It was the latest addition to his growing fleet, a brand-new Oldsmobile of some sort, white with a royal blue trim and W-TAXI CO. written inside the stripe. "Maybe, on my way to the airport, I'll take a drive past Best Price and look for this Rurik guy," he said. "What does he look like?"

I hesitated here. Despite all his twelve-step philosophy—and believe me, Walter was heavy on the slogans—he was not taking this breakup with Geralyn well. He had a lot of pent-up anger that he was itching to redirect.

"What are you going to do if you find him?" I asked.

He shrugged, as if he hadn't thought about that yet. But I knew better. Back when he was a drug dealer, Walter had made his own rules and meted out his own justice, and despite his many years of rehabilitation, he wasn't above slamming a little justice down someone's throat. Especially if that someone was a pornographer who abused teenage girls.

"That wouldn't exactly help my story," I said.

He shrugged again, as if to say that it was hard for him to

care about my story, when I, like the man who had stolen his former fiancée, was a member of the media.

"You're not doing so great at detaching," I told him.

He gave me an unapologetic look, resigned to this personal failure.

"Live and let live. Remember that?"

He took a long swig of coffee, and we were silent as the waitress came to our booth to drop off our check. I grabbed it before Walter could. He was making a good living on the combination of his Providence and Boston cab fleets, and always tried to pay for everything. But I was solvent now. In the black.

"My turn," I said.

He shrugged again.

"Enough with the shrugging," I said.

"Well, you won't let me go punch the guy."

I looked at Walter, normally so reasonable, so wise. He was leaning halfway back in the booth, with one leg up, his boot actually on the seat, and unconsciously slapping his right fist into his open hand. Usually, he was presentable in a cowboy sort of way, but now his hair, a little thin on top, needed a shampoo, his *Easy Rider* mustache drooped, and the one-day whiskers on the side of his chin had sprouted a few gray hairs. He looked like he'd been held hostage in his own taxi.

My first thought was that I probably should get him to a meeting. I'd have to go home and look one up. AA, Substance Abuse, my old Gamblers Anonymous meeting. It didn't matter. Walter could find the philosophy and structure he needed in any of them. My second thought was more self-serving.

"Hey, I know how you can help me nail Rurik," I said.

"How?"

"You must have taken a few fares to Allens Avenue." I was

talking about the red-light district of Providence, an industrial section along the waterfront that had become a regional hub of the sex industry, with an explosion of strip clubs, bathhouses, adult video stores, and sex toy shops.

"Like half the businessmen I pick up at T. F. Green." That was Rhode Island's major airport.

"So those shop owners, they know you?"

"They don't *know* me." He sounded insulted. "But they've seen me waiting outside in the cab."

"Can you introduce me to them? So I can ask them a few questions?"

"You're going to go interview them? And you think they are going to tell you anything?"

"You'd be surprised sometimes what people will tell you. Not about their own businesses, but about their competitors," I explained.

"And no one gets pissed off about that, I'm sure." Walter was heavy on the sarcasm. "Hey, if you are going to start hanging around these scummy neighborhoods, you've got to make good on your promise. I'm headed there this afternoon."

Walter is always forcing me to make promises. It took me a moment or two to remember which one he meant.

Then I got it. The gun promise. Ever since the Salazar murder, Walter has been after me to learn how to use a gun. A couple months ago, he bought himself a new nine-millimeter semiautomatic and started going to a shooting range in Attleboro on a regular basis. He wanted me to come as a guest. Had I actually promised?

"I can't go today, because I'm going sailing with Matt, but I'll tell you what. I'll come with you to the shooting range next week if you do me a favor."

He offered a besieged expression: *What now?*

"You ask around, see if these stores have any of this kiddie porn and if they'll tell you where they get it."

His eyes, a mute gray, now lit with amusement. "Yeah. Right. I'm going to walk into one of these shitholes and identify myself as a total perv."

I could see his point. "Okay. How about you chat up some of these businessmen you take there. See what kind of stuff they're buying?"

"Most of these guys are doing this on the quiet. They're not real eager to tell me all their sexual quirks."

"But they're from out of town. They must be asking you where to go for this shit. You could ask what they're looking for."

He stroked his mustache, a habit when he was thinking. Then he offered a deal. "You come with me to the firing range, and I'll see if I can work it into the conversation."

6

They say you can tell time by the wind in Narragansett Bay. And true to form, we had a morning calm, until predictable early-afternoon breezes filled the sail. Like magic, we picked up a beautiful southwesterly and rode it all the way to Newport.

Matt, who'd had a hellish week, let me man the helm while he dozed off in the cockpit. He'd worked late every night on a case he'd lost. So I let him sleep until we made the lower harbor and I needed his help to drop the mainsail.

Newport Harbor was always busy. Even in May, before the official start of the season, the docks were filled with yachts and commercial fishing boats. Luckily there were plenty of available moorings in the harbor.

It was cocktail hour, and after we tied up to the mooring, we were going to go ashore for dinner. I was hoping that Matt would let me stop by the Marriott—which I knew had a public computer and wireless connection in the lobby—to let me check for messages from Lexie.

But mooring the boat was proving more difficult than sailing it. As predictable as the morning calm, late-afternoon gusts—often called a harbor hurricane—began buffeting the boat. Maneuvering in a tightly spaced mooring field was tricky. Since I was better with a boat hook, Matt took over at the helm while I ran up on deck.

We were amidst midsized sailboats and powerboats tied to moorings about twenty-five feet apart. All were swirling with the wind. Kneeling, I had to lean over the bow to try to hook the buoy and pull the mooring line out of the water. The chop lifted and dropped us, spraying me with salt and wrecking my aim. When I missed the buoy, our Bristol kept pushing forward. It headed straight for a gleaming black yacht with a lightning bolt painted across its beam.

Three men jumped up onto the deck. "What the fuck!"

"Reverse!" I yelled to Matt.

Sailboats don't really reverse. The small prop doesn't have much bite. Matt threw his might into the rudder, yanking the boat to starboard just in time. Our bow skimmed past the black-hulled yacht, with the men on deck still screaming, "Asshole!"

We headed farther out into the harbor, to an isolated mooring with no other boats around. On the second go-round, I was able to hook the buoy and pull the line up to the bow.

"Holy shit, that was close," Matt said. After he'd cut the engine, he'd run up to the bow to help me secure the line to the cleat.

"Yeah." My heart was pounding so hard, I felt like it was going to rip through the Lycra of my bathing suit. The muscles in my arms were shaking, but I felt exhilarated, too. Nothing like a raucous wind.

But when I looked up at Matt standing at the mast, my elation faded. His sunglasses, hanging on Croakies, had dropped to his chest, and he was squinting in the direction of the black yacht. He had a strong jawline anyway, but now it jutted forward and his Adam's apple protruded. Something was wrong.

"Did you know one of those guys on that boat?" I asked.

"I know the boat. It belongs to a defendant," he said. The prosecutors in his office gave the word a slightly French pronunciation, with an accent on the last syllable. An informal expression of disrespect.

"Not Pauley Sponik?"

Sponik called himself a personal trainer, but really, he was a thirty-something drug dealer. Yesterday he had beat Matt in court with a motion to suppress. A perennial pain in the ass, he always managed to slip off the hook, largely because he had access to big sums of cash and the best criminal defense attorneys.

"Pauley," Matt confirmed.

When people think of Newport, they generally think America's Cup races, Cliff Walk, and the Vanderbilt Estate. But until it was recently torn down and reconstructed, the city had a very troubled housing project, Tonomy Hill, which incubated all sorts of crime in the city's north side. Pauley Sponik had grown up there, but he'd stepped up in the world, to larger, more lucrative crimes. He pretended to be a personal trainer, but was believed to be compiling quite an empire: drugs, bookmaking, escort agencies, you name it. Once, a few years back, *People* magazine ran a photo of him with his arm around one of the more troubled former Disney actresses right before she went back into rehab.

I scrambled across the bow to the port side to see if I could make out the men on the yacht. I wanted to get a good look at the weasel that had destroyed Matt's week and was now threatening to destroy our weekend.

The Bristol was four or five boat lengths away from the yacht, a fifty-foot vessel that looked brand new. I had to wait until the wind spun the vessel toward us, but finally, I could make out the men. One tall white guy with rock-star hair who looked like he hit the gym a lot, another white guy with thick legs and a beer belly, and a heavyset black man leaning over what appeared to be a cooler.

"The tall one?" I asked Matt.

"Asshole should be locked up for life." I took that as a yes.

From this distance, I couldn't make out any facial features, but the tall one looked too tan for early June, and he had something in his hands. Something he lifted to his face to peer through. Binoculars. Binoculars pointed this way.

I quickly turned my back on the yacht and moved away from the rail, back toward Matt, who was now struggling to fold the mainsail.

"He's watching us with binoculars."

Matt glanced at the vessel and then at me. I was wearing a bikini, which suddenly made me feel terribly exposed. "Let's get everything battened down, and get the hell out of here," he said.

Newport's waterfront has a series of wharves, an energetic mix of high-rise hotels, marinas, restaurants, and shops. All of this is designed to be quaint, with lots of awnings, flowerpots, and nautically themed art.

It was a short walk from the launch pier to Bannister's Wharf.

Because the night had grown cool, we eschewed the outdoor waterfront dining at the Black Pearl to take a table inside at the rough-hewn tavern, which reiterates the pearl motif with woodwork painted a glistening black and walls decorated with nautical charts.

But even after two beers, Matt wasn't really relaxed. We'd ordered oysters and littlenecks, but he picked at them, his back stiff against the wood slats of the booth and his eyes darting past me to the door every time it opened. The Black Pearl was a busy place. The door opened every couple of minutes.

I knew that Matt did not want to wind up drinking in the same bar as Pauley and his cohorts, but I was sort of curious. I wouldn't mind a chance to see a celebrity scumbag up close. "You shouldn't let this guy wreck your evening," I said. "It wasn't your fault."

An odd sound came out of Matt's throat, as if he was choking something back. A clam neck? But there was something deliberate about the way he coughed into his fist. An effort to shut himself up.

I thought maybe he was stifling criticism of the new prosecutor in his office who had drafted the faulty search warrant, which was the reason the guy had walked. Police had found a cache of twelve semiautomatic handguns on Pauley Sponik's property, but the judge had ruled that the warrant limited the search to the house and did not include the shed where the handguns were found.

"You didn't write the warrant," I said.

Even this early in the evening, the crowd was three deep around the bar, the tables all filled, and a line of people waiting. Matt looked up as if he expected every tourist in the room to be listening to our conversation.

I grabbed the last oyster on the plate and squeezed lemon all over it. I remembered something Matt had said once about Pauley being politically connected. Something about his cousin owning a chain of motels and his current girlfriend being related to a congressman.

Or was it a judge?

Suddenly, I knew what Matt was trying not to say. There was a reason why the criminal charges against Pauley Sponik never stuck. It occurred to me that if the webcam story fell through, Pauley would make a killer profile, a front-page lead for the Sunday *Chronicle*.

"Someone should take a look at how many times this guy has slipped through the legal cracks," I said. "Point out the pattern of leniency in all his cases."

Matt's eyes sought mine. "We have a deal, Hallie."

He was referring to the deal we struck before we moved in together. As a prosecutor, the security of information was paramount. If it were suspected that he couldn't keep his mouth shut and that confidential information were leaked to his girlfriend, the *Chronicle* reporter, none of his colleagues would be willing to work with him. His career would be over.

To make our relationship work, Matt had sacrificed his high-profile job in Providence and relocated to the Newport office. For my part, I'd agreed not to cover any Newport stories, no matter how tempting. "I didn't mean I would write it," I said, although it was *my* kind of story.

"Any exposé comes out in the *Chronicle* about this guy, they'll figure it came from me." By *they* Matt actually meant his boss, Aidan Carpenter, the attorney general.

Matt pushed the empty plate of clams to the edge of the

table. The argument was over. I knew he was right. I had to hold up my end of the deal, but I couldn't help thinking that until Pauley Sponik's political connections were illuminated in the press, the judges would just keep ruling in his favor, and Matt would keep losing.

The waitress arrived with our entrées, swordfish and baked cod. With our stomachs filled, our mood improved and the workweek finally dissolved. Matt stopped watching the door, and I stopped worrying about my next story.

The half-Italian part meant Matt tanned easily in the sun, and in this light, he looked something of a pirate, with his dark hair windblown and needing a cut. I put my arm on his and could feel the heat of the sun still on his skin.

Matt and I had never spent an overnight on the sailboat, and now I was suddenly very eager to get back to the V-berth before the exhaustion of a day in the sun knocked us both out. We skipped dessert and coffee, and headed straight to the launch dock.

The launch, a large, open powerboat that acted as a water taxi ferrying people to and from their moorings, arrived and departed from a long dock that also accommodated the variety of commercial boats. In the peak of summer, this dock might be a madhouse, but tonight, it was a quiet spot near the water.

To comfortably accommodate the crowds, there was a waiting area fashioned nearby around the dock. There were flowers in pots, wicker chairs, and several long wooden benches. Alone, we had our choice and took the bench nearest the water. At first, we merely sat side by side as Matt pointed out a few of the faraway commercial fishing docks that proved, despite all the contrivance, that Newport remained a working port.

But the longer we waited for the launch, the longer Matt stretched out on the bench. Soon he was lying lengthwise with his head in my lap.

Maybe because of the colder air, the sky was cloudless and full of stars. Matt began to teach me about the constellations. He was trying to get me to see the "leg" of the hunter. He reached back to take my hand and point my finger directly overhead. "That's Rigel." This star was the namesake of his brother's sailboat.

I squinted upward.

"Look, right there." He moved my arm slightly. "It's one of the brightest stars in the sky."

"If we had our own boat, what would you name it?" I asked playfully.

"Hallie," he said.

"No, you wouldn't."

"Yes, I would, it's a great name for a boat." He tilted his head back to meet my eyes. "Maybe *The Hallie,* or *Hallie's Lead,* how about that?"

Now he was teasing me, but I loved it. I ruffled his hair with my fingers and countered, "How about we name it for you. We could call it *Guilty Verdict?*"

"Too harsh," he said. "Sounds like a powerboat."

I agreed. Then I had a better idea. "How about *Conviction?*"

"Too fucking far-fetched." A male voice startled us.

Matt sat up swiftly. We both turned around.

Standing with his two friends was Pauley Sponik. He was wearing what looked like silk pants and a collared shirt, only the shirt was completely unbuttoned to reveal a rain forest of black chest hair and a pierced nipple. In his hand, he had a plastic cup filled with clear liquid. The two guys we'd seen on the boat were behind him, with the same cups in their hands.

Matt sprang up from the bench, so that he was standing with his back to the water, arms folded in front of him, glowering at Pauley.

"Oh, sorry, did I interrupt something?" Pauley's gaze shifted to me as he took a deliberate inventory of my body parts before he asked Matt, "Were you going to get some?"

"Fuck you, Sponik," Matt said.

But Sponik only smiled. Not at Matt, but at me. He had an enormous mouth with a major overbite and very large white teeth.

Perhaps he thought that made him attractive, because he took a step closer and bent toward me so I could see that over-bite close up. He smelled of cologne and rum, and I tried to back away.

"I wouldn't be too sure your star here can get it up anymore."

I twisted away from him. He stepped closer and put one of his large tanned hands on my bare shoulder. He opened his mouth so I could see that the teeth were capped. "Fuck you, Bucky," I said, trying to pull away.

But his hand was glued to me. His two friends laughed. From the other direction, I thought I heard the sound of the launch engine in the harbor.

"Take your hand off her." Matt reached for him with a clenched fist.

I stepped back, freeing myself from Pauley's hand. "Leave him alone. It's all right," I said to Matt.

Pauley smiled at me, as if he found this somehow endearing. "I think this means she wants me," he said to his friends.

This really pissed me off, but I forced myself to smile back, as if maybe for even a nanosecond this could be true. Then I said, "Like I want head lice. Or a case of the crabs."

I felt Matt grab my arm. "We're getting out of here." He pulled me past Sponik toward the dock, where the launch was just pulling up.

We stepped over the gunnels into the boat. Matt said something to the launch boy, who immediately revved the engine and began backing up the boat. The engine drowned out most of what Sponik was shouting. The only thing I could make out sounded a lot like: "You bitch."

"What the hell were you thinking?" Matt asked as we were propelled across the dark water to our mooring.

I didn't actually know what I'd been thinking. But I knew what I was feeling. A surge of adrenaline.

"Sorry," I said. But I wasn't sorry. I felt alive to the fingertips. "You get in a scuffle like that, it could end up page one," I told him.

"I don't give a shit. The man is an animal. He could have hurt you," Matt said.

"I'm okay," I said. But I could still smell rum and Pauley's horrible cologne.

The launch boy, who was about eighteen, was trained to ignore embarrassing conversations in close quarters. He kept his hands on the wheel and his eyes glued to the sea ahead of him.

In the moonless night, the harbor was dark, lit only by the mast lights, which looked like faint candles atop the sailboats. In the open launch, we picked our way through the array of moored vessels rocking silently on the water.

The farther we got from the lights of shore, the blacker the harbor, but with the adrenaline rush, my vision on the water was unusually clear. And my veins were still vibrating with the excitement of the encounter.

I shivered.

Matt misread the shiver and gave me his jacket. Then he put both his arms around me to offer more warmth. "We're almost there," he said. "And don't worry about that asshole, Pauley. I'll get him locked up for life, if it kills me."

7

"**What did the** police say?" Whitney asked that next Wednesday, when I picked her up after school.

She had just buckled herself into the passenger seat and turned to me with hopeful eyes. They were pale green with reddish lashes, rimmed with way too much eyeliner. But the hope made her seem more vulnerable somehow.

I had to explain that the editor wouldn't let me go to the police, and that police weren't about to listen to me when there was no missing-persons report from a parent or guardian.

Turning away from me, Whitney began fishing inside her laptop bag. She pulled out a cigarette, lit up, and sucked on that thing as if trying to extract all the nicotine in a single inhale. Then, she opened the window slowly, punishing me with her smoke.

"I'm sorry," I said.

She didn't respond, or even look at me. She exhaled out the

passenger window, gaze trained on the street. A half-dozen girls in the plaid St. Olivia's kilt crossed slowly in front of our car. One girl wearing three-inch high heels that clomped like horse hooves on the asphalt noticed Whitney in the car and waved. Whitney pretended not to see her.

I needed a place to talk in private, someplace comfortable where I could try to regain her trust and pry the details of her webcam experiences out of her. A place that didn't remind her that everything she told me would be in a newspaper. That ruled out the newsroom. "You want to go back to that coffee shop?" I asked.

"Too many kids from school," she said stiffly.

"You want to go to Roger Williams?" This was the city's largest park.

She turned to me with a sudden ferocity. "Do you even really care about Lexie? Or are you just another user like Rurik?"

I felt a twinge that burned through my ribs. Reporters were the biggest users of them all.

The thing I hated about my job was that you had to get people to trust you. I was especially good at getting people to trust me—which hadn't worked out so well for all my sources. Especially in the Salazar investigation. But I couldn't think about that now. Instead, I said, "It's like this. I work for a newspaper, and I have a job to do. There's no getting away from that."

She stared at me, trying to gauge these words, convert them to a plus or a minus. She halted, without decision.

Was there anything worse than working a fifteen-year-old? I was programmed; I leapt right in. "You don't want to go to police yourself and tell them what you know. I understand that. But without you as a witness, the only way police will listen to me is if I put the story on the front page—and to do that, I need to know how it all happened."

The ash on her cigarette had grown so long that it spilled onto the floorboard. She ground the ash under her shoe, opened the window, and threw the butt onto the street. "Okay," she finally said. "Drive me home, the house is empty. We can talk there."

We sat down on stools at the granite counter that divided the great room from the kitchen. Whitney's house was on a side street off the Boulevard, not far from where Matt and I lived. She had assured me her parents wouldn't be home from work for at least three hours and her brother was at baseball practice, but I still kept my eye on the window that had a view of the driveway.

I left my digital recorder inside my backpack, but pulled out my notebook and pen. Whitney regarded the notebook with suspicion. I reassured her that I'd give her a fake name in the paper and never reveal her true identity—no matter what. "The more you can tell me about Rurik and these videos, the more details you can give me, the better chance I have of tracking him down and of proving that he's a bad guy."

"He's a bad guy, all right," Whitney said. As she got up and walked to the refrigerator to get herself a Diet Coke, I realized how thin she was, how scrawny the legs underneath the maroon kilt skirt. Perched on a pair of espadrilles, she hunched forward and leaned on the refrigerator door for balance. "You want one?" she asked.

"No, thanks." As I waited for her to fill a glass up to the brim with ice, I glanced over at a laptop set up below what looked like a cookbook shelf. It had a large screen, a webcam, and a sort of auxiliary drive that looked like a hardcover book. I'd also spotted a laptop in the great room, on a small desk near the plasma TV. Apparently, Whitney's father was some sort of software consultant.

When she finally sat down again, across from me, I said, "I need to know exactly how Rurik goes about being a bad guy. How he works. How he goes about getting young girls to . . ." I stopped myself, searching for a more delicate way to say *strip for the camera*. "Pose."

But even this disturbed her. Her gaze dropped to the countertop. There was a long, painful silence. "It starts off easy," she finally said. "It doesn't seem like any big deal."

"Can you explain it to me? A step-by-step kind of thing?"

But here the computer made a dinging sound, and Whitney's head jerked up. She pointed me toward the refrigerator. "Go stand over there and don't move . . . and don't say anything."

I grabbed my notebook and pen off the counter. For good measure, I kicked my backpack across the floor to the refrigerator, hoping like hell Whitney was accurate about the range of the webcam.

Whitney touched a button, and suddenly the head and shoulders of a woman in her late forties appeared in a window about a third the size of the laptop screen. She had the same narrow face, but with glasses. I couldn't tell whether her hair was brown or auburn like Whitney's, but her voice, which came out of the speaker, had the same low timbre. "Hi, honey. Josh has a game tonight."

"I figured."

"I left chili in a Tupperware in the refrigerator. You can heat it in the microwave and make some biscuits."

"Yeah."

"Don't skip dinner, Whitney." There was a tension in this command that made me scrutinize Whitney a second time. She was definitely underweight. "And your homework, have you started it?"

"Almost done," she said.

There was a moment of silence that suggested that her mother didn't believe her. I wondered if her mother could actually detect a lie in her daughter's eyes via webcam, or whether Whitney just always lied. Then her mom said, "You know, Dad's going to the game, so I could skip it if you want. If your homework's done, you and I could go out for dinner. Have a girls' night."

Whitney blew that off: "Thanks, Mom, but I've got too much math tonight. Go to the game, I'll see you when you get home."

There was silence again, and the two of them stared at each other, waiting, I think, for the other to say good-bye. Finally the mom said, "Okay, I'll be home by eight thirty unless there's extra innings, and we can go over the math if you want."

"Does she do that every day?" I asked after the screen had gone dark.

"Yeah," Whitney said. Then, just in case I had any questions about who was in charge, she stepped beside me, opened the refrigerator, and pulled out the Tupperware container full of chili. She walked to the sink and spooned it down the disposal.

I duly noted her defiance in my notebook. Also the family's use of the webcam as a parenting tool. A thought occurred to me. "Is this the webcam Rurik gave you?"

"This one my father bought," she said, pointing to the kitchen computer. "The one Rurik gave me I put upstairs in my room."

"Do you actually have a laptop in that bag?" I pointed to the fashion accessory that she carried her cigarettes around in.

"Not usually. It's upstairs. My brother and I each have one."

For my story, I needed the geography. I wanted to be able to describe her computer setup and the room where Whitney took her clothes off and posed when her parents thought she was doing her homework. "Can I see your room?" I asked.

She shrugged, and I followed her up two sets of stairs to a renovated third floor that might once have been the attic. It was a big room, but with a low, sloped ceiling over the two windows that faced the backyard. A bra and a pair of her underwear had been discarded on a white furry throw rug, and the queen bed was unmade. Another heap of clothes blocked the door to a bathroom. I finally spotted the laptop, which was on a white laminate desk in the corner, along with a webcam, printer, and cordless phone.

Whitney flopped down on the bed, which was underneath the low-ceiling part of the room. I took a seat across from her, at the desk. I touched the eyeball of the webcam and made an internal comparison to the equipment I'd seen at Best Price. I'd look it up on the Web later, but it looked like one of the more expensive models.

"Why did you want one?" I asked.

"I *thought* it would be a good way to meet boys."

"And was it?"

She snickered at this. "Like as soon as you get it, you start to get messages from all these new guys who want to be friends. Some of them tell you they are sixteen. But they're all like thirty or forty. But we talked back and forth, messaging and stuff. A lot of them were okay. Nicer than Rurik."

"Nice? How?"

"I don't know. Just nice." She was on her back on the bed, directing her answers to the ceiling instead of to me.

"I need to know how they were different from Rurik."

She stared up at the ceiling some more, grabbed a pillow, and bunched it under her head. I hated that I couldn't see her face, her expressions, but figured maybe it was easier for her to talk this way, spilling her guts to the ceiling instead of to an adult.

Finally, she said, "I guess because they wanted to know all about you. They remembered things you told them. You know. And they'd send you presents and stuff."

"What kind of presents?"

"Cool stuff. CDs. Some of that really nice body lotion from Body Works. Anything I asked for."

"What did you have to do?"

There was a long pause. I remained waiting until the silence itself was painful. "At first they just wanted to message, you know. Talk about stuff," she finally said.

At first were the key words. I underlined them in my notebook. "And then?"

There was another silence as she conducted some sort of internal debate. Finally, she sat up and pulled herself to the edge of her bed. She wasn't so much looking at me as looking past me, to the computer screen on the desk. "One of them offered to send me a hundred dollars if I just took off my sweater and sat in front of the webcam in my bra. I figured what the hell? I walk the beach in a bikini top and that's the same as a bra, right?" Her tone challenged me to argue, but I remained silent.

"The next day, he sent me a hundred-dollar gift certificate to the mall."

I had to quash a wave of flulike nausea. Force myself to ask the questions as if this were all matter-of-fact. "So it was easy money?" I asked.

"At first."

"And then?"

But here, she stopped again. She was still wearing her St. Olivia's uniform, and her gaze dropped to the plaid kilt spread across her knees. "Do you have to write all of this in the newspaper?"

"Not everything you tell me will be in the paper, but I need to know the whole story, so I know how to tell it."

"You want to see some of the stuff they bought me?" she asked. And without waiting for my response, she got up from the bed and walked over to the closet and pulled out a pair of cloth sandals with silver heels. An entwined *C* logo in black and silver patterned the cloth. "Aren't these psychotic?" she asked, waving them at me.

Psychotic apparently meant "cool." I studied the shoes. CHANEL was written on the insteps, for those of us who might have otherwise missed the fact that these were from an expensive designer. She handed me the shoes and dug farther into the closet and pulled out another pair. These were four-inch-high slingbacks with some sort of fake jewel across the open toe. These said JIMMY CHOO on the instep. "You want to try them on?" she offered.

What I wanted to do was photograph them with my cell phone camera. These would make killer art for the story. And I could also check their value on eBay. I placed the jeweled high heels on the desk next to the first pair and slipped my cell phone slowly out of my backpack. "Would you mind if I took a picture of these first?" I asked her.

"They're awesome, aren't they?" Consumer pride had apparently overtaken caution.

I nodded my admiration, snapped the picture quickly, kicked off my Hush Puppies, and slid the high heels on my feet. I made a big deal of admiring them before I asked, "And these guys sent you these for just taking your top off?"

She looked at me like I was crazy. "These are eight-hundred-dollar shoes."

I slipped them off my feet and, to show the required respect for footwear, placed them carefully together on the desk. "What did you have to do?"

She ignored the question. "If my mom saw these, she'd wonder where I got the money." Grabbing the shoes from the desk, she accidentally knocked my cell phone onto the floor. It landed underneath the radiator.

As I was extracting it, I found a dollar bill rolled up with what looked like powder on it. I looked up. Whitney, who was hiding the shoes deep in the closet, had her back toward me. Cocaine?

"Sorry," Whitney was saying as she sat back down on the bed. "I'm such a klutz."

"No problem," I said, but my brain was whirring. Did this explain her weight problem, or was Rurik jacking these girls up on drugs to get a better performance? I glanced around the room, looking at it in a whole new way. *Did she use that mirror on the night table to cut up coke?* I wondered. Or did she do it in the bathroom, turning on the shower to make sure no one came in?

"So what did you have to do to get the shoes?" I repeated.

"We made out for the camera," she said. "Me and Lexie. It was a goof."

"With your clothes on?"

"Sometimes. We did one on a beach, once. But that one wasn't that bad. Rurik called it a teaser."

"A teaser?"

"Just to get them interested."

"And other times?"

She didn't answer again.

"You took your clothes off?"

She nodded.

"And you went further than kissing."

"It's not like we were lesbians or anything. We did it because they got off on it. Not because we were into it."

My hands couldn't write fast enough. When I'd caught up my notes, I asked, "You get anything else from Rurik besides shoes?"

She didn't answer.

"He ever give you drugs?"

Still there was no response.

"Because if he gave you any drugs, the cops would definitely want to go after him on that alone."

Finally she said, "He always wanted Lexie to do coke. He said the guys liked us to look real skinny. But Lexie hated drugs. She said her mother had been an addict and that prostitutes are always junkies. She wouldn't do drugs."

"And you?"

"No, never." Then her gaze dropped to the floor. A long silence followed.

"Okay, but just . . . sometimes a line of coke made it a little easier," she finally said.

I had to quell another deep wave of revulsion. My brother Sean had died from cardiac arrhythmia caused by cocaine use. "When did you start doing these videos?" I asked.

"About a year ago, maybe." She still wasn't looking at me.

"And the coke?"

"Just a couple of months."

"And you got into this after you met Lexie on the Buzz?"

"Don't blame Lexie. She got all pissed off about the drugs. And the other stuff—she got me into it, but I'm to blame. It was my choice. We all thought it was kind of cool. You could get tons of money—"

"*We* all?"

She blinked the pale green eyes. "Lexie and me. Just Lexie and me. And after we became friends, *real* friends, Lexie wanted me to quit. She kept warning about Rurik and the drugs. In the last two or three weeks, she was on a rampage. Making me promise I'd stop going to the apart—" She cut herself off.

"Apartment? What apartment?"

She'd gone further than she wanted to.

"I thought you did this here." I pointed to her computer.

"The stuff I did alone. But . . . Lexie wouldn't come here. She was afraid of running into my mom. And there was this apartment we used to go to. That's where we'd do the web-cams together. Where we . . ." Her gaze drifted to the closet.

"Where?"

"Where we made extra money."

"For videos?"

She hesitated. "Sometimes Rurik would send over a couple of his friends. You know, to watch, while we did it. They gave us cash."

I had to struggle not to let shock or disgust show on my face. But I couldn't stop my brain. Couldn't stop from thinking, all this for *designer shoes*?

Maybe my gaze had shifted to the closet, or maybe Whitney

could just read my mind. Because she said, "Lexie thought the shoes were stupid."

I didn't know how to respond to this, so I just nodded.

"All she wanted was the money," Whitney went on. She sounded bitter about this. "And she never spent any of it. Not even for a soda at the mall."

I remembered what Whitney had said about Lexie wanting to run away from Rurik. "So maybe she just finally saved enough money to do it. To run away."

"No way," she said, standing up abruptly from the bed. She crossed the room, brushing past me to get to the desk, and opened the center drawer. She pulled out a cosmetic bag with a large poppy appliqué. I unzipped the bag.

"Oh my God," I said. It was filled with one-hundred-dollar bills. Seven of them.

"This is Lexie's money," Whitney said. "She had me hold it so Rurik couldn't steal it from her. If she was planning to run away from him, she would have gotten this from me first."

8

Seven hundred dollars in cash. Eight-hundred-dollar shoes and cocaine. I left Whitney's house feeling that I wanted to rip every last bit of her computer equipment out of her house.

It was too late to go back to the newsroom, but too early for Matt to be home. I went back to the condo, alone in that weird empty hour of the afternoon, hyped up on anger and determination.

I tried to go over my notes from my interview with Whitney but was too restless. Having left my notebook on the dining room table, I began pacing to the corduroy couch in the living room, going back and forth, trying to figure out my next move.

I was going to alert the world to that dirtbag Rurik. Shut down his operation and hopefully send him to jail. The hardwood floor creaked with my outrage. To the couch and back again.

I thought of something Whitney had said. She hadn't had an address for the apartment, but she had remembered the color of the building. If I could actually find that apartment, I could convince Dorothy to let us put it under surveillance.

I grabbed my notebook from the dining room table and began flipping through my interview notes to the end, where Whitney had been talking about the apartment.

Providence, I had written, with a question mark. Second floor. Tall house. Three-decker with another question mark. Yellow, maybe gold. Rusty mailbox. Big driveway. Dead end.

Then below, I'd scribbled: *See bay.*

I squinted at that a minute before I remembered. She'd said it was possible to see the Narragansett Bay from the bathroom window. The ugly part, she'd said. With the tanks.

She must have meant the Port of Providence, the industrial section at the southern tip of the city, where big white tanks full of gasoline and heating fuel rose along the waterfront. A vast industrial complex now monitored by Homeland Security.

It had occurred to me that Walter might have a good idea of the residential neighborhoods in the Port of Providence area. He drove cab, for God's sake. How many dead-end streets could there be with a view of the tanks?

I took my cell phone out of my back pocket and skirted around the dining room table to the bay window, where we got the best reception.

The window looked out on Elmgrove Avenue, a busy side street that fed into Wayland Square, a retail area with a bookstore, pharmacy, and overpriced market. From my old apartment building, which was across the street, I'd had a good view of the square, but from here, I couldn't see any of the stores, only the cars desperately hunting the side streets for parking.

I got Walter's voice mail and hung up.

One of the cars below, a Camry, late-'90s shade of blue, made an illegal U-turn at Angell Street to drive back down the other side of Elmgrove. The car slowed in front of our building, then sped up.

I'd seen a blue Camry parked in front of Whitney's house when I'd left there a half hour ago. Was it the same one?

As I was standing there frozen, a foot away from the window, I happened to spot another blue Camry whizzing down Angell Street. This one was newer, a more periwinkle blue than the teal, but it reminded me that every other car in Rhode Island was a Camry, for God's sake.

And a lot of cars slowed down to view the Victorian architecture of this building, the cool turret, and period-detail painting. Probably I was overreacting.

But then the original late-'90s Camry appeared again, making its third swing past the house. There wasn't a hint of an open parking space on either side of the street, and yet the car traveled at a snail's pace. It came to a halt directly below.

I could see someone, a man, craning his head, looking upward. I pulled away from the window.

I had no idea how big Rurik's operation was, but there had to be serious money at stake. Not to mention, if caught, he'd either be deported or sent to jail as a sexual offender. He had plenty of incentive to want to shut me up.

Or at least try to intimidate me.

The cell phone was still in my hand. It rang. It was Walter calling me back.

"What's up?" he asked.

A lot of things. Only now I heard myself say, "I'm ready to make good on my promise."

"Why?" Walter was immediately suspicious. "What's going on?"

I told him about the blue Camry that was now disappearing into the square. "I think maybe you're right. It might be useful to learn how to use a gun."

"Can I try this one?" I pointed to a pretty silver .22-caliber pistol that was in Walter's fishing case of handguns. It was between a .38-caliber revolver Walter strapped to his ankle when he drove cab and the nine-millimeter Glock that he had bought himself for Christmas.

We were at the American Firearms School in North Attleboro, a warehouse of a building with a dozen shooting stations, each with its own target on a pulley system. It reminded me vaguely of a bowling alley, only everyone wore yellow safety glasses and ear protection and had to shout their greetings over the bullet fire.

"I brought that one for . . . ," Walter said. We both were wearing ear protection that looked like a pilot's headset. I heard his words as if through upholstery.

"What?" I asked.

"Just for learning!" he shouted again. "For learning. Not good protection." Then he said something else I couldn't make out.

The range was deep, going back about one hundred feet. Walter pushed a button, and the pulley brought the paper target back ten feet, which appeared to be beginner distance. At a small table opposite the range, Walter readied the gun. Carefully pointing it to the floor, he walked it over to me. Then he demonstrated how to use the little red laser beam to aim.

I took the gun, aimed carefully, and pulled the trigger. I felt a little rush as the bullet fired from the gun. And then a bigger one when I realized it hit the bull's-eye.

Walter was not so impressed. He'd already loaded the nine-millimeter Glock and was handing it to me.

This gun was bigger, blacker, and not pretty at all. It was also absent the helpful red laser beam. I aimed at the target just as carefully, but it took more strength to pull the trigger.

The muzzle of the gun lifted out of my hand, and the force of the propulsion sent a shock wave up my arm. The bullet missed the paper target and hit the metal target holder instead. The whole apparatus fell to the ground.

The shooting range was a busy place. People on both sides of us stopped to see what the hell had happened.

Walter was laughing.

I gave him the finger.

He took the gun from me and demonstrated how to push the heel of the gun deeper into my right palm. Then he placed my left hand over the three fingers of my grip to increase the pressure. "Steady," he mouthed.

The trigger was easier to pull the second time, but after about a half hour of coaching, I still couldn't shoot a bullet that actually hit the paper. If I could have thrown the gun in frustration, I would have, but I wasn't allowed even that much satisfaction. There was a whole safety process. I had to open the slide, point it to the ground, and hand it carefully back to Walter.

On the way out, he picked up some brochures about firearms courses. I was stunned to learn how long it would take before I could legally own or use a gun for protection. "Forget it. There's a reason I run road races and don't play tennis," I told him. "I have absolutely no eye-hand coordination."

"Come back with me next week, just one more time, and I promise you'll get a lot better."

I couldn't believe that Walter really thought I'd ever improve my shooting. I was starting to suspect that he was lonely since his breakup with Geralyn and just needed company.

I relented. "I'll give it one more time. But you've got to do one thing for me."

"This sounds like it might be in Washington Park to me," Walter said as we bypassed our exit and headed toward the Port of Providence.

Washington Park was a mostly middle-class neighborhood on the southeastern edge of Providence. The part I was thinking of, toward Narragansett Boulevard, had large Victorian homes and an occasional carriage house. It didn't seem the kind of neighborhood where you'd go for a live sex show.

Walter turned onto Allens Avenue, which was a much more likely location. It was an ugly exit from the city, an industrial thoroughfare that was under major reconstruction with the relocation of the highway overhead. There were cement abutments, partially constructed overhead ramps, and a lot of large windowless industrial buildings that had been converted into strip clubs.

"So in an average week, how many total perverts do you drive here?" I asked.

"Not every guy I drive to a strip club or even a porn shop is a pervert, you know. They're just male, that's all."

"How many?"

"I don't know. Depends on the week. And if there's any kind of convention in town, could be ten. Could be fifty."

"Ick," I said.

There was a long silence as we waited at the light. I had another thought. "What percent of men you know watch porn on the Internet?"

"A hundred."

"A hundred percent? Come on."

He shrugged. "Guys I know, anyway."

"You're telling me that a hundred percent of the guys you know would pay to watch young girls—"

"I didn't say that. Not kiddie porn. There's enough other porn on the Internet, and most of it's free."

"Well, that's a relief, I guess."

We continued south on Allens Avenue, and the boatyards and strip clubs began to disappear. A few residential side streets emerged. It occurred to me that the beach video of Lexie and Whitney had been free, a teaser to drive customers to the cash business, the live webcam shows.

"Turn here," I ordered.

Because of the way the bay elbowed, nearly all the houses on the left side of this street would have a view of the tanks from their back windows. One of the three-family houses was painted yellow, but it had a neat, owner-occupied look to it, with a swing set in the yard. There was no rental sign or rusted mailbox.

We were in Walter's cab, and since it was Saturday, people were in their yards. Heads turned as everyone tried to figure out who was getting dropped off or picked up. One guy who was weeding a patch of grass near the sidewalk stood and pretended to hail us. Walter ignored him.

He turned the car around in someone's driveway. Then instead of returning all the way to Allens Avenue, he made a left. We came upon an entire grid of side streets that dead-ended with a metal barricade and the bay. Blocks and blocks of houses, all with potential bathroom views of both the water and the industrial tanks. At least two dozen of these were multifamily homes, and at least ten were painted some variation of yellow.

We drove up and down five or six streets that all dead-ended on the bay but could not find a yellow house with a rental sign or a rusty mailbox.

"Fuck this," Walter finally said. "You need to call that girl again. We're never going to get anywhere this way."

Walter and I stopped at the Sea Plane Diner for lunch. I had a BLT and a short phone conversation with Whitney.

She said she thought the street was "one way" but wasn't completely sure. I repeated some of the street names to her—they were all named for the states—but she recognized none of them.

"You think if we drove together around these neighborhoods, you'd be able to point out the building to me?" I asked.

"Maybe," she said. It was almost two o'clock in the afternoon, but it sounded as if she'd just woken up.

"You doing anything after school on Monday?"

"I've got a detention," she said.

"Afterward?"

"My mother is taking me to some stupid therapist."

Hopefully it was a therapist skilled enough to convince her to address her webcam adventures and her cocaine use. "How about tonight around seven o'clock? Before it gets dark?"

There were a few minutes of silence while she considered this.

"My parents will be at Josh's baseball game. You can pick me up at my house."

It seemed like we'd been up and down every state in the union at least three times. Oklahoma Street. Washington Street. Nevada Street. We were in the right neighborhood. That much Whitney knew. She recognized the crowded two-families, the multitude of swing sets, and the steady sea breeze that fluttered the wind socks and chimes on every other front porch.

But after a half hour of driving around and smoking no fewer than three cigarettes, she began to question whether the apartment had been in a yellow house after all. "Maybe it was more of an ivory color," she said. "This color." She pointed to her shorts.

They were more of a pale pink, I thought. It was a warm evening, and in the teenage tradition, she was wearing almost nothing. A sleeveless racerback top, the incredibly short shorts, and metallic purple flip-flops.

"Maybe the industrial tanks were farther away than you thought," I suggested. The white cylindrical storage tanks that rose from the Port of Providence could be seen from any number of neighborhoods south of the city. And probably from some parts of Warwick, I thought dismally. We would never find this apartment.

Whitney shrugged, as if to say she really had no concept of distance. It occurred to me that she'd probably been so high on alcohol and cocaine when she was here, the apartment could be in Boston, for all she knew.

It was past seven thirty, and the day was fading into a dusty gray light, but I decided to give it one last try. We headed farther south on Allens Avenue to what appeared to be the last bayside street still in Providence. It looked like all the others to me, but Whitney lifted out of her slumping position and began peering intently out the window.

"We're getting close." She stamped out her cigarette in the ashtray.

We drove down to the very end of the street, where a tall wooden barrier and a metal fence blocked off the bay. The last house on both sides of the street would have a waterfront in their side yards, but you could probably see the storage tanks from the upper floors of every house on the block.

"That's it," Whitney said. "That's the house."

It wasn't yellow or ivory, but an ugly mustard color, with a faded 4-RENT sign plastered to one of the lower windows. The building looked like a run-down boarding house, with missing clapboards, a bowed front porch, and an exterior staircase in the back. There were at least four floors, and judging by the multiple and rusted mailboxes on the porch, at least that many units.

"This is where Rurik brought his friends? You're sure?"

She tossed her cigarette butt out the open window. "I'm sure."

I'd been writing in my notebook and taking down salient details. Correct address, phone number on the 4-RENT sign, number of cars in the small adjacent parking lot. Now I looked up.

She was no longer looking out the window, but down into the car, past her lap. At first I thought she was staring at her painted toenails, but then I saw the small bruise on the side of her thigh. It looked like a thumbprint.

"You okay?"

She put her palm over the bruise. "Yeah." The tone was defiant, but not particularly convincing.

She lifted her gaze to one of the upper floors of the building, where a yellowish light flicked on behind a drawn shade.

Then her head came down swiftly, as if she couldn't bear that view. But she wouldn't turn back to me, wouldn't let me see her face.

"Did any of those guys ever do anything to you?" I asked softly. "Did they ever do more than just watch?"

She didn't answer.

"These men, they could be prosecuted just for being there. And police could put Rurik in jail, if you'd give them their names."

But she shook her head before I even finished. "I don't know their names. Besides, these guys are like really rich. They know people."

"*Knowing* people doesn't help when you're a sex offender."

There was another silence. And then: "I deserve what I got. I . . . I got other girls to come with me . . . young girls . . . who shouldn't have been there."

"None of you should have been there. And whatever mistake you might have made, you're too young to deserve this," I said. "These guys. They—"

"I made money," she said softly. "A lot of money."

"That doesn't give them the right . . ."

She lifted both hands, splayed, to silence me.

I wanted to repeat that it wasn't her fault. That she had the power to put these guys in jail. But her left hand was still lifted up, warning me not to try to reach her.

She closed her eyes, as if looking inward with loathing. It was too painful to watch. I shifted my gaze back to the house and the small paved lot beside it. One of the half-dozen cars parked there was blue. A Camry.

"Does Rurik drive a Camry?" I asked.

"What?" Her eyes opened wide with alarm.

"Look, over there. That blue car, does that look familiar?" I asked.

She peered at the car only a moment. "Let's get out of here."

I pulled past the house toward the barricade and made a U-turn at the end of the street. But then I realized what I'd missed. I put the car in park.

"What are you doing?" Whitney asked.

"I'll just be a minute." Grabbing my pen and notebook, I got out of the car and walked about ten feet into the driveway and quickly copied down the license plate numbers of the cars. Then I turned, ran back to the car, and jumped inside.

"What the fuck were you doing?" Whitney screamed at me. She had slouched down so that her entire lower body was on the floor and only her shoulders leaned against the seat. "Get the hell out of here."

"All right. All right." I put the car in drive.

I drove fast down the street, but had to stop at the intersection of Allens Avenue, waiting for a break in the traffic.

"Just go," Whitney said.

"What are you worried about?" I was checking behind me in the rearview mirror; no one was following us.

"I saw him," she said.

"Who? Rurik?"

"I saw him, upstairs in the window. He snapped open the shade and was looking down at the car. He saw you take down the license plates."

"Are you sure it was Rurik?"

"Are you kidding? I could see his bleach job the minute he opened the window. I ducked before he saw me. But it was definitely Rurik. I saw him. And he saw you."

9

"**Who are you** looking for?" Matt asked.

"What?" I pulled away from the window and let the curtain fall from my fingers.

"You've been at that window all morning, Hallie."

The bay window in the dining room had the best view. You could see the cars on both Elmgrove Avenue and Angell Street. "I'm just checking to see if the rain has finally let up."

"Right."

Matt had been making coffee in the kitchen, where he'd apparently been keeping an eye on me through the archway. Now he was standing on the other side of the table, with two mugs in his hand. He placed them on one of his legal pads so they wouldn't leave water rings and stood, waiting for a more believable answer.

He didn't have a lot of time to wait. Although it was Sunday, he had pulled the weekend shift and had to be to work in half an hour. I left the window to grab my coffee from the table. He waited while I took a sip.

I considered telling him about Rurik. The Camry I'd seen before. The bleached-blond head watching me take down license plate numbers outside his awful apartment. "What would you think about my learning to use a handgun?"

"You're kidding, right?"

I explained to him about going to the shooting range with Walter yesterday, and about how I'd take a comprehensive course, and get licensed and everything.

"Are you crazy, Hallie? I don't want a gun in my home. And why the hell do you feel like you need one? What's going on?"

Still, I hesitated. I'd completely freaked Matt out last time when I'd gotten into trouble with the Salazar investigation. If I told him about Rurik stalking the condominium, he'd insist I file a complaint. He might even get state police to follow me around.

"Nothing. Walter's just really into the gun thing. And he's lonely, you know, since his breakup with Geralyn. He's trying to get me into it, so he has someone to go to the shooting range with him."

His eyes flashed with irritation, which he struggled to conceal by walking past me to the window. He scanned the street below for an unnecessary length of time, I thought. As if to accent that he didn't believe me.

I told myself that there was no need to alarm Matt. There hadn't been any blue Camry below, either last night or this morning.

"I hate this," Matt said, finally turning away from the window. I pretended not to know what he meant.

"That you can't tell me when you feel threatened by some-one."

"No one has threatened me," I said.

"I hate that you won't let me do anything to protect you. That you feel that you need a gun."

He was so plaintive, so sincere. All he wanted was honesty. I should have just come clean about Rurik. Should have dealt with whatever Matt wanted to do to protect our home. But I thought first of the story, and how I'd never be able to do sur-veillance on that apartment, never capture the comings and go-ings of the young girls if I had a state police cruiser on my tail.

So instead, I walked to the window, slipped my arms around him, and gave him the only promise I had to give. "I hated shoot-ing, honest. And I have no reason to get a gun. I promise you, I won't bring one into this house."

That afternoon, Matt called me from work. "I've got to stay late. Do you know who's got the weekend shift at the paper?"

It was almost two o'clock. We were supposed to leave for din-ner at my mother's in Worcester in an hour. I was in the kitchen unloading the dishwasher, and I had a handful of spoons. I dropped them into the drawer.

"Jonathan Frizell is covering." I knew this because origi-nally I'd been scheduled to work, too, but when I'd found out Matt was on call this weekend, I'd had to switch. This was to try to prevent a situation that led to me going to Matt for in-formation in an official capacity. "Why, what's going on?"

There was silence on the end of the phone. An overly princi-pled silence, since I wasn't about to call our online editor to get a news flash on the Web site *before* the press conference. But maybe this was retaliation for not confiding in him this morning.

The silence meant it had to be a decent story. Shit. Leave it to real news to break on Frizell's weekend. I overturned the silverware rack and shook it over the counter, trying to loosen a fork that was stuck. It fell to the floor and landed underneath the butcher block table. "Is it an arrest?"

He wouldn't even give me this. "I'm going to have to miss dinner at your mother's tonight. Can you give her my apologies?"

Missing dinner at my mother's was no big deal. More of a big deal was that of all the people I could have switched with this weekend, I switched with Jonathan Frizell. It had to be some sort of major arrest for police to hold a press conference on a *Sunday.* "Can you tell me if it's front-page material?"

"For a Monday?"

Although posited as a question, this was actually an answer. A reminder that even criminals and drunks took it easy on Sundays, which made Monday a tough news hole to fill. Anything that required a press conference would make Monday's front page.

I told myself it didn't matter. I was too busy with my own investigation anyway—which was certain to be a much bigger story. This reminded me that I should check my e-mail messages. Whitney had given me a new e-mail address for Lexie, and I'd written to tell her that I was really a reporter and offer any help she might need. I let Matt get back to work, picked up the fork from the floor, and returned to the dining room, where I'd set up my laptop. I scanned through my messages, but it was mostly spam.

I nearly stopped breathing three-quarters of the way down the list when I spotted this e-mail return address: 4YOUROWNGOOD@mail.ru.

Since the paper now ran our e-mail addresses after pretty much every story, I got all kinds of crazy e-mails from readers. But I knew from experience that the capital letters usually meant the entire message would be in capital letters. A diatribe from some angry whack job.

Lots of times I deleted them without opening the e-mail. But not today.

There was no salutation, no name.

It said: *Stay away from the girls. Butt out.*

Whenever I looked up from my desk the next day, Jonathan Frizell was marching from one end of the newsroom to another with his stout body erect and that insufferable expression of self-importance on his face. He was hovering over the City Desk, harassing Dorothy, or dashing back and forth to the Online department, no doubt conferring with Corey Weist as well.

There had been no arrest, but at the press conference last night, Providence police had warned that there was a new "killer stream" of heroin flooding the state. Four junkies had died of overdoses in six days. All were believed to be shooting the same 70 percent pure heroin, supposedly imported from Afghanistan.

The story had been page one, but under the fold, at least. The high number was unusual, but heroin overdoses were nothing new in Rhode Island, which was right along the pipeline from New York to Boston.

I thought about something Lexie had told Whitney: that she'd seen a lot of prostitutes become junkies. At least she was smart about drugs. If Whitney was to be believed.

I was hoping that the word got out quick, the overdoses ceased, and the drama of this story evaporated. I needed the entire investigative team ready for surveillance on that apartment. If Jonathan got too deep into this, he'd blow the whole thing out of proportion with special features on everything from the growth of drug use in the suburbs to the economy of Afghanistan since the Taliban. He'd be useless to me.

Later that afternoon, Frizell managed to finagle a news meeting with Nathan, the editor in chief, and Corey, who was now invited to every meeting. For God knows what reason, the publisher, Ian Clew, came down from the fourth floor, too. The four of them huddled together on the near end of the conference table. Jonathan, who was facing in my direction, tilted his head, squinting between the tropical fish cutouts pasted to the glass. He was trying to see who was around to witness what a big deal this story was.

"You heard back from Bennett on any of those license plate numbers?" Ellen asked. Trying to get a better view of the Fishbowl, she'd wandered over to my desk.

"Not yet," I answered.

Inside the Fishbowl, Ian Clew, who was deceptively boyish, even in designer suits and those thin-soled Italian shoes, seemed especially animated. He gesticulated with his pen and flipped through something that looked like a chart.

"Why is Ian coming down for news meetings?" I asked.

Ellen's husband was an editorial writer, with an office on the fourth floor. He often knew things. "That new issue of *Rhode Island Monthly* came out today."

I shrugged. What the hell did that mean?

"The one with Jason Keriotis on the cover. The one with the article where he brags about how he's captured all the local online revenue for the Buzz. And that print media is dead. Ian wants to bury him."

"Ah." Now I remembered Dorothy telling me about the upcoming issue and its effect on Ian's psyche. At least he was actually drawing a connection between online ad revenue and improved news content. That was a good sign.

"Look down at your keyboard," Ellen ordered. "Jonathan's watching us. Don't give him the satisfaction."

We huddled in front of my laptop screen, pretending to be reading something together. Then, immediately, we shifted our focus back to the Fishbowl.

Ellen said, "Maybe what we need to do is barge in. Expand this heroin thing into a team investigation, so we all get an angle on it. Your boyfriend have any idea where this shit is coming from?" Everyone in the newsroom now referred to Matt only by this distinction. He no longer had a name; he was now only *your boyfriend*.

"If he did and he told me, do you think I'd be on this side of the Fishbowl right now?"

Ellen had pale, almost blond eyebrows that faded into her face. But she had the ability to lift just one in a perfect expression of cynicism. "Oh right, I forgot, you guys don't *share* information."

Just then Dorothy stood up at the City Desk and marched down the center of the newsroom. As soon as she poked her head into the Fishbowl, everyone at the table stood up at once.

"Some new development. Probably an arrest. I'll go find out," Ellen said. She made her way to the City Desk and grabbed

Dorothy's assistant. After a couple of minutes, she returned with the scoop.

"No arrest," she said. "Another OD. Real sad. Some teenager."

I got a real cold feeling deep in my stomach. "Girl or boy?"

"A girl. Some little tenth-grader at St. Olivia's."

10

The death notice said Whitney had died "suddenly" late Sunday night, but there was no mention of an overdose. The funeral would be Thursday at St. Sebastian's Catholic Church. Calling hours at the East Side funeral home were Wednesday evening. Donations could be made in Whitney's name to the St. Olivia's scholarship fund.

"Are you all right?" the intern asked.

I was standing next to the fax machine with Whitney's death notice in my hand and a scattered pile of discarded faxes around me on the floor. The intern was new and I didn't know her name, but it was her job to sort through the death notices, and I had just made a terrible mess of them.

I dropped to my knees to pick up the faxes, eyes on the floor. There were a dozen sheaves of paper. Half of them carrying the story of a life expired. Except that all those other lives were older lives. Much older lives.

"Is it that girl at St. O's?" I heard the intern ask.

That afternoon, the principal had refused to come out of an inner office. She'd sent word, via the receptionist, that she was not prepared at this time to make a statement to the press. "Can you just tell me the name of the girl who died?" I'd begged. "Just a name and I'll go away." But I got nothing except an escort out of the building.

"Here, let me help you with those faxes." Dorothy was suddenly standing over me. I was still on my knees, the papers scattered everywhere. She crouched beside me, picked them all up, and handed them to the intern. Then she put her hand under my elbow to guide me to a standing position.

"Did you know that girl from St. O's?" she asked.

I handed her Whitney's death notice.

She sat on the edge of the intern's desk and read it. For a moment, she appeared puzzled. Then the connection flickered in her eye. "Not your source?"

I nodded.

"She was a junkie?"

"She *wasn't* a junkie."

"Didn't you tell me that this dirtbag pornographer *gave* her cocaine?"

"But she didn't do heroin," I heard myself explain. "She was adamant about that."

I had this weird disembodied sensation, oddly analytical of my own response. Of course Whitney would lie to me. I was an adult, an authority figure. Fair game.

Dorothy didn't say anything, but the look in her eyes reiterated that I was being naïve. Then, as her news brain began clicking, her expression changed. "That Rurik guy? You think he might be the source of this potent stuff that's killing everyone?"

"She didn't say anything about him being a dealer."

Dorothy glanced at the intern, then past her to the quad of desks where several city reporters sat together. Her gaze shifted farther back into the newsroom. Finally, back to me. "You probably aren't up to calling police on this, but I need someone to look into it, so I'm going to have to pass this information to Jonathan."

Maybe she did this intentionally, knowing that the best way to jostle a reporter out of shock was to try to take a story away from her. But in a sudden, jerking motion, I grabbed the death notice out of her hand.

I owed it to Whitney to find out exactly what killed her. "This is my story now," I said. "I'll call police myself."

The Providence Public Safety Complex rises over the highway with three stories of steel and glass and a triangular atrium, reminiscent of a bow of a boat, steering right into three lanes of traffic.

Inside, it's a stark, cold building, with lots of granite and security, a feeling of rules that could not be broken. Major Carl Holstrom was already waiting for me in the lobby when I got through the metal detector, and he had to use a special set of keys at least twice before we made it up to his office.

Holstrom, who ran the investigative division, was not a particularly large man. But he still loomed large, with a stiff posture, a just-under-the-skin aggression, and a low brow over blue eyes that perpetually scanned the room. We'd gotten off to a rough start when I was covering the Mazursky murder a couple of years back. But since then, I'd earned a begrudging trust. This meant that he took my calls; it did not mean that he answered my questions.

Even as he led me to his office, he checked his watch. This was to remind me that he had many more important things to do than waste time with a reporter.

I had no intention of keeping him long. All I wanted to know was whether police knew for sure that Whitney had overdosed on the high-potency heroin, and if they'd made any progress in finding out where this heroin was coming from.

Carl's new office was a huge upgrade from the one in the old police building. Here, he had a corner office with a view of the Gothic towers of the Cathedral hovering over the highway. Holstrom sat down behind a mahogany desk. The chair I took was actual leather.

"So where's Frizell? I thought he was covering this?"

"He needed a little help," I said, trying to sound nonchalant. I didn't want to tip him off that I'd been working on a separate investigation involving Whitney. "And I'm curious about the girl. I heard she went to St. Olivia's?"

"Believe me. She wouldn't be the first East Side girl to go down the wrong path."

"Was she shooting it?" I'd been thinking of the rolled dollar bill under her desk, and that maybe, maybe, Whitney had snorted heroin, mistaking it for cocaine.

Carl swiveled around in his chair to a credenza behind him and picked up a file, probably from Narcotics, placing it before him on the desk. He leafed through several papers to get the details on the case. "Says here that she was found with the works on the floor next to her."

I was trying to process this picture of Whitney. Saturday evening she'd been wearing a sleeveless shirt. Could I have missed track marks in her arms?

Carl Holstrom was now regarding me with a look of curiosity. "Probably got hooked up with some dirtbag boyfriend who taught her the ropes," he said slowly.

"Right," I said.

He was watching me intently now, eyes alert.

I tried to sound matter-of-fact. "And you think it was the high-potency stuff?"

He nodded. "The toxicology reports will take a couple of weeks, but the ME seemed to think it was likely." Then he dipped his head back into the file for a minute. "And it says here only two glassine bags found on the scene."

Even with my limited knowledge of heroin use, I knew this was a small dose. Maybe Whitney hadn't been lying to me, maybe this had been her first time.

For an instant, I saw her standing in her bedroom, fondling her Chanel shoes, feeling smart and street tough, ready for the world ahead of her. Then it dissolved and I was in the police station talking to a cop about her death. I scribbled into my notebook, pretending I was still writing. I needed another minute to compose myself. "Any leads on where this stuff is coming from?" I finally said.

"Be a lot easier if one of these ODs survived," he said. I took this to mean no.

"Who found her?" I finally asked.

I had been picturing Whitney at home, sitting on the toilet of her bathroom, legs sprawled in front of her, nodding for eternity, and hoping that it wasn't her poor mom who found her. But Carl still hadn't answered. Something was up.

"Was she at home?"

Finally, he looked up from the file. "Look, she was victim number five in less than a week. There's definitely some bad heroin out there. That's your story."

When a cop tries to define your story for you, you know you've hit some kind of nerve. "*Where* she was found dead is pretty basic. I assume this would be in the police report." This was my way of reminding him that the information was public record.

"Don't you think her parents have suffered enough?" he responded.

Okay, so there was definitely something big here we needed to report. "I will keep that in mind when I take this information back to my editor, but I can't just ignore the news."

He wasn't going to tell me any more than he had to, so he offered only what was required by law: He pulled a sheaf of paper out of a file and pushed it across the desk.

I picked it up. It was handwritten instead of typed. Slanted writing that lost strength at the end of each word. *L rest. r,* I read. *Mall.* It took me a minute to piece it all together. Whitney had died where she loved to live. At the mall.

I read this three times, and still the data would not compute. Why the hell would Whitney go to the mall to do heroin? A drug she'd claimed to fear. "What time of day was this?"

Carl explained that the cleaning crew had discovered her after hours. In the ladies' room. Already dead. The needle, works, and empty glassine packets on a cold, impersonal tile floor.

And all by herself in a bathroom stall? "Isn't it weird that she was alone?" I asked.

"Junkies have a habit of not sticking around when things go south," Carl said dryly.

"What did she tell her parents?" I asked.

He looked at me, confused.

"Before she left for the mall, I mean? What did she tell them?"

"I don't know. I could take a huge leap here. That she was going shopping?"

"By herself? Or was she meeting someone?"

I'd forgotten to sound matter-of-fact. The watchful look returned to his eye. "You'd have to talk to the parents to find that out. You're awfully interested in this girl," he said.

"She's fifteen. Dead at the mall," I said. The public-place aspect of the story made it bigger. Holstrom knew that, which was why he'd stalled in giving that information.

"No. There's more to it than that."

Our eyes met. Carl had guessed that I was working on a bigger story. That I had more information than he did. "People are dying here, Hallie, and if we can cut off the source of this shit, we can save a few lives."

I could hear Jonathan Frizell's supercilious tone clear as a bell. If we come across someone drowning in the pond, our job is to take the picture, not save the victim. But this was a fifteen-year-old.

"Hallie?"

Dorothy would kill me for giving information to the cops. I hated this about my job. Always reporting that the world was coming apart, never doing anything to stop it from unraveling.

"The syringe, can you get prints off it?"

His eyebrows lifted. "Why?"

"Look, she was a source. Telling me things people don't want in the newspaper. It's possible someone might want to shut her up."

"What kind of things?"

"Nothing to do with heroin trafficking," I said.

"You got a name for that 'someone'?"

Yeah, I had a name. But I couldn't give it to him. I shook my head.

"How about a physical description?"

A scrawny middle-aged man bleaching his hair blond so that he'd look younger to teenagers. You can find him at the Best Price. More than anything I wanted to help Holstrom find Rurik and lock him up. Throw away the fucking key. "I have no idea," I had to say.

Carl stared at me a few minutes, trying to figure out what I was holding back. Then he shifted gears. "So what? You think someone followed her to the mall and stuck a syringe in her?"

"I think it's possible."

"This *someone*—you think she could have been dealing for him?"

Whitney could have been lying to me about trying heroin, but I couldn't see her dealing it. "Not from what she said to me."

"Was she worried about this *someone* you keep talking about? Was she scared enough to run away?"

This was a new twist. "Why do you ask that?"

"Can we go off the record?" he asked. "I don't want to see this in tomorrow's paper."

I nodded.

"She had seven hundred dollars in cash on her," he said.

Seven hundred dollars was the exact amount of money she'd been holding for Lexie.

The absolute worst part of being a reporter is when you are assigned to invade a family's shock and grief to ask them how they "feel" about the tragic death of a loved one.

Having lost my brother Sean, I know how these people feel about it, of course. They "feel" that all their organs have been ripped from their bodies and they are left as a shell of their former selves. They "feel" that at this time of all times, they deserve some privacy. And they "feel" that you are some sort of bottom-feeder, jumping to exploit the horrible event that has forever altered their lives.

But since Whitney had died in a public place, there was no way to avoid this story. Dorothy wanted me to contact the cleaning person who found her, the corporation that owned the mall, and Whitney's parents.

Back at my desk, I decided to get the worst part over first. If I used a newsroom phone to call the O'Connors' home, her parents would see the *Chronicle* come up on caller ID and let the answering machine take the call. Then I wouldn't have to talk to anyone. I could leave a message with my phone number and ask them to call *me* if they had anything they wanted to add to the story for tomorrow's paper. When they didn't call back, I could simply say "the family declined comment" and officially be off the hook.

Luckily, the O'Connors' home phone number was listed in the directory. Even as I punched in the numbers, anxiety shot through my veins. Certainly a family that routinely communicated with each other via webcam had caller ID on the phone. And certainly at a time like this, a helpful relative would be screening their calls.

The phone had a thin, high-pitched ring. I wondered if the voice mail was rigged through their computer service. I imagined the number coming up on a computer screen as well as the phone itself. *The Providence Chronicle,* someone would say out loud. *What kind of vultures are they?*

The phone rang four more times. What if the family had turned off its answering machine? Then I'd have to keep calling back all night, harassing these poor people until deadline.

"Hello?" the real voice, a male, startled me.

"I'm . . . ah . . . really sorry to intrude at a time like this," I stuttered. "My name is Hallie Ahern. I'm calling from the *Chronicle*." I paused, expecting him to hang up.

But he didn't hang up. He waited.

"I realize you probably don't want to talk right now, and I want to start by offering my condolences. I'm assigned to write the story about . . ." I stopped and had to force myself to push out the next words. "About Whitney's death. And I didn't want to just write what the police said. I wanted to give the family a chance to comment."

There was silence at the end of the phone.

"If you want to. Of course, I totally understand if you want your privacy, but I wanted to give you the opportunity—"

"My sister wasn't some junkie," he said.

Ah. Her brother. I grabbed a pen. What was his name again? Jordan? Joshua? Was he eighteen years old? Old enough to quote by name? "I'd be happy to write that in the story. Can you tell me your name and age?"

It was Joshua. And he was eighteen years old. Fair game.

"So this was an awful shock then."

"She wasn't perfect. But she didn't do heroin." I noticed here that he didn't say that Whitney didn't do drugs, but specified heroin. I felt a flutter of hope: Did this mean that Whitney confided in him?

"Do you know if she was supposed to be with friends? Or who she was meeting at the mall?" I asked.

"She lied to my mother. We found that out. We think she was really meeting that weird girl from . . ."

I heard a female voice behind him. "Who are you talking to, Joshua?"

"Someone from the *Chronicle*," he said.

"Oh, Joshua." Even muffled, you could hear the pain. Then there was the sound of a phone shifting hands.

"We have nothing to say to the paper at this time. Absolutely nothing."

It was Whitney's mother. I recognized her voice from the webcam.

"I'm so sorry for your loss," I said. But she didn't hear me. The phone was already dead in my hand.

The Providence Chronicle Online

East Side Teen Dies of Overdose

St. Olivia's to Offer Counseling

BY HALLIE AHERN

staff writer

PROVIDENCE—A tenth-grader at St. Olivia's School in the East Side was found dead early Sunday morning in the women's restroom at the Centre Mall, an apparent victim of the high-potency heroin that has killed four other people in the last six days.

Whitney O'Connor, 15, of the East Side, was pronounced dead at the scene by paramedics. Major Carl Holstrom of the Providence police force said results from an autopsy were not available last night.

In a statement yesterday, officials at St. Olivia's said O'Connor was a "quiet" teenager and a well-liked student who did not miss class or show any other signs of problems.

"Whitney had a lot of good friends who will miss her deeply. Our sympathies go out to her parents and brother during this difficult time," Sister Maryann Sarto, the school's headmaster, said in a statement.

The youth's family declined to comment last night.

The school, which is offering grief-counseling sessions to students all week, will hold a service at the school's chapel for students, parents and other community members.

Police said they were investigating several leads into the source of the high-potency heroin, but have no arrests. They also said there were no other reports of drug or alcohol problems at the mall, which employs a well-staffed security force to monitor teens' behavior.

A spokesman for the Longvell Corporation, which owns the Centre Mall, did not return phone calls last night.

To post an online tribute to Whitney O'Connor, click here.

11

The next afternoon at work, Frizell got a tip that police were keeping an eye on a low-level dealer from Providence who might have sold the high-potency heroin to one of the overdose victims. But Angelo, who led the Narcotics division, refused to confirm the tip or say if it had been an investigation into Whitney's death that produced the lead.

I immediately called Carl. "So what's going on?" I asked.

I heard a shuffling of papers.

"We heard you've got a possible suspect."

There was no answer.

"Okay, can you tell me, off the record, if it had anything to do with Whitney?"

"No, Hallie, it didn't."

"You didn't get any fingerprints off the syringe, then?"

There was another long pause.

"Off the record?"

"Yes."

"We got her prints off the syringe."

A shock? Not really. But I still didn't want to believe that Whitney had lied to me—or that at fifteen years old, she was already into heroin. I thought of that bruise on her leg, the force involved. "Could someone have—?"

Anticipating my next thought, Carl cut me off. "And except for a small black-and-blue on her leg, there weren't signs of any bruising. Nothing consistent with being forced, physically, to inject a needle."

"So case closed?"

"Unless you've got any evidence you'd like to share with me . . ." This was facetious. Reporters never shared. "It's a sad story," he continued. "But this poor girl did this to herself."

"So we've got one dead source, one missing—and nothing much from police," Ellen said, summarizing the bleak status of our investigation.

The team was gathered in the Fishbowl, waiting, as usual, for Dorothy. Sitting at the table with my back to the windows, I had a full view of the newsroom, and could see her standing at her desk, arguing with the regional editor. This meant we'd be waiting a long time.

"You must be at least a little relieved," Ellen said. She was sitting directly across from me with Jonathan to her left, and Bennett and Ryan a few empty chairs away at the far end of the table. "At least now you know her death didn't have anything to do with that guy seeing you take down the license plate numbers."

"Yeah, not everyone gets murdered because of you," Jonathan said. "It's *fairly* rare."

This was a reference to the Salazar investigation, and totally uncalled for.

Ellen shot him one of her ice-blue looks, and he retracted from the table, pushing out his chair, crossing his arms protectively over his chest. He looked to Bennett and Ryan for support. Ryan, who had one foot up on an empty chair, rejected the plea with a rare narrowing of his eyes, shaking his head like he just couldn't believe Frizell. Bennett looked up from the printout he was studying. "Was that supposed to be funny?"

There was silence, and then, grudgingly, Frizell offered a half-assed apology. I accepted it swiftly, mostly just to get on with it, but also because Frizell had hit on the truth. I *was* relieved. I've dealt with a lot in the last couple of years, but I didn't think I could handle being responsible for the death of a fifteen-year-old.

After a minute, Bennett slid the printout across the table to me. It had been mailed to him from his source at the insurance company: a list of car registrations, names, and addresses from the Division of Motor Vehicles.

"Four of those license plates belong to tenants in the building," he said. "And one of them was a rental car."

"Let me guess—the Camry," I said.

"You got it."

"So we go back and watch the apartment house," I said. "See if there's any more activity. Any teenage girls going in and out."

"That's the thing," Ryan said. He dropped his foot onto the floor and sat up straight in the chair. He was a tall guy with big feet, and the small room echoed with the importance of this gesture.

"What?"

"I called that phone number you gave Bennett for the rental office, and the woman told me unit four was newly vacated and available for rental next week."

Which meant Rurik had cleared out of there after he'd seen me snooping. And now, we had nothing. No sources. No place to set up surveillance. Nothing, except a grainy video we would be reluctant even to mention unless we had a lot more proof that it was connected to a larger crime.

"Sorry, kiddo." Ellen reached across the table and patted my hand. Her eyes were sympathetic, but her tone was brisk. The message was clear: Time to move on.

"We could use this Whitney girl's death as a lead-in," Frizell was saying, "and then look at the heroin problem nationally. They think the heroin is coming from Afghanistan again, by way of Nigeria."

This Whitney girl? I was damned if I was going to let her be reduced to an anecdotal lead in Frizell's dissertation on drug running. "Didn't we have a story on the northeast corridor trade just last fall?" I asked.

"We did." Dorothy's voice suddenly intruded. She tossed a legal pad and pen on the table and took a seat to my right. "And I don't know if any of you have noticed, but there have been no new overdoses here in what? Three days. Reader interest is already waning."

"Five people died," Jonathan reminded her. "A nice upper-class girl from the East Side." This was a rather transparent gesture to line me up on his side.

"You're so hot on this heroin thing, you can follow the police investigation," Dorothy told him. "Cover the bust, if they ever get one. But as for the rest of you"—she swiveled toward me—"Ian wants us to stick to the original story. It has *juice*."

She gestured to Ellen. "You go talk to all the tenants in that building and the neighbors, too. One of them might have seen the girls coming and going. Or they might have heard something. Or have information on where they went."

Then she ordered Ryan to go back and ask around Best Price to see if Rurik had showed up there recently, and to check with Warwick Police to see if any parents had ever complained. "And go back to that rental agency to see if you can get the name that was on the lease of the rental unit."

To me, she said, "Give Whitney's parents a week to grieve and then go talk to them. Find out what they know about their daughter."

"That oughta be fun," Ellen said under her breath.

But Dorothy wasn't finished. "And that girl—the one you were supposed to meet at Best Price—"

"Lexie?"

"What happened to her?"

I began to explain her disappearance from cyberspace, but Dorothy cut me off. "You think she's dead? Or out of state?"

I thought of what Whitney's brother, Josh, had been about to say before his mother had cut him off. Whitney had lied to them: She'd really been off to meet her *weird* friend at the mall. That sounded like Lexie. And police had found seven hundred dollars on Whitney's body. "I'm not sure, but my gut tells me that she's still in Rhode Island somewhere."

"Then go find her," Dorothy said.

I went back to cyberspace. This time with Bennett, who knew about tracking people down through their computers.

Since he was a computer-whiz guy, Bennett had his own

office—unheard of for a reporter—which was in the *Chronicle* library. It was a large office with a tall Palladian window, a distant view of Kennedy Plaza, and a door that shut out the hushed conversations of the library staff and the nonstop printer at the database terminal.

We were sitting side by side at his desk so early the next morning that the sunlight through the window was still faint and none of the library staff had arrived yet. Bennett had done some preliminary research. He told me that a lot of child porn was traded through Limewire and other sharing software. But pedophiles tended to trade their collections for free. For Rurik to make money on this cam-girl operation, he had to be selling either videos or live performances as a subscription service. This meant that somewhere there had to be a Web site taking orders and a vendor processing payment.

The first step was to find the Web site. Bennett tried an ordinary search through Google, plugging in a few choice keywords, like "young teenage girls," into the engine. But this produced too many pages of porno sites to sort through. His secondary plan would take more time. All images, including the beach video I copied, left a data string, which included the URL address and several lines of data. Hopefully, this would lead us back to the Web site.

The video clip I had of Lexie and Whitney, the beach shot, was actually too innocuous, too "soft" to be of use. But if we could find more explicit photos or video clips of Lexie, Whitney, or any other recognizable underage Rhode Island teen on the Web site, we were golden. Not only could we document the crime, but Bennett, being a computer geek, had a host of computer geek friends. And one of them, he was pretty sure, might be able to hack into the Web site, up the snout of the computer

host, and into the e-mail accounts that identified the paying customers.

The process was illegal, of course, which is why Bennett
didn't do the actual hacking himself and why we didn't discuss
it with Dorothy. At this point, I didn't care about the privacy
rights of child pornographers or their clientele. All I cared
about was shutting down Rurik's operation and finding Lexie.

"Do these guys download the videos onto their own home
computers?" I asked.

"The stupid ones do. The smarter ones download it right to
a flash memory stick," he said, pointing to the two-inch storage device hanging off his own USB port. "You can get rid of
it a lot easier than a laptop."

At home, the summer evening dimmed around me as I studied Lexie's profile on the Buzz, searching for clues.

There was a poem about friendship that she must have
copied off the Internet somewhere.

> *Friendship*
> *Wear it.*
> *Like a shawl on the shoulder*
> *Worn in the wind.*
> *The intricate laces, weightless*
> *And warm.*

It was the way teenagers always idolized friendship: weight-
less. As if there were never any conflicts. As if a friend couldn't
send you down a completely destructive course.

Ominously, the listing of all Lexie's "friends" had been

deleted, as were the postings on her bulletin board. As if her connection with the outside world was now permanently eliminated.

Then I searched through MySpace, Facebook, and all of Yahoo's special weird and kinky sex groups. But there was no sign of her.

It wasn't until a car alarm on Elmgrove Avenue snapped me out of cyberspace that I realized how the day had vanished. Only my laptop screen illuminated the dining room.

I stood up and began flicking on lights. Matt was working late for the fourth night in a row, and the condominium felt empty.

It was after ten, and unusual for Matt to be gone so late. Unless he was preparing for a big trial, he was usually home by seven o'clock. But he wasn't talking about having a big trial, or complaining about the hours, or even a difficult judge.

Ever since Whitney died, I'd been having trouble with my sleep, again. I didn't wake up in a panic the way I had after my brother's death, but I was restless. I'd drift off okay, but then wake up at odd hours. Sometimes I could go right back to sleep, but other times my mind would rev up as if it were the middle of the afternoon.

That night, Matt got home after midnight and was so exhausted, he just crept into bed. I left him sleeping, got up, and went into the kitchen to make myself a Frosted Brown Sugar Cinnamon Pop-Tart, which I buttered. Then I poured a glass of milk and went back to my laptop.

I sat down at the dining room table and clicked back into the Buzz. Still no messages from Lexie.

After wandering into a few chat rooms, I found myself doing a search to see if Whitney's profile was still online. It was, lingering after her like a ghost. Her photo looked as if it had been deliberately staged to make her look even younger and more innocent, as if she'd been coached. She was wearing a pink pajama top over her St. Olivia's kilt and was about to toss a stuffed animal either at the camera or across the room.

I thought of the small bruise that had been on her leg. Her fingerprints on the syringe. And the way she completely ignored her mother on the webcam, pouring the dinner she'd left down the sink.

I had gone to Whitney's funeral, but the church had been so crowded that I had to stand in the lobby, where I couldn't hear anything or feel like I'd taken part. Suddenly, I felt a strong need to express my grief. I logged on to the *Chronicle* Web site and clicked on what was one of the *Chronicle*'s attempts to draw traffic to its Web site: the online guestbook for the mourners who read the obit page.

I scanned through several entries, which were full of grief for the loss of a child. I stopped at this page.

CHRONICLE ONLINE

GUEST BOOK FOR

Whitney O'Connor

(1993–2008)

Entries are free and are posted after being reviewed for appropriate content.

June 5

Debra, Ron, and Joshua,
Our thoughts and prayers are with you and your family at this
time. The parents and families of St. Olivia's will miss Whitney
terribly. We are all thinking of you.
Maureen and Kevin Maguire (Lincoln, RI)

June 5

Dear Mr. and Mrs. O'Connor
We are so sorry for your loss. Whitney was much loved by her
brother and all of us here in Bishop Hendricken community
feel for your family at this difficult time. May God give you
courage strength and peace.
The Rev. Michael Kearny
Bishop Hendricken High School

June 4

to the family of Whitney,
it was terrible ur daughter didn't deserve to die
i will miss her and am so so sorry
you dont no me but i was 1 of her bst friends
anonymous (Providence, RI)

Page: 1-2-3-(4)-5-6-7-8-9-10-11-12-13-14-15

An anonymous friend with no concept of punctuation.

Could Bennett do some kind of search on this? Find out if it was routed through the same ISP? If she was still in Warwick?

And then, another thought occurred to me. If this *was* Lexie, and she was making entries on this Web site, she felt guilty.

I remembered something else Whitney had told me. That Lexie had felt guilty about trying to entice younger teenagers into this life. That's why she'd tried to blow me off when I wanted to meet at Best Price. She'd thought I was fourteen.

I'd sent Lexie about two dozen unanswered messages, but now I sent her one last plea.

"I need to talk to you about Whitney," I wrote, and typed in my cell phone number. "Don't let other young girls die this way."

12

I **sat in** my Honda, parked a half block down from Whitney's house on the opposite side of the street, waiting for her mother to pull into the driveway. Whitney had told me that her mother got home around six o'clock, about an hour before her father, and because I'd checked the sports schedule on the high school Web site, I was pretty sure Whitney's brother, Joshua, would still be at baseball practice.

It was a quiet leafy street, between two busy thoroughfares, and the cars that used it as a cut-through drove through wildly, as if thumbing their noses at the painstakingly restored Victorians and imposing colonials with their deeply green fertilized lawns.

Two houses away, a woman about my own age was planting impatiens underneath a tree. She was sitting on the ground with about a dozen flats of flowers around her. They were all pinks and purples. I watched her gently pull the plants apart and plant them in pretty alternating colors.

Not for the first time, I wondered what it might be like to be a professional gardener, working outside in the summer, creating a pleasing landscape. A simple, positive profession that did not require you to slink down in your car as you attempted to catch a poor, grieving mother by surprise.

The Honda Element, a distinctly boxlike car, was not neutral enough for this neighborhood. For one thing, it was a bold orange color. For another, it looked bound for a California beach. I felt like everyone who lived on this block would know I had invaded.

I've always hated interviewing the survivors in a newsworthy death. But at least when you interviewed people right after the fire, or car accident, or shooting, they were numb. Two weeks after the tragedy was worse. The physical shock had worn off, and the day-to-day reality of the loss was just settling in.

But this was my only shot at actually getting Whitney's mother to talk to me. I'd tried to call her twice and had only gotten her machine. So now I was forced into a surprise attack.

"Sometimes people *think* they don't want to talk to us," Dorothy had insisted. "You've got to give them an opportunity to change their minds."

Translation: *You've got to wear them down.* Relentlessness was a key quality in a reporter. Sneakiness was a tool of the trade.

From the death notice, I learned that Whitney's mother's name was Debra. And from a quick Google check, I found out that she was a graduate of Providence College and had a big job at one of the downtown accounting firms. The search also pulled up road race results that listed her as a runner, like me. I'd gone so low as to call her accounting firm at lunchtime, pretending to be someone organizing a road race. Her secretary told me that Debra O'Connor was "at lunch." This confirmed that she'd returned to work since Whitney's death, and that I might be able to catch her returning home tonight.

Several Camrys ripped through the street, although none of them were blue. A number of SUVs, one of those smaller, compact Cadillacs, and a remarkable number of Honda Accords. A Mercedes drove slowly past me and pulled into the driveway directly across the street from Whitney's house. An older woman wearing a business suit stepped out of the car. Then, instead of going inside, she walked down the driveway to pick up a newspaper circular lying near the sidewalk. She exchanged greetings with the woman planting the impatiens. Then she glanced down the street and spotted me sitting in my bright orange car.

An intruder.

Immediately, I turned and gazed at the house directly to my left, at a front door guarded by two spear-shaped evergreens. I stared hard at the door, then at my wrist, and back to the front door, as if I were growing impatient, waiting for someone who was late.

The older woman peered at me another moment, then put the circular under her arm and headed up the driveway into her house.

Another twenty minutes passed as I watched the woman planting her impatiens. She was using both peat moss and topsoil and was adding too much fertilizer. I also wanted to tell her that she was planting the flowers too close together and not giving them nearly enough room to grow.

I tried to think about what I'd say to Debra O'Connor, how I'd open the conversation. There were no real "icebreakers" when you had to ask a mother about the death of her fifteen-year-old, no way to ease into asking if she knew any of the people who had recruited her daughter to pose naked in front of a webcam.

A BMW station wagon turned into the street from Butler, and I felt my whole body tighten. A high-end mom car. The car headed toward me at tortoise speed. From my rearview mirror, I watched it approach. There was a lone woman at the wheel. Her hair was styled, her look professional. I recognized the glasses from the time I'd seen her talking to Whitney via webcam.

As the car got closer, I could see the sadness of her forward gaze, the resignation in her shoulders.

Debra O'Connor pulled into her driveway alone. Just the way I had planned it.

I reminded myself that my duty was to the newspaper's readers. That I had to be aggressive. I grabbed a notebook and pen out of my backpack with my right hand and, with my other, got ready to open my driver's door and spring across the street.

Sometimes a survivor wanted to talk about the victim, wanted to eulogize the loved one in print. And who knew, maybe I could get Whitney's mother to see the threat that the Internet and webcams posed to all young girls. Enlist her in a cause.

Moving slowly, Debra O'Connor got out of the car, carrying a grocery bag and an enormous tote. I climbed rather than sprang out of my Honda, and although heading toward the house, stayed on the sidewalk on my side of the street, in front of her neighbor's house. Luckily the woman was so involved in her plants, she didn't even look up as I passed.

Debra O'Connor put the grocery bag on the front step and searched inside her tote for something. She pivoted back to the car, slid behind the passenger seat, and grabbed something. She returned to the front walk with keys in her hand, but then stopped, dead in her tracks. She stood there, not five feet from the door, motionless.

I should have already run across the street by now. I should be approaching her. But instead I retreated, taking a step closer to my car. It was as if the swell of her sadness broke across the street and pushed me back to the shore.

A minute went by, and Debra O'Connor just stood there, shoulders sloped, arms hugging her elbows.

And then, I understood.

She didn't want to go inside. Didn't want to face the house, emptied of her daughter.

After another minute, Debra O'Connor picked up her grocery bag and turned around and with a slow, beaten step, moved toward the car in the driveway.

This was it. Time to run across the street and catch her before she had the option of slamming a door on me or rolling up a window. If I sprinted across the street, I could still get her before she got to the car. While she was still stunned by the assault, I could beg her to talk to me. Tell me what she knew about her daughter. Ask if she knew anything about where I could find Lexie.

My feet wouldn't move on the sidewalk.

Giving this poor mother "a week to grieve" was not enough. She wasn't ready to talk to a reporter. She didn't want to discuss her daughter's heroin overdose, or hear about her webcam activities or how she'd managed to buy herself those Chanel and Jimmy Choo shoes.

A sprinkler started up, and a whoosh of spinning water rained on me. The neighbor had finished her planting and was watering her flowers. Instead of running forward to escape, I walked backwards toward my car.

Out of range of the sprinkler, I watched as Debra O'Connor slipped into her car. I listened to her door slam and the engine start. I remained motionless until the BMW station wagon backed up the length of the driveway, turned down the street, and disappeared into Wayland Square.

At lunchtime in the middle of the week, the shooting range was a lot less crowded.

Although we still had to wear the protective headgear, it wasn't quite so loud. This meant I could hear more of what Walter actually said, and I could ask more questions.

I learned how you had to carry the gun from the table to the station with the slide open, so that everyone could see it wasn't loaded. How you had to point it at the ground. How you had to push it deep into your palm to stay steady. How to determine the dominant eye. Aim carefully.

I even learned that there was a score system. Some sort of formula using the numbers on the paper target and the distance. Walter, who was shooting in the station next to mine, was apparently getting higher and higher scores. I was beginning to understand the attraction of his new addiction.

But after half an hour, I was able to hit the paper target only twice on the very rim, and at five feet. I hated the nine-millimeter Glock more than ever.

"It's too big, too ugly, and the recoil scares the crap out of me," I complained to Walter when I gave him back the gun.

Even Walter, who desperately wanted a shooting buddy, had to admit that I wasn't getting any better.

"We'll have to innovate," he said.

"What?"

He walked over to his tackle box of guns and came back with a little leather case, the size of a wallet. Apparently it was some kind of holster, because he pulled out a tiny four-inch handgun.

"It's adorable," I said.

He loaded it and gave it to me.

"It's a Seecamp. It'll fit your small hand better. Go ahead, shoot it."

He was right; it fit into my hand perfectly. The trigger had a lot of resistance, but I squeezed off a shot. The little gun felt like it exploded in my hand. The bullet hit the paper target, and I felt that rush of power again. But I had no more sense of skill with this gun than with the Glock, and I gave the cute gun back to Walter, somewhat disappointed.

As we were leaving the building, heading across the parking lot, a man getting out of a Ford Escalade called Walter's name.

"Oh shit," Walter said under his breath.

The man was in his late thirties with ratty black hair to his shoulder and a big silver peace sign on a strap of leather around his neck. He was all moving limbs, with an unbridled energy that launched his Gumby-like body across the lot to stop us in our tracks.

He grabbed Walter's hand and shook it. "Fucking A, Walter."

"Hey, Pez," Walter said without enthusiasm.

Pez? Like the candy? Pointedly, Walter did not introduce me to him.

"Long time, buddy. What the hell you doing here? You belong here?"

He meant the firearms school. Walter did have a membership, but he didn't own up to it. "What are you doing here? They can't let people like you in, right?"

Pez laughed, as if this were a joke, but I got the feeling Walter meant it.

"I'm meeting a guy. Collector. Gonna let me shoot an assault rifle. Maybe sell me one. Pretty fucking cool, huh?"

"Pretty cool," Walter said, but his eyes narrowed, as if he'd seen something terribly wrong with this picture.

Pez apparently caught his drift. "Oh, that thing. I had some luck and slipped out of that. Helluva lawyer. Although fucking guy left me broke."

I gathered they were discussing Pez's criminal record, or maybe his lack of criminal record. Convicted felons were not allowed to shoot at the range.

"So what are you up to now?" Walter asked.

"Ah, you know, I'm all over the place. A little of this. A little of that. Developing retail space mostly. I work for a guy with some real capital looking to diversify. How about you?"

"I drive a cab now," Walter said. I noticed that he didn't take the opportunity to explain he'd done so well that he actually owned the cab company. Owned two cab companies.

"Good for you," Pez said, handing him a card. "We should catch up."

"Yeah." Walter took the card but did not sound eager, or hand him one of his cards in return. "But I'm living in Rhode Island now. You're probably still in Boston, right?"

Pez shook his head. "Nah. Just moved to Rhode Island, too. South County. Nice oceanfront. Jake, Woody, and I are all doing commercial real estate."

These names seemed to disturb Walter. He glanced at his

watch. "I got to get her back to work," he said, still failing to introduce me. "Nice to see you again."

I waited until we were back in the cab to ask who Pez was.

"He was a business associate. High up in the food chain." Walter's eyes were on the rearview mirror, making sure Pez disappeared.

I guessed that they had been drug dealers together. And that Walter might have bought his cocaine from Pez. Or maybe from Jake and Woody.

"And he's no fucking real estate baron," Walter was saying. "That's all code."

Walter put his key in the ignition, but did not turn the engine over. He twisted his mustache three times, a nervous gesture. "Jesus Christ," he muttered to himself. "As if Rhode Island didn't have enough dirtbags already without Pez." Then he looked at me.

"What?"

He didn't answer. Instead, he got out of the car and went to the trunk, and returned with something. He slipped back into the driver's seat, checked his rearview mirror again, and he put a wallet-sized holster in my hand. The adorable four-inch handgun was inside. He also dropped a package of ammunition onto my lap.

"What are you doing?"

"It's for you. Stash it in your apartment. Your nightstand. This holster fits in your back pocket. Don't put it in your backpack, where it'll get lost. Bring it with you if you're going anywhere near that Rurik guy."

"Without having a license? Are you kidding me?"

"Look. Dirtbags like Pez are running around the state armed

to the teeth. And they'll kill whoever gets in the way of their business interests."

"So?" Walter's logic was eluding me.

"So, it'll take you three months to get a license, and that Rurik guy could kill you by then."

"No one is going to kill me."

"Like you don't have a way of pissing off the wrong people?"

He was talking about the Salazar investigation. A near-death experience.

I thought of the blue Camry. I thought of Whitney. I thought of how easy this gun would be to hide.

It was so small, playlike in its holster. It would slide easily into my back pocket. I'd been held at gunpoint before. I could do without that choking fear of being utterly helpless.

But I had promised Matt. He was a prosecutor, for God's sake. An officer of the court. If I got caught carrying an unlicensed gun, it would reflect on him. Even if he just stumbled across it in our bedroom, our relationship would be over.

I handed the gun and the ammunition back to Walter. "I'll take my chances, unarmed."

It was after midnight again when Matt crawled into his side of the bed.

It's an hour of the night when no one should be allowed to think. The lights were out in the bedroom, but my thoughts were spinning like some sort of disco lamp. Ryan hadn't gotten ahold of the landlord who had rented the Providence apartment to Rurik. None of the neighbors Ellen interviewed admitted to having seen any young girls enter the apartment unit. And Bennett's hacker buddy had not been able to get any tracking information off the video clip.

I probably should just have let Matt go to sleep. But I was so wound up, I could barely keep my legs and arms under the sheet. I kept seeing Dorothy's look of reproof when I told her I hadn't been able to approach Whitney's mother, couldn't shake myself of a new worry. I was losing my competitive edge.

Somehow, all this anxiety suddenly became Matt's fault. "I know you have a big *important* case, but you could have called and let me know you were going to be late," I said.

"I'm sorry," he said. "But I've been working late every night this week, I thought you—"

"Whatever."

"Are you mad at me?" Matt sat up and turned on the light, illuminating our bedroom, the mismatched nightstands both piled high with newspapers and books.

His hair still needed to be cut, and he looked like he'd forgotten to shave this morning, both of which I found terribly appealing. The air of perpetual fatigue that he'd been wearing for the last several months was gone, and he was looking at me, intently, sincerely baffled. "I really just didn't think—"

"No, I'm not mad." I was actually happy for Matt that he was working late. It meant a big case was coming up. Hopefully something he could win. Something that could reverse his string of defeats.

So why was I giving him such a hard time, anyway? Because I couldn't sleep? "I just miss you."

He took a moment to decide whether he believed that, but then he smiled and slipped both arms around me. I turned my face into his chest. Inhaling his soapy lime scent, my mind finally stopped spinning. He kissed the top of my head and stroked my shoulder.

It felt like forever since we last touched. Matt flipped off the light and kissed me, a deep, urgent kiss that obliterated the long week it had been since we'd last made love. It was sex-on-a-school-night, tender, direct. Afterwards, it was hard to remember the anxious thoughts that had kept me from sleep.

Matt held me in his arms, and I relaxed into his long limbs. He promised to ask his brother if he could borrow the boat. "Maybe he'll let us take it on an overnight again," he said. "You seem like you could use a getaway."

Was I that transparent? "It's just the story I've been working on."

"A big *important* story?" he asked, teasing. Then in a more serious tone: "The story that's got you looking over your shoulder?"

"I'm not looking over my shoulder anymore," I said. "But I'm not getting anywhere on it, and it's a story that needs to be told."

"Then you'll figure it out. You always do."

I closed my eyes and, for a full minute, allowed myself to feel his confidence in me. But then I opened them again. "Sometimes, even though you know it's all there, it slips through." I splayed my fingers and looked through the sieve.

"Welcome to the prosecution," he said dryly.

We were both silent again.

"So what? You can't get anyone to go on the record?" he asked.

"I only have one source, and she's a kid—"

"Your source is a *kid*?"

"A teenage girl."

"Is this connected to that OD you wrote about? Or that Best Price pervert you told me about?"

Another time, I might have dodged this kind of question. But it seemed beyond the point. "Both," I said.

"I thought Frizell was doing the follow on the overdose stories."

"He is. This is a different angle."

He looked at me, perplexed. He opened his mouth to say something and shut it again. Maybe because it was so late, or maybe because he didn't want me to start asking about his big *important* case either, he decided not to press for more. Instead, he offered what turned out to be very useful advice.

"If you want to know about kids, the best thing to do is talk to other kids."

At four thirty in the afternoon, the day's sun was still remarkably strong, scorching the metal bleacher seats I was sitting on and making me feel desperate for Gatorade.

Online, I'd checked the athletics schedule at Bishop Hendricken High School in Warwick, where Joshua played baseball. The team had an away game today in Coventry. I hoped both that Joshua would be playing today, and that it was early enough in the afternoon that his parents couldn't leave work to go watch.

I'd arrived in the bottom of the sixth inning. Most of the parents of the boys on the home team sat together on the other bank of bleachers, and several fathers stood together near the first base line. I'd managed to find a picture of Whitney's father online and was relieved that he didn't appear to be among them.

Sitting on my bleacher, there was only one mom, her

elementary school–aged daughter, and a grandmother. They rooted loudly for Coventry, and for a boy named Travis, who had struck out when he came to bat, just as I'd arrived.

I searched the field until I found Joshua O'Connor playing second base. You couldn't really see his features underneath the baseball cap—let alone match it to the photo of him I'd seen on the family screen saver. But luckily, all the last names were stitched across the backs of the uniforms.

Whitney had said that Lexie wouldn't come over to her house, but I still thought it possible that Josh could have met Lexie, maybe dropping Whitney off somewhere or picking up his sister at the mall. And that day on the phone, he seemed like he *wanted* to talk about his sister. *Wanted* to right the record.

So here I was, waiting for the game to end and hoping to catch Joshua for ten minutes before he had to get on the bus back to school. I was also hoping that he wouldn't make a scene when I approached him and that some infuriated school official wouldn't have me hauled off private school property for trespassing.

"Do you have a brother on the team?" the little girl asked me. She was about eight or nine years old, wearing a white Red Sox shirt with a juice stain on the front.

"I just like to watch baseball," I told her. This was not a lie. I was an ardent Red Sox fan, plus I'd spent many an afternoon as a kid watching my brother Sean playing high school games like this one.

The little girl stared at me in that unabashed way kids have, as if she could stare at me all day long. I asked her about her shirt, and she started telling me that she didn't really like baseball and that she played softball. She was telling me about her last game and then a boy at bat for the home team sent a line drive down the third base line. The spectators roared as the hitter took a double. Diverted by the cheering, the little girl returned to her mother and grandmother.

I tried not to think about how much time I might be wasting if Joshua refused to talk to me. Or about the pain I might inflict on him simply by asking him to talk about his sister. Instead, I kept reminding myself that I'd spent more than a year trying to find the real explanation for my own brother's death, and that only learning the truth had brought peace.

I thought about this all through the end of the sixth and seventh innings, when the pitcher for Joshua's team swiftly retired the side. To try to escape the heat, I moved to the far end of the bleacher, where there was now a couple of inches of shade from a nearby stand of trees. I waited while the teams shook hands, returned to their dugouts, drank the Gatorade I coveted, and sat through the coach's postgame breakdown. Finally, as the boys headed off in the direction of a Snack Shack, I jumped off the bleacher and followed them.

Joshua was a tall boy, about six foot, and so thin that the uniform pants slipped low on his hips and bagged at the ankles. Luckily, he was walking alone when I pulled alongside him. "I was wondering if I could talk to you a minute?" I asked.

He looked at me quizzically. Was I a teacher? Someone's sister? A mother?

A half-dozen other boys and several parents were passing us on either side, a horde headed to the Snack Shack. I avoided introducing myself. "I was hoping you could help me out."

His eyes were the same color as Whitney's—a pale, clear green. They narrowed with suspicion.

"I'm trying to find someone," I pushed on.

He waited.

"Someone who knew your sister."

"Who are you?" he asked.

I had no choice but to tell him.

"Are you the same reporter who called me the day—?"

"I'm sorry for having bothered you," I interrupted. "For bothering your family. We have to do that. When someone young dies, suddenly, in such a—" I was going to say *weird way,* but stopped myself. "When there is a tragedy like that."

The pale eyes darkened, and he began shaking his head, as if remembering the offense all over again. I thought he might walk off. Or start shouting at me.

"I'm really sorry. I had to write a story about your sister's death—since it happened in such a public place."

"The fucking mall," he said.

I nodded.

One of his teammates—the catcher, I think—walked back with three hot dogs and a piece of pizza. He thrust one of the hot dogs into Joshua's hand. "They're running out," he said, eyeing me.

"Thanks," Joshua said, but his tone dismissed his friend, who left and rejoined another group of teammates.

"Everyone feels sorry for me," Joshua said, gesturing to the hot dog. "That's the part I hate."

I told him that I'd lost my brother, too.

"Yeah, did he OD at the mall?" The question was derisive.

"No," I said. No public embarrassment, although there were similarities. "But it was a drug overdose, too."

He must have seen the pain flash in my eyes. "I'm sorry," Joshua apologized. "I was being an asshole."

"But you're right, everybody's loss is different."

He shrugged, looked down at the hot dog, untouched in his

hand, and then in the direction of the empty ball field. A group of boys were already heading back toward the bus in the parking lot. "Thanks for not putting what I said that day in the paper," Joshua said.

A point for me. I nodded, accepting his thanks. Good time to press on: "Whitney was helping me with a story before she died. And it could affect a lot of kids. A lot of kids Whitney's age. And I'm trying to find out about—"

He interrupted me. "Whitney was talking to a reporter at the *Chronicle*?"

"Off the record. I promised her I wouldn't use her name. And I'm going to keep that promise."

He was not impressed. "About what?"

"About the Internet. The friends she met on the Buzz. And—"

"Oh no. Oh shit," he said, shaking his head.

He knew something. Or had had his suspicions. I could tell by his response.

"Joshua, please. I need to find a few of these people trolling the Internet for young kids. Stop them from doing what they did to your sister."

He searched my eyes. "You mean the drugs?" But I got the feeling that he *didn't* mean the drugs. He was probing to find out how much I knew.

"There's another part of it." I hesitated. "Whitney ever talk about a girl named Lexie?"

A dark look came in his eyes, and I realized then that if I'd seen the video of Whitney and Lexie on the beach, there was a real good chance that he'd seen it, too.

"You have any idea where she lives?" I asked him. "Or have a cell phone number for her? I need to talk to her for my story."

"Why?"

"This guy, Rurik. I think he's the one who got Whitney the drugs, and he gets young girls to . . ." I wanted to put this in the gentlest terms possible. "To take their clothes off for the webcam. I won't write about Whitney, I promise. But I want to expose this asshole. Nail him. And I think Lexie can help me do it."

He shook his head. "I don't know anything about this girl."

"Would you be willing to check Whitney's room? Maybe she has Lexie's number scribbled down somewhere. In an address book or back of a matchbook."

"You want me to search through my sister's things for you?" He sounded insulted.

"O'Connor!" Now it was the coach yelling for him to get on the bus.

"Look. I waited for your mother to come home from work the other day, and I was going to ask her about Lexie. But she still looked pretty upset, and I wanted to spare her any more—"

"You can't tell my mother about this." His voice was in full alarm.

"I won't. Just help me."

"It'll fucking kill her, you can't—"

"I won't."

He turned, started walking toward the bus, gesturing for me to follow. "And you won't ever use Whitney's name in the paper?"

"I promise."

The coach was waving both hands over his head for him to hurry. He picked up the pace.

"Will you help me? Search her room for me? Check her laptop—"

"The police took her laptop," he said. "And she must have

lost her cell phone that night in the mall because the cops didn't find it . . ." Here, his voice broke. ". . . anywhere."

She *lost* her cell phone the night she died? More likely it was stolen by whoever she was meeting that night, whoever knew she was dying and was worried about the cops finding the phone numbers programmed into the phone. But I didn't say this. The coach was leaving the bus and heading our way. I quickly dug into my pocket where I'd stashed a stack of new *Chronicle* business cards. "If you find anything, will you call me?"

He took the card reluctantly. "Just don't call *either* of my parents for *any* reason," he said. "And I'll see what I can do."

13

For more than a year after my brother Sean died, I struggled with insomnia. If I was lucky enough to fall asleep, I awoke at one in the morning, the hour he died, with my heart racing. It led to a sleeping pill addiction, and then, as part of my recovery, my dedication to early-morning running. Five miles a day exhausted my body to the point where falling asleep each night was a guarantee.

But recently, my restlessness at night has morphed into a new tic. I'd started waking up progressively earlier and earlier. For a week now, I'd been up before the sun rose. I would be back from my run and showered before Matt had even hit his snooze alarm.

So I was a little surprised when I got back to the condo the next morning, dripping with sweat, to find Matt not only awake, but already dressed. He was standing in front of the bureau mirror in the bedroom, looking unusually groomed and especially handsome, combing his hair with the kind of concern that could mean only one thing.

"Big day in court?" I asked.

He didn't answer. "I made coffee," he said, turning his attention to his top drawer, where he was hunting for something.

I stared at his suit, blue linen, clearly his best summer wear, and a brand-new custom-tailored dress shirt that his mother had given him for his last birthday. Whatever case he was working on would be documented by court records and public information. Why was he being so secretive?

"Can you help me?" he asked, pulling out a pair of cuff links and handing them to me. I grabbed a towel from the chair and toweled off the sweat before taking the cuff links.

As I stuck the cuff link, a silver sailor's knot, through the wristband, I noticed Matt's reflection in the mirror. His shoulders were squared, and he stood with a command posture.

Something about his expression reminded me of how he looked when we first started going out. What was it? The air of authority? And I realized what it was. Matt looked confident again. He looked like he knew he was about to win.

Something fluttered in my chest. Love? Pride? Or maybe just pure animal attraction. I put the other cuff link through the other wrist and kissed him. "Whatever you've got going on today," I said, "good luck."

At work, Bennett Castiglia was waiting for me.

It was now about eight fifteen, which was still early for the newsroom. As I walked past the empty reception desk and stopped to pick up the day's paper from the stacks on the floor,

Bennett bolted out from the library and shoved an envelope into my hand.

"You found the Web site?"

He shook his head. "I think he may have shut it down. We can't find anything."

That was bad news. But he was smiling.

"You found Rurik?"

"I found Atlanta Antiques."

I ripped open the envelope and pulled out a copy of a canceled rental check. The name of the signature was unreadable, but it was written from a company called Atlanta Antiques, in New Bedford.

Bennett said, "According to a listing I found on the Web, the company actually has a warehouse and retail store in New Beige."

This was the nickname for New Bedford, a city about forty minutes from Providence on the southeastern shore of Massachusetts. A former whaling capital and mill town with scores of empty industrial buildings. Lots of locations for a porno studio.

"Can you drive?" I explained that since Rurik had already identified me in my bright orange Honda Element, transportation to the location required someone else's car.

He glanced at the clock. Bennett was a computer guy. An Internet guy who didn't like to leave his desk, let alone the building.

"We can be back here before lunch."

Bennett had never been a beat reporter, never hung around a police station, or gone to a poor neighborhood to write about street gangs. He had very clean fingernails that looked buffed, and he played piano for a choral group.

"Please?"

Maybe it was a sign of how desperate we were for this story. How aware we'd become that we were reaching a dead end. But after one last glance at the clock, a sigh, and a shrug, Bennett turned back to the library to get his car keys.

You know you're about to bypass New Bedford when you come to the highway billboard promoting the free needle exchange.

"It's just a very medically progressive city," I said to Bennett, who was already regretting his decision to chauffeur me. "Turn here, this is the exit."

It was the wrong exit, but after several turns, we ended up just inland from the fish-processing plants on a side street filled with a half-dozen old factory buildings with boarded-up windows.

We headed up the one-way street and found the address. The building, set back from the road, was about fifty feet wide, with a large swath of asphalt in front of it. This parking lot was empty except for a big white truck with a flat tire in front of the receiving area. A sign over a door on the far side of the building said ANTIQUE STORE.

There was clearly no warehouse activity. Since it was just a little after nine o'clock, an hour before most retail stores opened, we figured it was safe to peek into the store windows.

We got out of the car and walked toward the sign and up to a small set of stairs with an elaborate wrought-iron rail. The door itself looked like an antique, carved oak with a fanlight above and sidelights on either side—clearly not original to the warehouse. There was a CLOSED sign hanging around the doorknob that looked faded from the sun. I peered inside the left sidelight while Bennett pressed his nose against the one on the right.

The glass was dirty, which gave the store a look of twilight. I could see a reception area with a cash register sitting on a desk. The desk was no antique, but metal and utilitarian. Beside it was a big modern office chair on rollers, like the kind we had at the newsroom. Two metal folding chairs leaned against a finished wall, and there was an empty soda can on the floor.

"Can you see through the door?" I asked Bennett, who had a better angle of an open door behind the register. I imagined it could be a showroom.

"No antiques," Bennett said. "Not much of anything."

Whatever antique store had once been here appeared to be out of operation. And if there was a porn studio, it would probably be deeper inside the building, away from the reception area. "You think there are windows on the other side?"

We walked down the stairs to the pavement and along the side between the warehouse and another vacant building. There were no windows, but toward the back, we found a small set of concrete stairs leading to a steel door with a rusty padlock. The padlock looked uneven, as if a screw were missing from the plate.

I climbed up the stairs to give it a try. Slipping my fingers under the padlock, I easily pried it open. It looked like someone had broken into the building before we got here and no one had bothered to fix the lock.

"What are you doing?" Bennett asked.

"I'm just going to open it a crack and see if I can see anything inside," I said.

"There's probably an alarm."

I fingered the rust on the broken lock, as if to say *I doubt it*.

He rolled his eyes. "This is breaking and entering."

"I didn't break anything," I said.

The door was heavy and wouldn't budge. I yanked on the handle twice and looked to Bennett for help. He shook his head; I was on my own.

I put both my strength and my irritation with Bennett into the next try, and the door swung wide open, nearly knocking me off the cement stoop. There was no alarm and very little light. In front of me was a long hallway with several closed doors, offering no view whatsoever.

I stepped inside.

"You're entering," Bennett admonished.

I ignored him and walked down the hallway, which was a finished area with speckled linoleum flooring and a hung ceiling. The ceiling tiles were yellow and sagging, and the linoleum was curling from what looked like water damage. The air smelled as if someone had peed on a campfire.

I followed the hallway to a door on the right. I tried the doorknob, but it was locked. A little farther down the hallway, there were two empty bottles of vodka, an empty Red Bull, and a crushed can of Chef Boyardee ravioli on the floor. It looked like vagrants had found a home here.

I stepped over the pile of trash to another door straight ahead at the end of the hallway. I tried it, and this one swung open. There was no camera equipment, just another metal desk, a small metal file cabinet, and two bedrolls that were partially burned. A pile of ash and wet paper lay on the floor next to a computer, with one of those large, thick computer screens they used to make in the '90s, and a processor the size of a small suitcase. The keyboard had several melted keys, and the top frame of the processor was warped, curving down into what had once been a floppy drive.

I felt something touch the top of my hair. I whirled around, but there was no one there. I saw an enormous cobweb I must have walked through. Something crawled on my head. I bent over, anxiously raking my hair with my hands until a small spider fell onto the floor.

"Hallie, come on!" Bennett shouted. He'd finally ventured through the door and now stood at the edge of the hallway. "Let's get out of here."

"One minute!" I said.

There was another door behind the desk, and I pushed it open. The warehouse was empty except for several large empty crates. There was no sign of fire damage here. And no sign of any camera equipment or lighting. Just an expanse of cement. Something squealed and fluttered above in the rafters. A poor sparrow trapped inside the building.

I backed up into the office.

On my way out, I decided to check the three-drawer file cabinet, which was completely empty. Then I turned to the desk. In the drawer, mixed in with a couple of pencils, a nail clipper, and a pack of rubber bands, was a small gold cross on a broken chain.

I picked it up and lay the cross on my palm. It was sized for an infant, and definitely Orthodox, more square than rectangular, with the "budded" ends. I turned it over, and it was inscribed with initials in a foreign alphabet. Russian?

Lexie's cross? The only thing she had left from her mother?

"Hallie!" Bennett yelled. "Someone's coming!"

I stuffed the cross in my pants pocket and ran like hell through the hallway, out the door to the cement stoop. I slammed the door behind me just as a man began walking up a weedy corridor of grass between the pavement and the next building.

He was in his midthirties, a stocky man with arms and legs that looked short compared with the width of his torso. Streaks of dirt or grease smudged a sleeveless T-shirt and long baggy shorts that made him look almost dwarflike. "You looking for someone?" he asked.

I tried to sidestep this question. "Has the antique store closed?" I asked.

He scrutinized us with new intensity. "Who are you?"

Bennett told him we were reporters for the *Chronicle*.

"And you want to write about a crappy little antique store?"

"Can you tell us who you are?" I asked.

"Jake Maury. I own this property you're sneaking around on. I guess I have a right to ask a few questions."

I decided to level with him. "I'm looking for a guy named Rurik."

"What you want with Rurik?"

"You know him?" I asked.

He looked as if I'd just insulted him with this question. "I asked you what you wanted with him."

"I'm hoping he'll help me with a story I'm writing," I lied. "About antique stores."

He laughed at this.

"I guess he's not in the antique business anymore?" I asked.

"As you can see, the antique business is gone, and wasn't much of a business in the first place. Which makes me wonder what the real reason is you want to talk to this guy you're looking for."

Here, Bennett exchanged a look with me. Jake did not appear to be a friend of Rurik's. Why not try the truth?

"We're working on an investigation that involves Rurik, and you're right, it has nothing to do with antiques. Can I ask if you've ever seen any camera equipment in the warehouse?"

He looked puzzled by this question, but shook his head no.

"Or any young girls?"

I knew instantly that this question was a mistake. His tone became defensive. "This has never been a whorehouse, if that's what you're asking. Not in my building."

"This isn't about prostitution," I said, to appease him. Of course, he wasn't going to own up to full-scale enterprise. Remembering the torched computer inside, I decided to test whether he would just deny everything. "How about computer equipment?"

"Yeah, for a store that sold old shit, they had a lot of computers. One of 'em they left in back got wrecked by a fire. They never came back to get it or nothing. But what the hell is this about, anyway?"

Since this jibed with everything I'd seen, I now did my best to look the landlord in the eye, which was tough because he was still glowering at me. "I'll level with you."

He folded his arms and waited. I fingered the gold cross in my pocket and took a chance.

"I'm doing a story about a young girl who I think might have been kidnapped. Maybe from Russia. I think she might be involved with one of the guys who worked for the antique store."

"The police looking for her?" he asked.

"She's an illegal. She doesn't exist as far as the police are concerned."

At the mention of an "illegal," a light flickered in his eye.

"You saw her?" I asked excitedly.

"No. Never saw no girl, but . . . these guys had the antique store for maybe three, four months, and I don't know, I think a couple of 'em were living here. In the back, sleeping here at night. Found a bedroll. And one of those camping stoves. I told 'em, I can't have that. Not zoned for people to live here. I'm liable if anyone gets killed in a fire."

My heart sank a little lower. Not vagrants, but Lexie, living in the back of a warehouse, eating Chef Boyardee ravioli out of a can.

"They never liked that I was around so much. Complained I was always 'checking on them,' but fuck them. It's my property. I can't have it. Can't have 'em living here in an industrial building," Maury was saying. "Then a couple weeks ago, when the federal immigration agents raided another factory, they bolted. Never heard from them again. I'm still waiting for the rent."

"You got a name of the guy who signed the lease?"

"There was no lease. They rented the whole fucking building month to month. Paid in cash, or with a temporary check. Never could read the damn signature on the checks. Then they took off without any notice. Douche bags."

"And you're saying they were all illegal immigrants?"

"I never seen no Guatemalans or Salvadorians. That's what we got mostly here. But Rurik had a slight accent. Russian or Polish, I thought. Although his English was so good, I figured he'd been in the country a long time."

"Did he run the place?"

"Nah. He drove a van. Picked up furniture, I think. This guy in charge was American. Name was Richard Betnick, I think. Or maybe Betnicki. Something like that. Like I said, I couldn't read the damn signature on the check. And the asshole gave me a phone number that's been disconnected."

Bennett interrupted. "If you find this guy's last name, it would help a lot. Can you call us?" He handed him a business card.

The landlord took it and stuffed it in his back shorts pocket without looking at it.

I tried another tack. "You have any idea where this guy Betnicki went?"

"If I did, lady, I'd have my last month's rent." Then a thought occurred to him. He gestured to my notebook and asked if I had something he could write with. I tore off a piece of paper and handed him my pen. He scribbled a phone number and handed it back to me. "I tell you what, if you find anything, you let me know where these assholes are, *you* call *me*."

14

None of the database searches turned up anything on a Richard Betnick or Betnicki. There was nothing on the *Chronicle*'s electronic archives or Lexis/Nexis, a search engine that let us into the archives of all the major newspapers in the country. There was no criminal record or listings in the Rhode Island court system.

We were in Bennett's office, sitting side by side in front of his computer again. I'd put the gold Orthodox cross in a plastic bag. We'd labeled it with a date and location as if it were police evidence.

Now, as Bennett punched some new Internet address into the keyboard, I stared at the tiny cross through the Baggie. The latch on the chain was broken and I pictured it being pulled from Lexie's neck. "You think this means she's dead?" I asked Bennett.

"I think it means she lost her necklace." His dismissive tone came as a relief. He added, "And if that is hers, we're definitely on the right trail."

Then he picked up the phone and hit his autodial. Soon he was pleading with a man named Connor, a source inside the insurance business, to look up Richard Betnick in the Division of Motor Vehicle records.

But Richard Betnick, spelled three different ways, was not listed in Motor Vehicles, either in Rhode Island or Massachusetts. And he didn't show up in any of the phone directories. No wonder the landlord wanted our help in trying to find this guy.

It was around two o'clock when we officially gave up for the day. I'd just left the library office and was making my way around the periphery of the newsroom to my desk, when Marcy Kittner, the state editor, flagged me down. She was sitting in the quad of desks behind City, going over a story with Jonathan Frizell.

"You still go out with Cavanaugh?" she called across the room in a whistle-pitched voice that cut through the television news and ringing telephones. At least three reporters looked up from their computer screens.

Mostly to silence her, I cut through two rows of desks to her desk. "Why? What's going on?" And why was Frizell, a member of the city staff, working on a story for the state editor?

"Was he headed for court today?" she asked.

"He didn't tell me," I said, which was true.

"But you live with him, right? You must have some idea if he's been working on something big?" she pressed.

Frizell rolled away from Marcy's desk toward me and looked up hopefully. "I'd like to give Risa a break and get home early if nothing is going on." Risa was his wife, and they had a newborn son. "If Cavanaugh is handling the arguments before the grand jury today, that probably means I've got to stay late because we've got a story coming on Pauley Sponik."

I felt my heart skip as I glanced at the calendar blotter on Marcy's desk. Last Friday of the month. This must be when the grand jury met in Newport County. That was what all the secrecy was about.

"You're expecting an indictment the same day?" I asked Frizell.

"Not usually," Frizell said, "but if it *is* Sponik, television is going to be all over this. And if Cavanaugh is handling it himself, he's gonna get the press release out the same day."

Since Frizell was merely using the information for planning purposes, it seemed a harmless revelation. "Matt *was* wearing court clothes when he left this morning—that's all I can say."

Back at my desk, my red message light was blinking.

The first message was from my mother, telling me there was an anniversary party for my aunt and uncle she wanted me to attend. The second was from Walter, asking if I'd go to the shooting range with him tomorrow afternoon, and the third was from the landlord we'd just met in New Bedford.

"Just talked to the UPS guy. He says he thought he heard one of them talking about moving the store to South County. He thinks maybe that means Rhode Island. And he could never read this guy's fucking signature either. So if you find him, you gotta call me with the address." Then he clicked off.

I swiveled to my computer and messaged Bennett with the information; then I called up Google, plugged *antiques* and *South County* into the search engine. I got twenty-five pages of hits and began scrolling through.

One of the sites was from a bed-and-breakfast in Newport. It listed all the antique stores within walking distance of Spring Street. It also gave the address, description, and hours of operation. None were named Atlanta Antiques. And after a check with some ancient phone directories, it seemed that all had been in business for several years.

A couple hours later, the phone rang, and I could see from the caller ID that it was Matt. He had to be out of court, and he would call only if he had a big success.

I jumped to pick up the phone. "Hey!"

He didn't bother with a greeting. "Did you say anything to Frizell today?"

I felt a sharp twist of something in my intestines. "What? Why?"

"Did you tell him I was going before the grand jury?"

"How could I tell him you were going to the grand jury today? I didn't even know that . . ." Until a half hour ago. But I didn't say that.

"Well, it's on the *Chronicle's* news blog today, and it's got Frizell's name on it."

I was going to kill Frizell; I knew this even before the *Chronicle* Web site loaded onto my screen. Right on top in the 24/7 news blog index, I saw *Something Up in Newport,* and with a deep-stomach certainty, I understood that I'd been screwed.

My finger felt numb as I clicked on the link.

Newport Grand Jury May Have Indictment Later Today

An inmate of the Rhode Island Adult Correctional Institution is testifying at today's grand jury proceedings in Newport County, according to sources close to the witness.

Although grand jury proceedings are secret, rumors are flying around Newport that today's subject matter is Pauley Sponik, a local businessman and former bad boy photographed in *People* magazine with celebrities.

Assistant AG Matthew Cavanaugh was on the losing end of a motion to dismiss charges he brought against Sponik for possession of handguns earlier this month. Judge Roland D. Towers said police had violated the scope of a search warrant used in discovering the guns.

Sponik claimed the guns belonged to the landlord and not to him.

Sources in the AG's Newport office say Cavanaugh has been devoting all his energies into "putting Sponik away for good," and said he expected an indictment from the grand jury would be a "slam dunk."

When asked if Cavanaugh was appearing before the grand jury today, a source close to Cavanaugh admitted, "He was wearing court clothes this morning, that's all I'll say."

Chronicle.com staff writer Mica Conway with reports by investigative reporter Jonathan Frizell.

For a moment, I was overwhelmed by my own stupidity. But my gut wrenched with foreboding. A story like this was going to destroy Matt's career.

Standing up with the phone still in my ear, I searched the newsroom for Frizell, who would be extremely lucky if I didn't kick him in the teeth. He wasn't at his desk. I panned to the other end of the room, to the Fishbowl, where editors had gathered for the afternoon meeting. Frizell wasn't there either.

"He said he just wanted to know if he had to work late," I told Matt. "If you were headed to the grand jury—then you'd probably be issuing a press release about the indictment tonight. I was so excited for you. . . . I didn't think he would—"

"No one could *ever* think Frizell would do anything *underhanded,*" Matt said with thick sarcasm.

"Matt, I'm so sorry."

"You have no idea how badly this screws me at work."

But I did know. I understood that if Matt got labeled in his office as a leak, a big mouth, a talker they couldn't trust, his reputation as a prosecutor would be destroyed.

"I'm so sorry," I repeated.

"I've got to go, the AG is on the other line," he said, and hung up the phone.

There was no indictment.

I didn't learn this from Matt, who didn't speak to me all night. I learned it from the *Chronicle* the next morning.

Matt rose early to go sailing with his brother. I was pointedly not invited. The newspaper didn't have any information, but I checked the Web site. There I found another story from Frizell, who apparently was working the weekend. This one said that sources "close to the defense" reported that the prosecution's star witness recanted his testimony. The story didn't name the star witness, but confirmed the indictment had been sought for Pauley Sponik.

So much for the *slam dunk.*

Although a part of me understood that Matt's real fury

should be directed at the sources in both his own department and on the defense who were delivering the bulk of the information to Frizell, I still felt horrible. I had broken our agreement. And for what? To help Frizell?

Even after a five-mile run on the Boulevard and along Hope Street, I felt no relief. My mind whirred with guilt. So when Walter called me again and asked if I'd go with him to the shooting range, I agreed. I might get some satisfaction pretending Frizell's face was photographed on the paper target.

Walter was in an unusually good mood on the ride home. We'd made friends with the guy in the next shooting station, who was the gun collector that Pez knew. He told Walter that he'd never invite Pez back again because he'd ignored all the safety precautions. Then he let us both shoot an AK-47.

It was significantly easier than the cute little handgun, but I was still feeling pretty low. Walter had not been sympathetic to my side of the story. He tried to cheer me up, telling me that Matt would "get over it," but he'd also added that I should know by now not to trust Frizell.

So we drove in silence for a while as I steamed, replaying in my mind the responses I should have given to shut down both Marcy Kittner and Frizell at the very first question. At the very first attempt to invade my personal life.

Walter kept shifting his eyes from the road to me. Finally, he said, "By the way, I asked all my drivers if they got any requests outside the regular old escort agency. No one had heard of anything featuring underage girls. Not in Rhode Island."

Shit.

"But then I chatted up the guy who owns the adult book

store when I was waiting on a fare. He said he'd never heard anything like that in Rhode Island either, but he did say there was a place in New Bedford—"

"New Bedford?" I sat up straight in the passenger seat. The heavy feeling I'd been carrying began to lift as I explained about tracking Rurik's license plates to the antique shop in New Bedford. And how the landlord said the owners might be opening a shop in South County somewhere.

Walter shot me a look. "Antique stores were the laundries of choice for some of the drug dealers I used to work with."

"The guys in Boston?"

"Yeah. But it could just be a generic thing. Antiques are great places to launder money because no one really knows how much you paid for the inventory or how much that shit should really sell for."

Then I had another thought. "You ever heard the name Richard Betnick?"

"Bet-nick?" He divided the word.

"Or Betnicki. The landlord said he couldn't really read the signature."

"You think it could have been Pez-nick. Richard Peznick?"

"Richard Peznick?" I had no clue who he was talking about.

"Pez."

"Holy shit. Did he say he was going into business in South County?"

"Yeah, with Woody and Jake. Two other pieces of shit."

"You think they'd be involved in child pornography?"

"I don't know. When I knew them, they were strictly drugs. But I guess it depends on how much money is in it. The one thing I can tell you is that if Pez is involved in this, he's definitely not the brains behind the operation. Or the capital. That guy can't keep his hand on a dollar."

"Can you call him for me? He wanted to catch up."

He looked ahead into the highway, resistant. Walter did not like to revisit his drug days. I knew I was asking too much, but I was desperate.

"He's not going to tell me anything over the phone," Walter finally said. "I'll have to go to a bar or have dinner with him." He made another face. "Even if he's not high, he's not anyone you want to spend time with. He's run out of brain cells, a blowhard to boot."

A blowhard was perfect. A blowhard talked too much. "Please," I begged. "It could help me find Lexie. Stop other young girls from getting involved with this Rurik guy."

He cut me off. "It could help you get on the front page."

"It's not just about me this time. It's about stopping these girls from wrecking the rest of their lives."

He looked at me a moment, evaluating my motives, before his gaze returned to the road ahead. "And you don't care where they run the story, right? Or if they promote it on the radio?"

"Of course I want it to get good play. That doesn't mean I don't care about the girls."

Walter said nothing, which pissed me off. Back in Boston, when I was struggling to stay off the Serax, Walter had understood that my career was part of my recovery. Lately, like every time Matt and I had a fight, Walter dropped another comment about how "single-minded" I was about my job. As if my job were just another personal problem. A topic for recovery.

"That's not fair," I finally said.

Walter took his eyes off the road to cut me a look.

I ignored it and pressed on. "And you're the one who was going to go to Best Price and take out Rurik. You want to get rid of guys like Rurik? Help me find where he's doing business, for God's sake."

"All right," he finally said, in a measured tone. "I'll call Pez. But you get anywhere near their operation, you either bring me along or you're packing that little gun in your pocket."

15

It was Tuesday, and I was sitting in the *Chronicle* cafeteria, having lunch with Bennett, when my cell phone rang.

"Eastern Atlantic Antiques," Walter reported. "But Pez says they're just moving in and haven't opened for business yet."

I reached across the table to grab Bennett's legal pad and pen. "Did he give you an address?"

"It's on a side street off Spring," he said. "In an area where there are a bunch of antique stores."

I began to thank him profusely, promising to do any favor he ever needed, when I stopped midsentence. "Spring Street? In Newport?"

"Yeah, between Thames and Spring." Walter knew about my agreement with Matt. That Newport was out of bounds. "You're going to have to tell him about this."

"Of course," I lied. Matt and I had not really talked about my info leak to Frizell yet. We were sleeping in the same bed, but there was a iceberg just barely melting in our condo. The temperature would go to zero again if I brought this up.

Across the table, Bennett was sprinkling vinegar on his french fries. He put the bottle down between us and cocked his head to one side, waiting for the update on my conversation with Walter.

For a minute, I considered sending Bennett to the antique store in my place.

But Bennett had proved himself useless in these circumstances, and Ellen and Ryan had worked last weekend and were off today on comp time. There was no way on earth that I could hand off this assignment to that asshole Frizell.

"Were you able to get anything out of Pez about the girls or a porn operation?" I asked Walter.

At the word *porn,* two reporters sitting in the next booth swiveled around.

"I couldn't ask him outright without letting on that I knew something," Walter said. "But I did ask why they moved the antiques from New Bedford to Newport."

"What did he say?"

"He said something about a landlord who hung around too much, and about one of their drivers who was pissing him off. And then he said something interesting. He might have just been trying to say he was still in the drug business, but he kind of leaned forward and winked. He said, 'In Newport, there's just a lot more people with money—and they'll spend it on all sorts of weird shit.'"

The sign for Eastern Atlantic Antiques was up, but the door was locked. Through the window, I could see several tall bureaus, a cedar chest, and what looked like an ornate headboard and footboard of a bed pushed together toward the back of the store. In the front, there was a ladder and a drop cloth.

I'd parked in one of the lots off of Americas Cup Boulevard and walked here, sweating through my standard reporter uniform, a khaki-colored button-down shirt and long pants. My legs grew heavier when I saw the building. It was not a likely location for the illicit sale of teenage sex.

For one thing, the building was not very deep, with little space for a back room, and no second floor. For another, the building was almost on the corner of Thames, a busy retail district. Cars fought each other for the limited parking on the street, and the shoppers who flooded the sidewalks could peer into windows and charge through doors.

"There's two or three other antique shops that are open just up the street," a woman about my own age told me. It was another warm day, without even a whisper of breeze off the water, and despite a crisp linen suit, the woman looked overheated. She carried what appeared to be a heavy tote bag embossed with the logo of one of those shops, Wishful Antiques and Fine Gifts.

"Do you work in one of them?" I asked.

She told me she was the store owner and pulled the tote bag sideways to better brandish the logo. A sharp afternoon sun glinted off the embossed gold.

"You know anything about the owners of this shop?" I asked.

"No one has met them." She sounded as if she spoke for the entire neighborhood. As if she'd polled every merchant on the street. "Are you looking for anything in particular?"

She meant a cocktail table or a dresser or a chair. In fairness,

I had to admit I wasn't a shopper but a reporter for the *Chronicle*. This admission either makes people back off immediately or take two steps closer. She took a step closer. "Oh, tell me you're not going to do a big feature about the competition, are you?"

"Nothing like that. I'm looking for a guy named Rurik. I think he drives for them."

Relieved, she stepped around me to see into the store window. "Oh. I guess it does look like someone has *finally* dropped off some inventory."

"Finally?"

"Don't get me wrong, I'd be thrilled if they never opened their doors for business, but they were supposed to be up and running by now. Word is that they got sidetracked by the motel project."

I had no idea what she was talking about.

"Supposedly, it's the same realty company that bought the Surfside up on 114." She crinkled her nose as if something smelled bad. "And God knows it'll take an awful lot of energy to rehab that old place."

The Surfside was as far away as you could get from the charm of Newport and still be on the same island.

Despite the name, there was no surf. No beach. Just the hot black tar of a highway clotted with chain stores, and a lot of traffic backing up at the light.

I got caught at that light in both directions, driving back and forth on the same strip of highway to try to get a look at the motel. But it was set far back from the road and completely surrounded by tall trees and overgrown shrubbery. All I could see was the name of the motel and a sign on the roof that advertised cable television.

Finally, I pulled into the strip mall next door and parked in front of the coin-operated laundry. I was hopeful that I might not even be in Newport anymore, but in the adjacent town of Middletown. That might buy me some leeway with Matt, although I doubted it.

The second I turned off the car and the air-conditioning, the heat became unbearable. I rolled down the window and listened for sounds of activity at the motel. But the shrubs between the two properties were thick, and the door to the laundry was open. All I could hear was the rhythmic thump of clothes dryers.

Or was that my heart pounding?

An out-of-the-way motel with lots of privacy for illicit sex and God knew what else. This *had* to be where Rurik had moved the operation.

I found my cell phone and called Bennett, asking him to look up the current ownership of the Surfside at the registry of deeds database. After he took down the address of the motel, he told me that the AG's office was to announce some new bust in Providence. Frizell was already on his way to the press conference, and Dorothy had just called Ellen in on her day off.

"So?"

"So there's no way she's going to assign any staff for surveillance unless you get something substantial."

Clicking off, I gazed through the passenger window, trying to see if there was a fence dividing the two properties or merely the shrubs. It was no big deal to just snoop around the motel at this hour, I told myself. Given the heat, work crews were probably gone for the day.

I stuffed my cell phone into one pocket and my digital

recorder into the other. Then, leaving my car parked in front of the laundry, I headed toward the shrubbery. I was relieved to see there was no fence to scale, just a few forsythia branches to survive.

Peering between the leaves, I couldn't see any cars. And there were no sounds of trucks backing up or power tools grinding. Just the whoosh of traffic from the highway.

I pushed through the shrub hedge, incurring only the most minor of scratches, and onto an empty parking lot. There were no cars, no construction vehicles, and much of the asphalt had been dug up so that the driveway had been reduced to gravel.

The motel was a typical design, a two-story building book-ended by cement staircases, with an ugly metal railing and overhanging roof. The exterior was some sort of fake stucco that looked like it had once been white.

There was no sign indicating that it was closed for renovation, but no signs of human life either. Still, I twitched when a car engine choked loudly on the highway. Anyone pulling up the motel's gravel driveway would spot me immediately.

I headed toward the nearest cement staircase, around the side, to the back of the motel. Here, I found large sections of the stucco exterior that had been pulled off the building and dumped on the ground. The entire railing had been ripped off the second floor and lay in pieces. I stepped over a pile of rusted metal to get closer to the first-floor rooms.

Each of the units had a small bathroom window and a slider that opened up to a slab of cement. None of the curtains were drawn. As I skirted along the back, I could see the standard is-sue decor: two double beds, a bureau, desk, and small wooden chair. Televisions and wall hangings had been removed, leaving empty Formica stands and exposed nail heads. The beds were stripped bare, and mounds of polyester bedspreads lay on the carpeting.

Midway across the building, there was a utility area filled with several unplugged ice and soda machines. Past this, another dozen units.

The first nine rooms were identical to the other side. The next two were completely stuffed with furniture and wall hangings, as if serving as a storage center. And then, on the very end of the building, I came across a room with its curtain drawn.

I got close to the slider and laid my cheek flat against the sliding glass, trying to see in through the sides. Nothing but faded green fabric liner. Hoping for a miracle, I tried the slider door. Locked tight.

I walked along the side of the building, around another ugly cement staircase and several more shrubs to get to the front of the motel. Although the room doors were solid wood, each unit had a small front window. A shoulder-height evergreen blocked the window of the corner room.

I tried the door first, but it, too, was locked tight. I pushed myself between the window and the evergreen to try the window sash. Stuck. I pounded on the upper corners of the frame to loosen it, and dug in with the heels of my palm. This time it opened, but only an eighth of an inch. I pushed again, and the window scraped open about a half inch more. It was enough for me to stick my hand under the frame and pull the curtain to the side.

Three leather couches were pushed up against a wall. The opposite wall was mirrored from floor to ceiling, divided only by a countertop with overflowing ashtrays, three laptops, and four webcams.

I felt both exhilarated and like I wanted to puke.

In the back of the room, against what must be the bathroom door, I saw a hinged screen, painted pink. In a corner, a tall pole mounted with lights leaned against a mini refrigerator. Three empty half-gallon bottles of vodka and a Diet Coke can were discarded on the floor.

I pulled out my cell phone first and aimed over the window sash to snap a dozen shots of the room, trying to get every allowable angle. Then I got my digital recorder out of my other pocket and held it over my head to capture the sounds of traffic on the highway.

That's when I heard the sound of tires on the gravel.

Shit.

I put the recorder back in my pocket and ducked under the evergreen, squatting with my back against a gnarled branch and my hands in the dirt.

I couldn't see the car through the dense brush, but I could hear the gravel spit louder until it stopped and the tires hit smooth asphalt. I heard the engine shut off and a car door open and shut.

A pair of legs appeared on the cement walkway, heading toward me. Male legs in pleated khaki pants, with sock-less ankles and boat shoes. Afraid my hands could be seen underneath the shrub, I lifted them slowly out of the dirt, and balanced on my knees.

The legs stopped in front of the unit door. A hand went into his front pocket and pulled something out. A key? He opened the door quickly and shut it softly. I could not see his face.

Another car engine approached. This one parked close enough that I could make out that it was white and sat high, on large tires. An SUV of some sort. These legs wore business pants and expensive, thin-soled leather shoes. Once inside the room, I heard a greeting with the first man, but there was no exchange of names.

My knees began to ache, waiting as two more cars pulled in. Three more sets of pants approached the room. Another key slipped into the locked door. The male voices inside the motel room began to rumble.

The refrigerator door swung open and slammed. Beer tops popped. Someone leaned toward the open window and blew out smoke. I crouched lower, dropping my head onto my knees.

"They're fucking late," the man at the window complained.

A new car spit gravel and squealed to a stop in front of the next unit, parking not twenty feet away. I felt my breath stop in my chest. This car was an out-of-date blue. About the length of a Camry.

The doors on this side of the car opened. These legs were young and female. Two sets. Tanned and bare. One in capri pants and glitter flip-flops. The other girl wore high-heeled mules and some sort of skirt.

As the legs approached the motel room, I got a better view. The skirt was short and fringed. I held on to my knees, desperate to maintain my balance. The girl did not lift her legs when she walked; the shoes scraped on the pavement.

I tried desperately to see her face, but I was crouched too low, bent too far forward. The girls stopped outside the motel room and waited. The glitter flip-flops had small hearts all over the soles. Shoes a Barbie might wear.

I heard the striking of a match and smelled cigarette smoke.

Another set of legs emerged from the car. These were male, in jeans; the shoes could be Nikes. "Put it out, you have no time for that now," a stern male voice said. The accent was Russian.

I swallowed air. Rurik.

"Just a sec," one of the girls said. Her voice thin and high. Maybe fifteen.

The other one giggled.

Behind him, another pair of female legs ran to meet them. These were shorter legs, pale. The shoes were spiked, black heels. As the legs got closer, I could see a Band-Aid on one heel and on her ankle, a small tattoo.

Lexie?

The door to the motel unit swung open, and the legs disappeared inside. Rurik's voice welcomed the men, issued orders to the girls to change their clothes. I strained to hear a single female voice, but they responded in a jumble. A door inside opened. The bathroom? Ice clinked in cups.

Then I heard the sound of the curtains being pulled, and Rurik's voice directly over my head. "Who opened window?" he asked.

I froze, head bent on my knees, praying to God he wouldn't look down into the shrub.

"I think it was open," another male voice replied.

"When you arrived? This window was open?" Rurik pressed.

My heart pounded against my thigh so loudly that I was afraid he could hear it. "Window was open?" Rurik repeated.

My arms were like rods clenched against my legs, and my head was so low, I could smell the dirt. It seemed like forever until there was an answer.

"What difference does it make?" a male voice finally said. "Maybe I opened it. I lit a joint and needed some air."

The window slammed shut.

For several minutes, I didn't dare move. I stayed put, the needles scraping the back of my shoulders, waiting for my breathing to return to normal. Then, when I heard the blast of Nine Inch

Nails, singing for permission to "desecrate you," I crawled out of the evergreen. Crouching low, I crept past the blue Camry and line of parked cars before I stopped and looked back.

The door of the room remained shut. No one had heard or seen me.

Hiding behind the last car, a Land Rover, I pulled out my cell phone again. This time I snapped the two nearest license plates.

Keeping tight to the building, I finally stood up. Then I ran like hell, back through the shrubbery to the safety of the laundry next door.

16

"**Where on earth** have you been?" Dorothy asked, looking me up and down.

It was almost six o'clock when I got back to the newsroom. I had dirt on my hands and face and scratches on the back of my arms. My hair was sweaty and tangled, and surely my eyes were wild. "Hell," I said. "I've been to hell."

We were standing just outside the Fishbowl. Nathan and Ian Clew were deep in conversation, and didn't see me as they filed out of the conference room, heads together. Several of the editors and assistant editors who trailed behind them eyed me and exchanged glances.

I was a mess. Torn up and not just on the outside. I'd struggled about what to do. Sitting in my car in front of the laundry, I'd dialed 911. Then hung up before it could connect. I knew Dorothy could fire me if I jeopardized this story by going to the police.

I'd decided I had to make the call anonymously, and drove up and down Route 114 in search of a pay phone. By the time I found one, outside a Kentucky Fried Chicken, twenty minutes had passed. I began to worry that the police would show up too late to make an arrest. The only thing I'd accomplish would be to make certain Rurik moved his operation somewhere else.

So instead, I'd driven back to the newsroom feeling dirtied by the whole experience. But I couldn't let that show. "We've got them red-handed," I told Dorothy, waving my cell phone at her.

"You've got photos?" she asked.

I pulled my digital recorder out of my pocket. "And sound."

She actually clapped her hands. "Ian will love this."

We moved to the conference table inside the Fishbowl, where Dorothy and Bennett huddled around me as I clicked through the pictures of the motel room. Bennett copied the license plate numbers, which he'd get his insurance company source to run down. I waited until Frizell and Ellen joined us before I told the whole story from the antique store to the motel to the evergreen where I'd hid.

Sitting across from me, Frizell took my cell phone and studied the photos. "I don't see any of the girls," he said.

I reminded him that I'd been crouching under a shrub. "All I would have gotten is flip-flops."

"Exactly."

He was telling me flip-flops were not enough. As if I didn't know that. Making porno by itself wasn't illegal; we had to be able to prove these girls were underage. "Obviously, we have to go back and watch the motel. Position a photog at the laundry next door and shoot with a telephoto lens. We've also got to go down there in a car that Rurik doesn't know so we can follow him when he drives the girls home."

"Is that all?" Frizell laid on the sarcasm.

What was his problem? I glanced at the others to see if they were also recording this bizarre behavior. But no one else looked surprised or confused.

Frizell decided to fill me in. Providence police had made an arrest today of a dealer caught with the high-potency heroin. Parents of the victims who had died from the drug had staged a rally at the press conference and were demanding murder charges. Ian Clew now thought the story had "juice" potential. He'd demanded an in-depth investigation of the Providence-to-Boston drug network.

The air that left my lungs seemed to deflate my entire body. I sat there at the conference table, desperately hoping that Frizell was merely being an asshole. I sought Ellen's eyes, silently pleading for her to tell me this wasn't true.

"I'm assigned to cover the bail hearing tomorrow," she said.

I'd been halfheartedly hoping that I could hand off surveillance to Ellen and keep my promise to Matt.

"Why can't Leo cover the bail hearing?" I asked. "Or Stacey?" These were the court and police reporters.

"For obvious reasons, Ian wants the investigative team on this," Frizell said.

I looked to Ellen, who shrugged. No way was she going to argue when the publisher specifically asked for her skills in a high-profile assignment.

"Ryan and I can do it," I said. "We really only have to watch the motel during after-school hours."

"I need Ryan to help *me*," Frizell said.

"These are young girls we're talking about. Destroyed for life. Don't any of you care about that?"

Ellen murmured something that might have been supportive, but I could barely hear her. Frizell was arguing that it wasn't about "caring." It was about "priorities" and "limited resources."

"We're talking about fifteen- and sixteen-year-old girls," I said. "This *isn't* our priority?" I turned to Dorothy. She sat with her hands clenched on the table and her bottom lip sucked in, as if she had to think real hard about this.

This pissed me off. I opened my mouth. Shut it again. Screaming at Dorothy might provide relief, but it would get me nowhere. I swallowed, took a deep breath, and tried another tack. "But we've got photos and video, too, remember? And sound." I waved my tape recorder.

She looked from me to Frizell, and back to me. Only she wasn't looking at me, but past me, through the glass wall of the Fishbowl.

I turned around and saw Ian Clew standing at the open door of Corey's office. Dorothy pushed away from the table and stood up. "Ian didn't know about this development in the cam girls' investigation. Let me try to catch him before he leaves tonight and see which direction he wants us to go."

We all swiveled in our chairs to watch as Dorothy walked through the newsroom to Corey's office. As she stopped at the door, standing just behind Ian, waiting for a break in the conversation, Frizell took a twenty-dollar bill out of his pocket and threw it on the table.

"Ian is gonna choose the heroin story."

"Bullshit," I said.

"You on?" Frizell asked.

God knows I'm a betting woman. But suddenly, I was enraged at his attempt at jocularity. As if we were poker buddies. I turned so I could look at him, allow him to see my utter disdain. "I don't trust you enough to gamble with you," I said. "So keep your money."

For a moment, he looked baffled, as if he had no idea what I was talking about. Then it came to him. "What are you talking about? I didn't quote you by name," he said.

"You lied to me. Tricked me. Totally screwed me at home. Matt is still furious," I said. "And so am I."

The others were looking at us, confused, so I explained how Frizell pretended he was just getting information for scheduling purposes when he was really going to use it online.

"For the Pauley Sponik grand jury story," Frizell said to the others, as if this were a viable defense.

Ellen shook her head at him, disgusted.

"I didn't quote her by name," Frizell repeated.

"You're a dirtbag, Frizell," Bennett said. "But I'll be more than happy to take your money." He dug into his pockets and threw a twenty on the pile. "Because Hallie's going to win this one."

But I wasn't so sure. Turning back to the glass, we could see that Dorothy had finally gotten the chance to step forward to speak to Ian, but he was standing with his arms crossed, not appearing receptive. Then, he leaned into her to say something, and the angle shaded his expression from view. They stood this way, in conversation, for what seemed like forever.

And then Nathan, who was facing us, became animated, interrupting Dorothy and gesturing with his hands toward the City Desk. She nodded and turned, making her way back to the Fishbowl. We all righted ourselves in our chairs and faced each other, as if we hadn't been watching her the entire time. Bennett threw a notebook over the two twenties, hiding the bet just as Dorothy appeared at the door.

"Okay, there's been another change in plans," she said. "Leo can cover the bail hearing tomorrow. You all will adjust your life schedules, because you're going to take turns watching that motel room, from two o'clock every afternoon till midnight. All through the weekend. Ian wants to break open this webcam story, and nail those pigs in Newport to the wall."

The condo was empty. There was a message on the answering machine from Matt, saying he was working late again, and not to wait up.

I felt both anxious and relieved. Anxious because I worried he might not be working late at all but staying away from the condo to avoid me. And relieved because I didn't want to face him after a day of sneaking around his back.

I glanced out the bedroom window at my garden. Even from here, I could see it needed to be weeded. But gardening had a tendency to slow me down. It was meditative. And I was in no mood to think. No mood to acknowledge my personal failings.

I pulled away from the window. I much preferred to ride the adrenaline rush, the excitement of my newsroom success, and the certainty that the team would be able to nail Rurik to the wall. If I could save Lexie, all would be justified.

Matt had left a pair of basketball sneakers on the floor beside his dresser. I picked them up and threw them into the closet, where I wouldn't be able to see them. Then I shoved his stack of legal newsletters under the bed. Finally, I turned my back on the bedroom entirely and shut the door behind me.

Desperate to celebrate my victory over Frizell, I decided to call Walter, who had the night off. I offered to take him out to dinner in thanks for his tip.

We met at Andreas, a Greek restaurant with comfortable booths that looked out on Thayer Street. I ordered myself a glass of retsina and clinked it with Walter's glass of iced tea.

Then between the cucumber salad and the lamb kebabs, I explained the whole afternoon, beginning at the antique store and ending in the newsroom battle.

"So, I'm glad you won," Walter said, but it didn't sound like he was glad.

"But what?"

"But you've got to either let the other members of the in-vestigative team take charge or—"

"I'm not bowing out of this assignment now. Not after all the work I've done and when I'm this close." I pressed my thumb and forefinger together, leaving about a sixteenth of an inch be-tween them. "This close to finding Lexie."

"Then you've got to come clean with him," Walter insisted.

"I might have told him tonight, but he's working late again," I said. This was entirely a lie.

"So later, when he gets home—"

"I'll try." But I had no intention of springing this confession on Matt tonight when he was exhausted. Mostly, I just wanted to shut Walter up.

I didn't want to talk about Matt. Or about the promises I'd made to him. I wanted to talk about how I was going to get Rurik and every one of those dirtbag clients who paid to watch those young girls. "You should see some of the expensive cars these guys drive," I said.

This managed to divert him. "You didn't see Pez's car there, did you?" he asked. "A Mercedes coupe?"

I shook my head.

"That's good, I guess."

"Hey, if he's involved with these people, businesswise, he's going to go down," I said.

"Oh, I know that," Walter said. "And it's not like I'd feel guilt pangs if Pez went to jail. I'd just feel a lot better about ever having hung with this dude if he's not actually an active pervert watching fourteen-year-old girls."

"You aren't going to believe who owns the Range Rover," Bennett said, grabbing me as I walked past the library late the next morning. Bennett was practically panting with good news. And his face was flushed.

"Who?"

He pulled me through the library into his office and shut the door. Before he would tell me, though, he sat down at his computer and called up a photo on Google Images.

"Did you see that guy there?" he asked, pointing to the enlarged photo.

"I didn't see anything but shoes," I replied before shifting my attention to the photo. It was the cover of *Rhode Island Monthly,* and the guy was Jason Keriotis, the founder of the Buzz, looking thoughtful with his hand placed on his chin.

I couldn't even say anything. I just stared at Bennett, and we both smiled with a sort of disbelief. If we could get photos of Keriotis going in or out of that motel room, we wouldn't only destroy this guy's reputation, but in a small state like Rhode Island, we could seriously hurt the reputation of the social network—especially among local advertisers.

"Ian is going to go out of his mind with joy," Bennett said.

The other two car owners were almost as good. One we confirmed as a forty-two-year-old high school teacher from West Kent. The other was a twenty-seven-year-old who worked in the accounting department of a cable television company.

It was one o'clock, and all the editors were still out to lunch. I was supposed to leave in half an hour to take Ellen and the photographer to the motel in Newport, show them where the room was, and how to set up in the laundry next door. But no way was I going to miss seeing Dorothy's face when she got *this* news.

The newsroom began to refill after the lunch hour. Soon, all keyboards were clicking and phones ringing. It felt like forever before we spotted Dorothy coming off the elevator. Bennett and I charged over, meeting her at reception.

She came back with us to Bennett's office, sat down in the chair I'd dragged in, and opened the file. There was a long pause. Then she looked up with that same smile I'd worn. Her eyes sparkled with journalistic wickedness. Then she picked up the phone to call Nathan. Within minutes, the two of them were headed up to the fourth floor to meet with the publisher.

17

I'd hit traffic on my way back from Newport. By the time I made it to the newsroom, the afternoon meeting was breaking up. Dorothy was standing outside the Fishbowl in conversation with Jonathan Frizell. She must have been waiting for me because she spotted me the moment I cleared reception.

She stood on her toes to wave across the newsroom. Not a hello wave. A two-handed extended-arm wave. A your-story-is-the-most-important-thing-at-the-*Chronicle* wave.

Assistant city editors were still milling around the Fishbowl, talking to Nathan. But Nathan didn't appear to be listening to them. His eyes were on me.

Dorothy was turning back into the vacated Fishbowl, so I crossed the newsroom to her. I was dying to hear how the meeting went, wanted to know the exact expression on Ian's face when he found out Jason Keriotis was one of those "Newport pigs." The assistant editors all dispersed as I cut through the aisle. Jonathan gave me a funny look as he walked by. What was it? Envy?

Inside the Fishbowl, Dorothy was already seated, head bent into a file. "How did he react?" I meant the publisher. "Was he blown away?"

"He was blown away, all right," she said. But there was something cautionary in her tone. Her eyes met mine warily.

"What?"

A moment passed before Dorothy could say it. "The lawyers have raised liability issues with the webcam story."

"What kind of issues?" The involvement of minors? Making sure the girls were underage?

She didn't answer. "We're pulling you off of it."

I couldn't possibly be hearing her right. "Pulling me off the story? It was my idea."

"Not just you," Dorothy said softly. "Everyone."

"You're pulling *everyone* off the story?" I couldn't believe it. "We can *prove* those girls are underage, it'll just take us a couple of weeks—"

"We don't have the staff to invest in this," Dorothy said. Then she coughed into her fist.

With some effort, she finally looked me in the eye. "The heroin story is hot right now, and that's got to be our priority."

"But Ian said—"

"Ian changed his mind."

"We get this incredible break—this incredible link to Jason Keriotis. Not to mention a West Kent high school teacher. And you want to forget about it. Kill the story? *Now?*"

Dorothy had a hard-blinking, unhappy look. And there was no emotion in her voice. "Look, you screwed up."

"I screwed up, how?"

"You took those photos of the motel room while on motel property. That's a privacy violation. We can't use those shots."

"Okay, so we go back another time and use a telephoto lens from the laundry next door. Or maybe from the street—"

But Dorothy wasn't listening. "And the license plates—those, too. Those were shot on motel property. We can't use those, either."

"Are you sure it's a problem if we don't use those actual photos in the paper?" I asked. I mean how did the paparazzi get all those topless movie star shots on private beaches?

But Dorothy wasn't listening to a word I said. "This story will just take way too much time and resources to prove."

"Just last night this was Ian's baby. It had juice. 'Online Dangers: Your Teenager Is Prey.' What happened to that?"

"Ian wants you in charge of the heroin story," Dorothy said.

Since when was Ian making assignments within the investigative team? And why reward me in any way if I'd really fucked up? "That's Frizell's story," I said.

"He wants you on it." Dorothy tried to make this sound like a vote of confidence.

But all this meant was that Frizell had nothing to do with this change in plan. Agitated anew, I stood up. I didn't know where Ian's office was on the fourth floor. And I'd never heard of another reporter taking her case directly to the publisher. But there was something drastically wrong here. Something that didn't add up. "I'm going upstairs to talk to Ian. I'm going to explain—"

"He's gone," Dorothy said before I got to the door. "On a flight back to California for meetings."

This was bullshit. I spun around. "I'm not letting up on this webcam story," I said. "I'm not letting this go."

I couldn't even look at her anymore, I was so disgusted. A

drum beat through my brain, pounded out my anger as I charged out of the Fishbowl and through the newsroom. When I was halfway back to my desk, Dorothy caught up to me. "You *have* to let it go," she said. She had me by the arm, in front of the Online department. A full staff looked up from the nonstop clicking of keyboards at their desks.

Dorothy's voice was low and full of warning. "The Ink and Mirror people are just looking for excuses to reduce the news staff and hire these young Web people. You defy Ian on this, he'll fire you. For *cause*. And he'll get away with it."

"I don't give a shit," I said, pulling away my arm.

"Yes, you do," she insisted. "Or you will when you calm down. Play it smart this time. Let it go."

I called Ellen from home the next morning. It was after ten o'clock, but I wasn't going back to the newsroom until I could plan my strategy. I needed to know the real reason Ian had killed the story.

"I've got the names of men who should be jailed and registered for the rest of their lives as sex offenders, and I'm supposed to forget about it? Move on to the next story?" I said.

"Yeah, but you got those names illegally."

"What?"

"Dorothy said you fucked up. You should know we're not supposed to take photographs when we're on private property. I mean it's a whole privacy issue."

I couldn't believe I was hearing this: Ellen toeing the company line. "Okay, maybe I screwed up, but we could go back and get them again, legally," I said. "Stand on the public sidewalk and snap the license plates as they leave the motel . . ."

"Well, Ian's all hot on this heroin story now, so I've got to go meet with some guy running the rehab clinic in Providence who knew one of the victims. I think it was supposed to be your story, but since you're not playing along . . ."

But I had stopped listening. *Not playing along?* It sounded as if she was blaming me. "Ellen, don't you care about these young girls?"

She didn't agonize over this one. "I never met them, Hallie. Not like you. Besides, caring is pointless." Her tone suggested that I was indulging myself by giving a shit.

"I can't believe this," I said.

"Hallie, it's not like we're going to change Dorothy's mind, so just let it go."

Let it go? The same words Dorothy had used. Usually Ellen sided with me, but of course, Ellen and Dorothy *were* longtime friends. I realized now that I would get nowhere. I took a deep breath, squelched my fury, and changed tacks.

"Okay, I understand your position," I said, "but you've got an ear on the fourth floor. Have you heard anything about why Ian went out to California?"

There was a long silence. She *knew*. But she'd been coached, prepped by Dorothy. I would get nothing. "He went to California?" She tried to sound surprised.

I called Bennett next. He hadn't even heard the story was canceled. "I wondered why I never got my file back."

He meant the file we'd given to Dorothy yesterday. The printout that detailed the license plates I'd photographed at the motel—and the owners of the vehicles. "Make me a copy and e-mail it to me, will you?" I asked.

"Sure," he said. "What are you going to do with it?"

"I don't know yet." I didn't tell him I'd violated privacy

laws by snapping those license plates on private property, just in case.

I heard the clicking of his keyboard. "It's on the way," he said.

I told him about the publisher's sudden departure to California, and he promised to try to go gather the scuttlebutt in the newsroom.

But before he could report back, I got the answer I needed from Walter.

A fare he'd picked up at the airport yesterday had left a copy of the *L.A. Times* in the back of his cab. In the business section, Walter had found a story that he thought I should read.

Fifteen minutes later, we were in my kitchen. I sat at the butcher block table, reading the article, while Walter made himself some tea.

Negotiations between the Ink and Mirror Media Group of Sacramento and the network of weekly newspapers around San Francisco recently broke down when the media conglomerate decided to shift directions.

"We don't need any more print acquisitions," said Lowell Harcourt, chief executive officer. "We need to enlarge our online presence. We're losing ad revenue to the Web, and we need to make a move to stem our losses."

"This isn't new," I told Walter. "They've been saying this shit about the online presence since they bought the *Chronicle*."

"Keep reading," he said.

Sources close to the Ink and Mirror Media Group say the company is in negotiations to acquire a number of the small regional social networking sites that have sprung up around the country.

The company is believed to be closing a deal in Rhode Island, where one local site has provided competition to MySpace and Facebook.

"Oh my God," I said softly.

"I think they probably mean the Buzz," Walter said. The teakettle was whistling, and he snapped it off.

But I could still feel the high pitch. In my teeth. The sharpness of it. This is why Ian had killed my story. It made perfect sense. He no longer wanted to destroy the competition. He wanted to buy it.

An hour and a half later, I threw the business section onto Dorothy's desk. I pointed to the article in the lower corner. "Did you know about this?"

Startled, she pulled away from her computer. "Jesus, Hallie—"

"Read it, please," I said.

Something crossed her brow. Guilt, maybe. Reluctantly, she grabbed her reading glasses from her desk and picked up the newspaper by its edge, as if wary of smudging the newsprint. She looked up at me when she was done. "This is an unnamed source," she said, impugning its credibility.

But I could see it in her eyes, knowledge. She was not shocked. She was not appalled. She was willing to do anything to protect her job.

"There's a fifteen-year-old who is dead," I said. "And another one who probably was kidnapped."

"We're not the police, Hallie. We don't solve crimes; we print stories."

"Apparently not. Apparently we don't print any story that might hurt our business plan."

My voice rose on *business plan*. The assistant editor at the next desk rolled away, distancing himself. Corey Weist, who was walking over from the Online department, halted midway.

Dorothy was handing me back my copy of the *L.A. Times.* "Try to understand that a newspaper *is* a *business.*"

If this were coming from Nathan, maybe I'd be less infuriated. But from Dorothy? A woman who had always put the ethics of a story first. The newsroom had grown hot, crowded by people who were all keeping their distance. Crowded by people all willing to do whatever the Ink and Mirror Group demanded.

I had walked away from a bad situation at that motel room. I'd made the decision *not* to call police because I thought they'd get there too late, blow the arrest, *and* screw up the story. I'd trusted the paper. I believed that we'd get the goods to expose this operation. And now my editor was turning on me. And worse, pretending that backing away from this story was actually the right thing to do.

I wanted to throw the *L.A. Times* back at her. Instead, I forced it under my arm. I would not scream. Instead, I kept my voice painfully low. "I'm not going to let this go, back off, or swallow one word of this bullshit," I said.

Her eyes met mine, but I could see nothing in them. She had anticipated my response and steeled herself for this moment. "Then I have no other choice, Hallie," she said. "I have to fire you."

18

By the time I got back home, I believed it.

I didn't have a job.

I was shaking on the inside, blood hot, fingertips cold, my brain pounding, but emotions numb. I recognized this as shock, like when I'd lost two thousand dollars at the blackjack table. The magnitude of it was just too big for my body to absorb.

I dropped down on the living room couch, barely aware of where I was. I stared without seeing. My eyes felt swollen, but I wasn't crying. I was still only halfway there. Dorothy had fired me. That I got. But why?

No one became a newspaper reporter for the money. It had always been for the mission. Pursuit of truth. Full disclosure of everyone and everything.

And now? I slipped backwards, replaying the scene in the newsroom, the dead look in Dorothy's eyes when she'd said those words. *I have to fire you.* She didn't have to fire me. She could have stood behind me. Fought for me.

I flicked on the television and proceeded not to watch it. My mind continued to churn as I thought of questions I should have asked or comments I should have made. Eventually, it grew dark in the condo, and I flicked off the television and turned on a lamp.

The only good thing in this horrendous day was that Matt had left a message on my cell phone that he was stopping to pick up pizza. A much-needed makeup pizza, he had said. As if he were willing to give it a shot and that maybe we could recover from Frizell's dirty trick.

I couldn't blame Matt for having avoided me when I'd been relieved to avoid him. When I'd been willing to ignore the promise I made him.

To get the story. The story that Ian had killed. The story that no longer fit into the *Chronicle*'s business plan. I'd been willing to sacrifice my personal life for that story.

The pursuit of truth. I snorted aloud.

Finally, I got up and went to the dining room to sit down at my laptop. But there were no messages in my mailbox. And when I heard Matt coming up the stairs, I flicked that off, too.

He arrived with a mushroom pizza and a six-pack of Corona.

"I've been really pissed off and frustrated at work," he began, "and I haven't handled this very well. I've just been avoiding you, and that's not fair."

Fair? The words stung.

"Has there been a lot of fallout from the grand jury story?" I asked.

"I got a memo. A warning from Aidan. He's not happy with me right now. It's a trust issue. Hopefully, I can prove myself. Get past it."

That didn't sound too encouraging. That sounded as if he were still deep in the doghouse. I felt a wave of guilt that Matt must have seen in my eyes.

"Look, you weren't the only source who leaked information to Frizell. And they can't be a hundred percent sure that he was quoting you about my court clothes," he said.

This valiant effort to reassure me had the opposite effect. Here he was trying to minimize my culpability in his struggles at work, while I'd been sneaking around his back. Effectively, no better than Frizell.

My appetite had dissolved, but I followed Matt and the pizza back to the living room, anyway. I knew exactly what I had to do. What I should have done the first time I'd learned that motel was in his territory.

"So what if you hadn't gotten fired?" he asked after I'd explained everything to him.

Then I would have turned the story over to Ellen or Frizell. Ryan? None of this was plausible. I said nothing.

We were sitting side by side on the couch, with the ignored pizza growing cold on the coffee table. Matt studied the inside of his beer bottle as he waited for some sort of response. When he got none, he finally met my eyes. "Are you saying that you'd still be lying to me?"

I wished to hell I could deny this outright. That there was no question that I would have done the right thing, no matter what. Instead, I looked down at my slice of pizza, which was getting cold and congealing on the paper plate, and felt a thorough revulsion. "I wanted to tell you," I said. "But when you weren't home, I put it off. . . . I shouldn't have put it off, I should have told you. . . ."

"So it was my fault?" He stood up.

"No. It wasn't your fault. It was my fault. That's why I'm telling you now, because I realize that."

But he walked away from me. As if he couldn't stand the sound of my voice. He paced to the dining room table. He still had the beer bottle in his hand. He put it down on one of his legal pads and turned back to me.

"I gave up the job in Providence, moved to Newport, which has—let's face it—sucked. It's been one failure after another. But it was our deal. I promised I'd do it to make this relationship work. And I was okay with that."

"You haven't been okay with it," I said. "You've been miserable. And we've been miserable—"

"Right. But I stuck by it." His brown eyes were both angry and sad. "For you."

I stood up, too, and began to walk toward him, but he held up a hand to keep me at a distance. "The first time there's a Newport story you want, you just completely ignore your end of the bargain," he said.

"I didn't mean for it to happen. When I first got this lead, the story led to New Bedford. Out of state, for God's sake, an antique shop in New Bed—"

"Please. When you figured out that it had moved to Newport, you could have told me. Or you could have handed it off to someone else."

"I just had to make sure the information checked out. I had

an obligation to my sources, young girls. One who I think was probably kidnapped—"

Now the brown eyes blazed. "It was all about doing the right thing, then, huh?"

"It was, Matt. These are young girls who are being ruined for life—"

"And you know it's going on in a local motel? And I can shut it down. And you don't tell me? No, Hallie, it wasn't about the girls. It was about making the front page."

"I had an obligation to the team. . . ."

"How about your obligation to me, Hallie? Was that ever in the equation?"

"Of course it was."

"I wish I believed you." He turned and walked to the bedroom, shutting the door behind him. I heard footsteps back and forth, drawers opened, and zippers ripped shut. When Matt came out of the room, he'd changed into jeans and a T-shirt and was carrying what looked like a gym bag full of clothes. "I'm going down to stay at my brother's for a couple of days, and then we'll have to decide what to do," he said.

Decide what to do? I had to struggle not to fall apart. Not to do the cheap thing and cry. "It's your condo. If anyone should leave, it should be me," I said.

"No, you stay here."

"Matt, please. I'm sorry about this. Really, I—"

He looked at me, and his expression softened. "I'm sorry, too," he said. "I'm sorry about your job, I'm sorry that we're fighting. And I'm sorry we just can't seem to make it work."

Then he grabbed his car keys off the dining room table and, without turning around again, headed down the stairs to the street.

I **awoke just** before four o'clock in the morning with a headache. I took a couple of Advils and tried to go back to sleep, turning from side to side. But no matter what ear I put on the pillow, I could feel sadness and regret pulsing inside.

I got out of bed and wandered to the dining room. I flipped on the laptop and went to the Buzz. Whitney's profile page had been deleted. For some reason, this made it all seem worse.

The battery light on my laptop started blinking. The laptop was company property and would have to go back to the *Chronicle*. But that hardly seemed to matter.

What mattered was that Matt would never forgive me. And for good reason.

I clicked to Lexie's page and felt relieved it was still there. As if this were an omen, that this meant that unlike Whitney, she was still reachable somehow.

Matt was right about everything else. I'd been compulsively ambitious pretty much my whole life. But he was wrong about this story. It wasn't just about the front page. It *was* about the girls.

I went for a run on the Boulevard and punished myself by upping my mileage, taking the run into the neighborhoods, allowing the sidewalks to pound into my knees.

There was no runner's high. No endorphins. I still felt like the world's biggest loser when I returned home, sweaty and tired and with a cramp in my calf that made me feel my best running days were behind me. But I was clear on one thing.

If this whole mission was about the girls, there was no reason to drop it just because I was no longer a reporter. In fact, if

I did that, if I *let it go,* as Dorothy had insisted, the *Chronicle* would have won the game.

If this was about the girls, it was up to me now to prove it.

I parked at the laundry parking lot next to the motel.

It was the next afternoon, a half hour before any high school or middle school let out. I turned on the radio to a talk station and slouched down in my seat, ready to wait.

I'd keep waiting in this parking lot as long as it took for them to come back to this motel with those men. As the day had gone on, I kept replaying my frustration with Dorothy, and my anger with the *Chronicle.* I'd made too many sacrifices for the paper, too many mistakes in my life. But I could make at least some of those mistakes worthwhile, if I could save Lexie.

So I was going to do what I should have done the first time. When the girls and the men arrived, I'd give them five or ten minutes to get rolling, and then I was going to call Matt. And if I couldn't get him, I'd call the police. I'd say that I heard someone screaming. Or I heard gunshots. Anything to get the cops there in record time.

It wasn't just about the story. It *was* about doing the right thing.

I had the radio on to a mid-afternoon political talk show. The cohost today was the *Chronicle's* political columnist, Charlie B. He was speculating about who was going to run for attorney general this year. "Last year, this time, everyone would have thought it would be Matt Cavanaugh, who was a rising star, but now, it's anybody's guess."

I snapped off the radio.

Matt hadn't answered his cell phone all day, and I had no idea when he was coming back to the condo. I didn't want to think about him. Or where I would move. Or how I had destroyed our relationship.

It was still a little too early for the girls to come, but I decided I should probably just check and see if there were any cars in the motel lot.

I squeezed myself through the forsythia hedge and onto the motel lawn. The lot was empty; even the crane was gone. The last of the stucco had been pulled off the building, and it looked naked and still.

There were no signs of life. Not even a crushed soda can or fast food bag blowing across the lawn. For the first time, I noticed the Dumpster. What looked like a brand-new Dumpster, set up on the far end of the motel, near where I'd hidden in the evergreen.

Any number of reporters have found their best clues in the trash. Discarded receipts, printouts, maps—you name it. There might be something in that trash that could lead me to a client list or even the online payment processor.

I slipped around the back of the motel the way I had last time. Only now, I moved quickly to my goal on the other side of the building. As I turned the corner, I slowed down, stopped to make sure the front lot was still empty. I listened for voices, but all I could hear was the traffic on the highway. The coast was clear.

Luckily, I was wearing an old pair of blue jeans, a cotton T-shirt, and my running shoes. The Dumpster was enormous, but one side of the retractable metal lid was open on its hinge. I stuck my foot in one of the ridges along the rusty side of the beast and hoisted myself up to hold my weight on my forearms.

As I peered down into the trash, the first thing I saw was my reflection. Cracked into three parts.

A broken mirror covered the heap of rubble. I smelled paint and cigarette butts and mold.

I saw a half-dozen broken bottles, an ashtray, an empty jar of maraschino cherries, and a long piece of Formica counter. The strength in my arms suddenly gave way, and I dropped off the Dumpster onto my feet. My entire body was cold.

This couldn't be happening. Not again.

I ran to the corner motel room and slid between the exterior wall and the shrub. I was afraid someone might have locked the window this time. But today, it wasn't only unlocked, it was open a crack. The curtains were already pulled to the sides. Standing on my toes, I had a perfect view.

The mirror in the Dumpster had been stripped from these walls, the Formica counter removed. The laptops were gone. So were the couches and lighting pole.

Two queen beds were in place, with a nightstand between them and a bureau in the corner. The operation had clearly been shut down, the only evidence of its existence, the trash in the Dumpster.

I dropped down to my heels and pressed my forehead into the wall. Then, as the lemony smell of detergent wafted out of the cleansed room, I felt a wave of nausea. Between yesterday and today, someone had tipped off Rurik.

Lexie was gone.

19

I sifted through the Dumpster as best I could with all the broken glass. But there was nothing of use there. No receipts, no papers, no hint of where Rurik and Lexie might have moved to next.

I returned home, feeling disgusting and desperate. A long shower took care of the disgusting part. But there was no washing off the desperation. Lying on the couch watching the Red Sox, I couldn't pay attention, couldn't care whether we got a hit or struck out. I sat up in the dark and debated opening one of the beers Matt had left behind. Drinking alone was never a good idea when you felt desperate.

"The Hokey Pokey" started playing somewhere in the back of the condo. My cell phone. I jumped off the couch, praying to God it was Matt.

I found the phone on top of the microwave in the kitchen. It was a number I didn't recognize. I flipped it open anyway.

It was Josh O'Connor. Whitney's brother. "Can you meet me?"

"Right now?" I asked.

"Yeah." Josh's voice was loud. I pulled the phone a quarter inch away from my ear. I heard voices in the background, as if he were in a car full of people.

"You find Lexie's phone number?"

Someone in the background was shouting his name. He told whoever it was to shut the fuck up. "You going to meet me?" he asked.

It was odd that he wanted to meet instead of giving me the information over the phone. But I welcomed an excuse to get out of the house. "Where?"

He gave me an address. A home in East Greenwich, which was at least twenty minutes away.

"Are you at a party?" I asked.

"Didn't your message say anywhere, anytime?" Now, besides being loud, his tone was belligerent. Like maybe he'd been drinking.

"I'm on my way," I said.

East Greenwich is an affluent suburb with a pretty harbor and a lot of colonial clapboard. But I never got close to the downtown historic district. Mapquest directed me off the highway onto my first right, where I passed a lot of modern buildings and a leafy golf club. Eventually I turned into a development full of large suburban homes, all with big porches and large lawns. Must have been a big sale nearby on those spiral-pruned evergreens in ornate planters.

A half block before I came to the house, I could hear the

music. The Black Eyed Peas, a chorus of hip, urban voices giving suburban teenagers just the advice they needed: to get "stupid" and "get it started."

A dozen cars filled the driveway, and another dozen were on the street. A volleyball net was centered on the front lawn, which was also strewn with discarded T-shirts and red plastic cups.

The porch had been decorated with evenly spaced baskets of petunias hanging from hooks. One of the hooks was empty, and one of the petunia baskets looked as if it had been lobbed over the volleyball net. It was lying next to a ball and several of the crushed plastic cups.

I stood on the porch for a moment, trying to figure out if I should bother to ring the doorbell or just walk in. Through the sidelight, I could see what looked like hard-drinking adolescents writhing to the bass of music that I could feel under my feet. In the spacious front hall, two girls wearing short skirts and midriffs were dancing together. One was rubbing her breasts into the other's back, and sliding down toward her hips. A bunch of boys stood leaning against the wall, gyrating in place as they watched with interest. Then two of them began to encircle the girls, who turned to face each other, eyes interlocked. Within seconds, each boy was pounding his crotch into a girl's backside.

I was standing there, not so much stunned as utterly transfixed. The movements looked practiced, professional even. As seen on MTV. Or more likely, YouTube or some porno site. As I was trying to figure out how old these teenagers were, and how long it would be before all their clothing was off, two other teenage girls opened the door and pulled me inside.

"We made him call you," one of them said as they dragged me through the dancers, who didn't seem to notice us barging past them to the kitchen. Here, a group of kids watched attentively as two boys stood at the end of the table, taking turns aiming a Ping-Pong ball at one of several red plastic cups filled with beer. Both missed.

On the other side of the kitchen, I could see a family room, where the music was coming from. A half-dozen teenage girls were dancing in front of a large screen, where a music video was projected from a laptop.

We turned the other way into a small library, which had lots of dark wood. Bookshelves lined the wall to the right and left, and a plasma TV was mounted over a fireplace directly in front of us. Several more half-empty plastic cups of beer sat abandoned on the hearth.

"It's so fucked up," the girl continued. She was tall, stocky, and wearing some sort of short dress that underlined her breasts in white ribbon. She reminded me of Heidi the Mountain Girl, only she was drinking a Diet Coke that smelled strongly of rum.

She told me her name was Rhiannon. "Josh's girlfriend is my younger sister—Danielle." She pointed to the other girl, who was digging through a quilted Vera Bradley bag on her lap. She was also blond and Germanic-looking, but leaner, and slightly less drunk.

"And *she's* a journalism major at Syracuse," Josh's girlfriend said, by way of introducing Rhiannon. "Second year."

"So where is Josh?"

Danielle peered into the quilted bag, as if he might be in there. "It's just so sad," she said.

"So sad," echoed Rhiannon. Both their eyes got wide and watery, and for an awful moment, I feared the beginning of a group crying jag.

"Josh?" I was forced to remind them.

Danielle dropped her quilted bag on the floor and said she'd go get him. As the sister and I took seats on opposite couches, Rhiannon told me she thought journalism was the noblest profession anyone could chose. It was all I could do not to vomit.

"Is there any chance you could recommend me for an internship at the *Chronicle,* this summer?"

Ah. The real reason they'd talked Josh into making the call. Why we had a meeting and not a phone call. I dug into my backpack for one of my now obsolete business cards and leaned across a small coffee table to give it to her. I found a pen and circled the cell number. No need to tell her about my current status; I could probably get Bennett to recommend her. "But we'll have to talk at another time," I said. "Like when neither of us is drinking."

She nodded. Then said, "Hey, you want a beer or something?"

I reminded her that, sadly, journalists weren't supposed to drink while they were reporting. Then I asked her if she'd known Whitney at all.

Her eyes got wide and teary again. "She wasn't a bad kid," she said. "But she needed a lot. . . ." She leaned across the table and lowered her voice. "A *lot* of attention. Josh was *always* worried about her. And now . . . now, forget it. He's totally guilted up."

"About what exactly?" I was curious how long he might have known about his sister's webcam activities.

But suddenly, someone changed the music and hit the volume. Someone had either dug into the parents' music or decided to go all eighties with the Talking Heads, "Burning Down the House"—which didn't bode well for the future of this party. Just as it occurred to me that I didn't really want to get caught in a police raid of a bunch of minors getting alcohol poisoning, the door opened and Josh appeared. His arm was around Danielle, who was physically supporting him.

It took a minute for his gaze to find me on the couch. "Oh yeah, that's her," he said, as if there had been an issue about my identity. Then he dropped to the seat on the couch beside me with so much force I worried about the furniture legs holding steady.

"He can talk off the record, right?" Rhiannon asked, flaunting her knowledge of newspaper terminology.

That was for sure. I nodded, but Josh wasn't even looking at me. His head was leaning back on the couch, and his eyes were closed. My own temples were throbbing from the music. "Off the record!" I shouted.

Startled, Josh opened his eyes, lifted his head. Then, he reached into his back pocket, pulled out a piece of paper that was folded lengthwise, and handed it to me. It was actually two pieces of paper. The first was graph paper, the kind you used in geometry. There were two initials on top that looked like LX. Underneath that was written *Whit* and *Kara*. Beneath these two names, the triangle widened to what looked like five other female names—all abbreviated. Below, there were a dozen more names that formed the base of the triangle.

I tried not to think what a great graphic this would make. How Dorothy would have gone crazy for this illustration. I noticed a note below the pyramid that said, "Callie still owed $75."

$25/friend—one time.
5 percent on all $$$ earned by your first three friends.
3 percent on all $$$ earned by each friend of your friends.
Up to 16 levels

I reread the note, and scanned back to the pyramid of names. Could this be a multilevel marketing deal? Young teenage girls recruiting each other into pornography over the Internet?

"I found that in one of her school notebooks," Josh shouted.

The pyramid suggested that Lexie was at the top of the food chain, getting money from everyone. Whitney, too, was near the top.

Suddenly I could hear her, that day in the car when I'd spotted the bruise on her thigh. *I deserve what I got. I . . . I got other girls to come with me. . . . Young girls.*

Is that what she had meant?

I made money . . . a lot of money.

I was a little queasy processing this. If all these girls were underage, this was worse than I thought. Teenage girls persuaded to recruit all their friends into pornography? All of them making a profit on it?

Next to Whitney's name was another girl, Kara. Was she still in operation? Still recruiting?

"Do you know any of these girls?" I shouted back. All three of them shook their heads. Then Danielle, who was still standing near the door, gestured that she would take care of the music. A minute after she left the library, the volume dropped to background level. I repeated the question.

"I don't know any of them. But I think they might all be involved with . . ." Even drunk, he couldn't bring himself to say it. "With that thing you were talking about."

It occurred to me that these other girls might not live in Rhode Island. This network could be national, in high schools all across the country. With men all over the world paying Rurik to watch.

Rhiannon was staring at the pyramid of names. "It was like

211

she was an Avon lady or something," she said. "Only what they were selling was pretty fucked up."

"You ever heard of any other girls your age doing this kind of thing?" I asked her.

"There's some sort of Ivy League cam-girl thing I heard of once. They strip for guys on the Web, or you know, and do each other. They try to sell them private shows. But the guys always want someone new. I heard that if you recruit another girl, you get a percentage of it. I'm not sure how much. Someone told me about it at a party."

"Ivy League, like Brown?" I asked.

She shook her head. "I think it was Cornell or maybe Penn. Anyway, I never heard of anything like this in high school, but, you know, there's a lot of weird guys out there."

No kidding. And a lot of enterprising young girls.

I flipped to the second page of paper. Here I found a type-written list.

1. *Five percent bonus for anyone signing up ten new girls by May 1.*
2. *Ten percent bonus for signing up girls under fifteen.*
3. *Fifteen percent bonus for girls willing to travel to RI.*

"You think you've got enough to write an exposé on this?" Rhiannon was asking.

If I actually still had a job at the *Chronicle,* maybe. But she seemed pretty earnest about the journalism thing, so I didn't have the heart to tell her what the real world was like. "It's a good start," I said.

I turned to Josh. "Can I take this with me?"

Josh waved it away. Like *get it out of my sight.*

I thanked him, folded the papers in half, and stuffed it in my backpack.

He glared at my backpack a moment, with that unseeing look drunks have, and then met my eyes. "The cops tried to say that Whitney was some kind of a drug dealer—because of all that money they found on her—but she wasn't any drug dealer. This was where she was getting her money."

If he wasn't drunk, I might have told him that I was fairly certain that was Lexie's money she'd been holding. Instead, I said, "Did you find anything with Lexie's phone number on it?"

Rhiannon looked confused, like she wasn't sure who Lexie was. But something lit in Josh's eye. "Oh yeah, right. I forgot about that." He reached under the coffee table for the quilted bag his girlfriend had dropped there and pulled out a purple cell phone. "This was Whitney's old phone. It's got a bad battery. So bad that the wireless people couldn't transfer her data to the new one she got last Christmas. But I think it might still be in there, if you can get it working again."

20

I **had to** go to two different Verizon stores to find one with a battery that would work with Whitney's nearly obsolete cell phone. It cost me almost forty dollars and an entire morning. But back at the condo next afternoon when I finally got the phone powered up and into Whitney's contacts, I felt like I'd won the lottery.

I clapped my hands together, the sound of victory a bit hollow as it echoed off the tile in the kitchen. The condo seemed large and lonely without Matt around. And I suffered from making my own coffee. But I swallowed some anyway, pretending it could be endured. I was determined not to think about the rest of my life—my relationship or my career. I was going to find Lexie and get her away from Rurik.

I grabbed a notebook off the table and began copying down all the numbers. Two of them matched the names on the graph paper. Kara had a New Jersey exchange. And Callie had a metropolitan Boston area code. A national home network of child porn. My stomach turned every time I thought of it.

I still wasn't sleeping well, but now I was fueled by coffee and sense of mission. I didn't know how I was going to do it, but I was going to shut this thing down. The first step was finding Lexie and getting her away from Rurik.

Josh's mention of the money found on Whitney when she died had given me an idea. If nothing else, Lexie appeared to be highly motivated by cold, hard cash.

The revving of my brain slowed enough to allow a solid thought to slip through. What were the odds that Lexie still even had that phone? That Rurik hadn't cut it off to prevent her from calling anyone?

Only one way to find out. I grabbed my cell phone and dialed. I tried not to be discouraged by the fact that it went straight into voice mail.

"It's me. Leave a message." The voice was soft and scratchy, and with just a hint of Central European origin in the inflection. The same voice I'd heard on Whitney's answering machine that day in the car.

Before I even identified myself, I charged into my sales pitch. "I have your money, Lexie," I said. "Seven hundred dollars Whitney's brother Josh gave me to get to you. Tell me where to meet you."

As if an afterthought, I said, "Oh yeah, and this is Hallie again. I need your help and I think I can help you, too."

I had eight hundred dollars left in my savings account and maybe one more check still to come from the *Chronicle*. But I was promising Lexie cash, so I needed to have it, at least to show her. I changed into a tank and shorts, stuck my ATM card into my running shoes, and attached my cell phone to my waistband. The ATM at my bank on the square was undergoing service, so I headed to the ATM on Thayer Street.

It was Saturday, and I swam against the tide of weekend pedestrians in Wayland Square to the relative isolation of Angell Street. I was jumpy inside, and ran indecisively, off the curb, on the street and up again. All the way, I was distracted by my churning thoughts and the feel of my cell phone on my waist. I stopped at least twice to make sure I had coverage and that I hadn't missed a call.

Thayer Street was quiet this time of year, but I still found a line of a half-dozen people who looked like summer session students from Brown University queuing up at the cash machine. A bunch of guys in baggy shorts and T-shirts were standing directly in front. They looked like graduate students, with that skinny-body, long sideburn, computer-nerd quality. One of them was checking his e-mail on his iPhone.

And then I realized that guy was no college student.

"Bennett," I said.

He turned around. A flash of surprise was followed by an awkward attempt to hide his sympathy. I could sense that our meeting was embarrassing him. "Hallie," he said, clicking off his iPhone and putting it into his pocket. "How you doing?"

"I'm fine," I said.

He nodded, but didn't look reassured.

"How are things in the newsroom?" I asked.

"In an uproar," he said. "Everyone's pissed."

"Really?"

"Frizell filed a complaint about the firing," he added.

"Frizell?" Now that was shocking.

"He said that he owes you," Bennett said.

The woman ahead of Bennett had gotten cash and was holding the door open for him. Bennett thanked her and then held the door. "And he thinks that management is vulnerable."

"To what?"

"Frizell says there's a clause in the contract about ethics violations. You should talk to him about it," Bennett said. "And he's gone to Ferguson. Have you gone to Fergie yet?"

Fergie was the union lawyer. I shook my head.

"Are you going to use the ATM any time today?" another guy asked Bennett.

"Yeah. Sorry," Bennett said to the guy. To me, he mouthed *asshole*. Then before he ducked inside the door, he said, "You know you should freelance that webcam story to your old paper, or to *The New York Times,* or something. Really piss the *Chronicle* off."

My cell phone didn't ring until I got back home. It was Walter, checking to make sure I was okay. This was about the fifth time he'd called after I told him that I'd been fired.

"Heard from Matt yet?" he asked.

"Nope."

"So try him again." Walter thought Matt was hotheaded and stubborn, but generally, he rooted for him.

"I've left three messages, apologizing, already. I can't call him anymore."

"Want to go to a meeting tomorrow?" Walter's solution for everything.

"No." I didn't want to go to a meeting tomorrow. I didn't

want a bunch of strangers, or Walter—or Bennett, for that matter—to feel sorry for me. "I'd much rather go to the shooting range and expel a little anger in target practice."

"Can't today." Walter explained that he had to go to Boston to resolve an issue with one of his cabbies up there. Almost as an afterthought, he added that he was to see Geralyn afterwards.

"Whoa. What?"

"She wants to talk about what went wrong in our relationship."

Geralyn had wanted to talk about what went wrong in their relationship for months now.

"You know, justify her cheating and everything," he added.

"Right."

There was a long silence. Finally, Walter deemed to elaborate. "Apparently, she broke up with the police reporter."

This was big news. "And?"

"And I'm going to listen to what she has to say. That's all."

I'd spent months advising him to forget about Geralyn. That she didn't deserve him, and that he should try to detach. But I could hear the hope in his voice. And if he was all about forgiveness, I wasn't going to argue against it. If Walter could forgive Geralyn, I figured there was hope for Matt and me.

As Walter began to detail how Geralyn's police reporter boyfriend had turned out to be the world's biggest asshole, completely jealous of her promotion to News Editor, I realized this was going to be a long story. I sat down at the dining room table and put my feet up on one of the other chairs. It was then I noticed my laptop, which was open on the table. It was still on RI Buzz profile page, blinking with a new message.

"Holy shit," I said.

"What?" Walter asked.

The message said it was from Dizzywon, Lexie's old screen name. "u can meet me at peecble markt on thames. R wl be gone"

I translated it for Walter. "She's saying that Rurik will be gone, and she can meet me."

"Ask her what time?" Walter said.

I messaged back with that question, my fingers tapping wildly. The Peaceable Market was a small sandwich shop, halfway down Thames, which was the main drag for tourists. I could be there in forty-five minutes.

It took forever for another message to appear. "Meet at 4:30 and bring my $ ok"

"Shit. I'm going to be in Boston then," Walter said. "Ask her if you can meet her tomorrow instead."

"No way."

"How do you know it's not a trap?" Walter pressed.

"How do I know this is really you?" I typed into the computer.

There was no response.

"What did she say?" Walter asked.

"Can you call me on my cell phone so I can hear your voice?" I typed.

We waited another five minutes. Still nothing. I checked her profile. "She's already offline."

"Call Matt. Get him to come with you," Walter urged.

"Yeah, right. He's not even speaking to me," I said. "Besides, it's a busy market, on a busy street. There will be people everywhere."

"I don't know, Hallie."

"I'll be fine."

"Don't go a-lone," Walter said, but he stretched each syllable, so I could understand his true meaning. "Let me give you something to bring."

He meant the four-inch handgun. "I'll drop it off. I can be there in a half hour."

"Let me think about it," I said. "I'll call you back."

I took a shower and changed into a T-shirt and a pair of khaki pants that had deep pockets. While I was trying to decide on shoes, I stood there, with the closet doors flung open, pretending I had a gun in my hand. I held one hand over the other, as if to steady the weapon. I closed one eye and aimed at the only cocktail dress I owned.

Then I reminded myself that the Peaceable Market would be full of people. I didn't have to worry about defending my life in a crowded sandwich shop.

But an image of that blue Camry driving back and forth in front of the condo kept playing in my head. What if the message came from Rurik, not Lexie?

I was hoping to convince Lexie to leave Rurik, and come back with me. I was hoping to get enough information to convince the cops to arrest Rurik, as well as to connect Lexie up with a social agency that could help her get back to her family in Russia. Even if she did show up at the market alone, Rurik could be in the shadows, following her.

Of course I wouldn't have to use the gun, I told myself. I could just keep it hidden in its tiny holster in my back pocket. Just for confidence. No one would know unless I used it. And I'd only use it in self-defense.

I put my hands together and aimed my pretend gun again. This time through the open bedroom door into the hallway. I felt a childlike excitement, but caught myself. Shooting a real live human being was not the same as hitting a paper target. Besides, what was I going to do? Draw the handgun like a cowboy? In the middle of Thames Street?

The best defense I had was to wear my running shoes. Stay alert and ready to run, that was the best strategy. I left without calling Walter back.

Even this early in June, Thames Street was already clogged with tourists and boaters on a sunny weekend. I had to drive around for a while before I found parking on one of the side streets.

I didn't want to be weighted down by my backpack, so I'd stuffed the envelope of cash into one front pocket, and the plastic bag holding the gold Orthodox cross into the other. I'd added a jean jacket tied around my waist, so I had extra pockets to carry my keys and cell phone.

Loaded down with the cash, I felt both heavy and oddly illicit as I hiked past the ice cream store and two tarot card reading shops on Thames, scanning the sidewalk as I passed. There were a half-dozen teenage girls milling about the stores, all looking vulnerable and foolish. But no sign of Lexie anywhere.

I figured I had to show Lexie I had the cash, but I was hoping like hell I didn't have to give it to her. That she would accept my offer of help instead.

Like nearly everything in Newport, the Peaceable Market strove for a nautical flair, with deep navy walls contrasted by bright white wainscoting, teak tables, and a big star cutout in the back of the chairs. There was a counter to the right and a room of tables to the left. It was quiet at this hour with only one party sitting down and three people in line at the counter.

Since there was no sign of Lexie anywhere, I slipped behind the people waiting at the counter, to an empty bench, up against the plate glass window that looked out on Thames Street.

Turning my back to the market, I stood with one knee on the bench scanning the street in both directions for Lexie, refusing to acknowledge the little voice that reminded me that she'd already stood me up once, at Best Price.

"Are you in line?" a male voice asked.

"No," I said, but the voice sounded vaguely familiar. I pivoted around to see who it was.

Pauley Sponik. He was a huge presence, tall and muscular, with a caged-animal energy that took over the room. His shirt was buttoned today, covering up the pierced nipple, but he wore exceptionally tight blue jeans and he reeked of that same cologne.

He gave me the once-over, with a smirk on his face. Did the celebrity actresses he hung with actually think he was good-looking? "Been sailing that *yacht* of yours today?" he asked.

I turned back to the window.

"Ignoring me? Come on, that's not polite."

I said nothing.

He walked past me to the Pepsi cooler and grabbed a handful of sodas, stepping in front of a tall woman in shorts and a Windbreaker to put them on the counter. I was hopeful that this meant our conversation was over.

But he turned back to me. "Just because your boyfriend doesn't like me, doesn't mean we can't be friends, right?" His tone was cloying, sarcastic.

I decided it was probably a good thing that I hadn't brought the handgun.

The counter girl sought to intervene. "Can I help you, Pauley?" she asked.

"I faxed my order," he told her. She hunted a moment and handed him two big bags and a smaller wrapped package in the shape of a small baguette. He pulled a big wad of bills out of his pocket and peeled off a fifty-dollar bill. "Keep the change," he said.

Hefting the bags, he returned his attention to me. "Let's keep in touch. Because someday, you just might want an exclusive, right?"

I felt my stomach tighten. This asshole had gone to the trouble of figuring out that I was a reporter. You should never respond to this kind of taunting. The smart thing was to keep your mouth shut. "Like when they reinstate capital punishment, just for you."

He laughed, as if I was just so amusing. "Maybe that *would* make a good story," he said as he brushed past me. Then, as I was still recoiling from his bare arm rubbing against my back, he turned around again. Hand on the door, with that smirk. "*If* you still worked for the *Chronicle*."

I froze.

The smirk broadened into a smile. He winked before swinging the door shut behind him.

I stood at the window, trying to bore my anger into the back of his head as he crossed Thames and walked down the side street toward the harbor. How did he know I'd gotten fired three days ago? Only a handful of people knew. And what the hell was he up to? Taking such trouble to learn about the woman who lived with the prosecutor. The prosecutor who was after him.

But all this turmoil in my stomach was quickly shelved. Out of the corner of my eye, I saw another figure coming down the sidewalk on Thames. It was a young girl with very short dark hair. She walked quickly, her eyes scanning the street in all directions as she made her way toward the market. She was alone.

She pushed through the door and searched the market. Her gaze landed on me and I nodded. "Lexie?"

Standing in front of me, she was less than five feet tall, and not a hundred pounds. But she looked older in person, at least seventeen, with a careful, measuring look in her eyes. They were set deep in a wide, Slavic face, paleness exaggerated by the hair color that looked dyed. The overall effect was exotic, almost Asian. Her pronunciation was tentative: "Hallie?" It sounded like *Ha-LEE*.

I nodded again.

"Sorry I am late. I had to watch the market for a while. And wait."

"Wait?"

"One of his friends . . ." Her words trailed off, but her eyes darted sideways, in the direction of the street.

It took me a moment. One of Rurik's friends, she meant. "Pauley Sponik?"

She made a face. "You know him?"

The question was, how did she know him? Was he a customer? "Sort of," I said.

"You have my money, yes?"

I nodded. "But I need to talk to you first." Two people arrived behind her and walked around us to the register. "You want to stay here and get something to eat?"

"Can I see?" She was not asking about a menu. She meant the money.

I dug into my pocket and lifted the envelope just high

enough so she could get a glimpse of the green bills and stuffed it back in. "Please, I need to talk to you," I said.

Her gaze traveled to my face, which she studied carefully. After a minute, she shrugged. "I have not eaten yet today. But I don't have much time."

"This won't take long," I promised.

We walked to the counter where I bought us each a sandwich, and after a short wait, we grabbed a table near the coffee station.

There were a dozen questions I had planned to ask her. To find out what she knew about Whitney's death. About the pyramid scheme. About where Rurik's operation had moved since the motel. But now suddenly all that was eclipsed. If I could get some dirt on Pauley Sponik, maybe it could help Matt.

"How does Rurik know Pauley Sponik?" I asked, as we settled into our seats.

She shrugged. "He is very rich, Rurik says."

"Are they in business together?"

I must have been too abrupt. Lexie had been unwrapping her sandwich, but now she looked up sharply. Her eyes searched mine. How much did I know?

I had to make a decision here, whether to come clean with her. I had no real reason to trust her, but I couldn't ask her any questions without letting on that I had some information. Besides, Rurik's swift removal from the motel must mean he already knew I'd followed him there.

So I explained that before Whitney had died, she told me about the webcam operation, and that I also knew about the private shows at the motel.

At the mention of Whitney's name, Lexie's eyes teared up.

She looked past me for a moment, with an expression I couldn't read. Sad? Frustrated? Maybe even angry?

"Is Pauley Sponik one of the guys who comes to watch?"

Lexie's pale face was hard to read, but she didn't seem unduly alarmed that I knew about it. "No. He never comes. He lets Rurik do the work."

As if Rurik resented this. As if . . . "Are you saying Pauley is Rurik's boss?"

She thought about that. "Pauley is the rich man."

"You mean Pauley Sponik finances the operation?"

The term *finances* might have thrown her. She didn't seem to understand what I meant.

"Pauley provides the money?"

"He owns the motel, I think." She took a bite of her sandwich.

I had unwrapped mine, but couldn't eat. My mind was whirling. This was huge. Pauley Sponik must have a stake in the company doing the motel renovations, probably obfuscated through some holding company machinations. But it meant that he was financing child porn. This could help Matt put him away for a good long time. If we could prove it.

"These guys who come to the show, how do they pay you?"

Her expression brightened. "In cash," she said.

"They give the girls all the cash? Or does Rurik take a cut?" I asked.

My tone was too aggressive. Her lips pursed, her eyes grew wary.

"Obviously I know they pay you in cash," I said, trying to sound nonchalant. I lifted the envelope out of my pocket as if to illustrate that knowledge, but I was trying to remind her that

I was still in possession of the payoff. "I was just curious about how generous Rurik was with you," I said.

Her eyes drifted to the envelope. "The men give all of it to Rurik. But these girls are American. And Rurik wants to keep them . . ." She stopped to search for the word. "Happy," she finally said, but she put her finger to her lips, indicating the real word was *quiet.* "So he is generous to those girls."

The last line was full of bitterness. A great motivator to tell all.

"And you?"

"He lets me keep just a little, *sometimes.*"

"Does Rurik kick the cash up to Pauley?"

Again, she didn't seem sure what I meant.

I rephrased. "Does Rurik have to give him envelopes of money? Make reports to him?"

She dropped her sandwich back on the paper plate and wiped her hands on a napkin. "I think I have told you enough, yes."

No, she had not told me enough, and I searched for some way to convince her that she needed to tell me more.

I pushed on, "Whitney told me that you wanted to get out of this. That you hated what Rurik made you do, finding the younger girls. This is your chance to start a new life. Get away."

"Whitney *wanted* me to run away. She never understands."

"Understands what?"

Her eyes met mine. "How far you need to go."

"I can help you," I said.

She didn't exactly roll her eyes, but her expression told me she'd gotten this kind of offer before, probably from Whitney. She struck a businesslike tone. "Getting my money will help me."

She was wearing a T-shirt and a short skirt. I could see that Whitney hadn't been lying about Lexie: There weren't any track marks in her arm. No signs of drug use or even bruising. Still, I was running out of cards to play. "Think about Whitney," I said.

Her expression got very still. Then she dropped her head, covering her face with her hands. She sat there like that a long time without saying anything. I thought she might be crying, but there was no heaving of her chest, no signs of sobbing.

"I'm sorry to bring up Whitney," I said. "I know you were good friends. But this is a rough life. It's not going to end up well if you stay with Rurik."

She lifted her head slightly and looked at me through her fingers, but said nothing.

"You said in your message to me that Rurik would be gone this afternoon. Can you just tell me how long he's gone?"

"He goes to Boston. For few hours."

"Is there anything, back where you live? Any kind of video footage of the girls that Rurik keeps. Or records of any kind?"

There was a flicker of recognition in her eye. Something she had seen. Something that suddenly made sense to her.

"How does he keep track of the money? The payments?" I pressed. "In a ledger? A computer?"

She hesitated, which only confirmed that I was on the right track. "Please, Lexie."

"He takes a lot of time on the laptop, with . . . what is the program? With all the lines in it and the numbers move."

"Excel?" I asked hopefully.

She shrugged again, uncertain. "Rurik is doing this all the time when I want to use the laptop."

This was probably how he kept track of the percentages

girls were owed when they recruited each other into the business. "The laptop, where is it now?"

"The boat, I guess."

"What boat?"

"Rurik moved us to boat, just for short time, he says, until we find another place. It's in harbor." She gestured behind her, to the water.

My heart began to pound inside my chest. "Is it Pauley Sponik's boat?" If it was Pauley Sponik's boat, that would provide the perfect tie.

She didn't answer, and I wasn't sure if she was holding back or didn't know.

I tried to remember the defining characteristics of the boat Matt and I almost hit that day in the harbor. It was a big boat, I remembered. A gleaming motorboat, huge and brand new. Then suddenly, I could see it, in detail. "Is it a black yacht? With a bolt of lightning painted on the side?"

I could see it in her eyes. Surprise that I knew this boat. This seemed to scare her, though, make her back away. "I am here to get my money," she said stiffly. "That is why I came."

"I'll give you the money." I pulled the envelope out of my other pocket to show it to her again, but I didn't hand it over. "But this really isn't your money. The cops took your money. This is my money. I got it out of my ATM today. I'll still give it to you, though, I promise. Just please, take me back to the boat."

"Are you crazy? Rurik would kill me."

"Not if you got away from him. You can come stay with me. I'll help you, Lexie. This is your chance to get away from this life."

She thought about this a minute. Then shook her head. "Rurik will find me. He will kill me."

"My boyfriend, he's a prosecutor." I saw by her expression that she didn't understand what that meant. "He works with the police. He can protect you. Make sure you are safe."

"Safe." But her tone mocked the word, the concept. And then, "Your boyfriend is police?"

"He works with the police. And if we go to him, we can get Rurik arrested," I said. "They'll put him behind bars. He won't be able to touch you."

"They will kill me like that." She snapped her fingers. "And if Rurik does not want to do it himself, Pauley has many others who work for him."

"If this is Pauley's boat, we can get all of them, Lexie. Bring down the whole organization. Put all of them in jail. If you just help me get that laptop."

Something flickered in her eyes. Hope? "Your boyfriend can do this?"

"If he has evidence, he can do it. But he needs evidence."

She narrowed her eyes, trying to understand.

"He needs proof. He needs the laptop. That's what will convict these guys. Send them to prison. But you've got to take me to the boat," I said.

She looked past me, through the window, out to the street, as if trying to imagine a different life. She couldn't seem to envision it.

"And I'll give you the money and help you start a new life," I pressed. "You can go back home, see your family again."

"I have no family," she said, her eyes returning to me.

At that moment, I remembered the gold cross. I felt around in my pocket, and pulled out the plastic Baggie. I handed it to her across the table. "This is yours, right?"

She fingered the gold through the bag. She pulled out the

cross and turned it over. Immediately the pale face grew bright, animated. "Where did you find it?"

I told her I'd been to the New Bedford warehouse. "I saw where you were living."

She had the gold cross in her palm and had turned it over again. She was so enthralled, marveling at its return, that I wasn't sure she got my point. That she understood how awful those living conditions were.

"Wouldn't you like to get away from that? From living in these awful places?"

"The boat is very nice place," she said.

"And how long do you think Pauley Sponik is going to let you live there?" I said. "The summer is coming. He'll want his boat back. You'll be living in the back of warehouses again, sleeping on bedrolls and eating out of cans."

Her eyes met mine, surprised again, by how much I knew.

"You don't have to live like that, Lexie. There are much better ways to live."

"How?" she said. "I have nothing."

"That's what I'm telling you. This is your best chance. Your ace in the hole. Police want to put away sexual offenders. It's a big priority. And they want to put Pauley Sponik in jail—real bad. You help them get the proof they need to do that, and they're going to help you in return."

Still, she hesitated, but I could see now that she wanted to believe me. Wanted to believe there was an escape.

"Make Rurik pay for what he's done to you." I invoked my last strategy. "If you don't want to do this for yourself, do it for Whitney."

Her eyes met mine.

"So that you don't end up like Whitney." I glanced at the gold cross in her hand. "Or like your mother."

She began to blink rapidly, and I wasn't sure for a minute whether she was holding back anger or tears. Whether I'd gone too far, crossed a line and pushed her away. But then, she pulled her cell phone out of her pocket and checked the time again. When she looked back at me, I saw resolve in her expression. "Okay, but we must go now. And we must be fast."

21

I thought a yacht like Pauley's boat, which would have a myriad of electrical luxuries, would be at a dock, connected to shore power. I was wrong. Lexie said the boat was tied up to a mooring in the outer harbor. Privacy over convenience.

This meant we had to pick up the launch, and we walked down to the same dock where Matt and I had studied the stars that night. The sun had disappeared and the sky was darker than it should be for five thirty. The air had a thick, heavy feeling.

Lexie sat down on the bench, but I was too nervous. I began pacing back and forth as we waited forever for the launch to pull up to the dock and the passengers to get out.

This underscored a troubling fact: You had to wait for the launch on both sides of the commute. On board the boat, it could be fifteen or twenty minutes from the time we called VHF radio until the launch showed up to ferry us to shore. Since the launch, an open boat that could carry up to fifteen people, always arrived with other passengers on board, we could even run into Rurik coming back to the boat as we were trying to leave.

I wished to God that I'd listened to Walter. That I had that four-inch handgun in my pocket. Even if I never shot the freaking thing, I'd feel a helluva lot better right now if I was packing it.

When the last passenger had debarked, Lexie stood up and looked over, waiting for me to make a move. Were we still going to do this?

Reflecting the sky, the harbor water was dark, murky blue, and the flag on the stern of the launch was dead still. "What time did you say he left for Boston?" I asked.

"He leaves at four o'clock," she said. "And he has business there. A meeting."

It was a good three hours to and from Boston and that was without parking the car. Still I hesitated.

I don't know if it was guilt about Whitney nudging her forward, or the promise of escaping Rurik forever, but Lexie no longer seemed reluctant, only determined. "It will take us only a few minutes on the boat." She held out her hand, gesturing for me to come aboard.

For a split second I thought about what Walter had said earlier. About a trap. Could this be an elaborate setup? A ruse to get me to the boat?

She saw my hesitation. "You want to wait here, and I'll go get the laptop?" she asked.

For a moment, I considered it. But there was too great a risk that if I let her out of my sight, she might change her mind and never come back. I stepped into the launch and took the seat beside her.

The driver, an eighteen-year-old boy, was wearing a yellow foul weather jacket. That didn't bode well. He looked at Lexie. "Back to the *Flash*?" he asked.

I understood this was the name of Pauley's boat. Apparently, the launch driver remembered Lexie, a pretty girl his own age. "And please, can we hurry?" she said.

Half a dozen other boaters piled into the launch, but the driver accommodated us. He maneuvered through the crowded field of sailboats and yachts moored close to shore, and sped straight toward the outer harbor.

One of the female passengers, a thin, weathered-looking woman with a sweater tied over her shoulder, began to complain when the launch whizzed right by her sailboat and didn't stop.

"It's the weather," the launch driver said, glancing up at the sky, with its heavy steel-colored clouds. "Want to get the farthest delivered first," he said. This was enough to shut the woman up until he made it to our mooring.

The *Flash* was moored in an isolated spot, far from any shore and alone among empty mooring buoys bobbing on the water. The next boat was almost a hundred feet away.

The launch pulled up to the stern of the yacht, which was an impressive vessel. At least fifty feet long, it had a good-sized open cockpit at stern, leading to an enclosed helm deck, and what looked like a large cabin area below.

Lexie immediately began climbing out of the launch and onto the yacht's swimming platform. The fare was two dollars per person, but I gave the launch driver a twenty. "We're only going to be a few minutes. Can you come right back here after you drop everyone else off?" I asked.

"Sure," he said. He glanced up at Lexie again, who was

already in the cockpit with her back toward him, before he slipped the cash into his shorts pocket. I scrambled up the swimming platform and onto the cockpit, but I got a knot in my stomach as I watched the launch pull away.

Lexie unlocked the glass door to the helm deck and turned to give me the all-clear sign. As expected, the boat inside was opulent, with teak flooring and paneling, and large windows on every side that made you feel as if you were lounging on the very surface of the sea. I entered the enormous salon, which was like a living room, with a large flat-screen television and an entertainment center on the starboard side, and a U-shaped sofa and cherrywood table on the port side.

Lexie marched through the salon, directly to the helm, forward on the starboard side. She leaned between two captain's chairs on pedestals that faced the dashboard and the sea ahead, and pointed to the teak surface of the navigation station, a small desk, just to the left of the wheel. "The laptop. This is where he keeps."

"Maybe he moved it?"

Lexie turned. I saw alarm in her eyes. There were two cabinet doors behind the navigation station. She pulled them open. Clearly there wasn't enough room there to stow a laptop.

"I'll check the cabin," she said, and slipped past another smaller, L-shaped sofa, opposite the helm on the port side, to the three-step companionway that led below, to the mid ship and bow, where there was probably a galley, head, and sleeping quarters.

The whole yachting thing was about coiling your line and polishing your brass. In contrast to Matt's brother's more modest boat, the salon was a mess. A half-dozen duffel bags were piled on the U-shaped sofa, wafting the scent of dirty laundry.

CDs spilled out of the open cupboard of the entertainment center and onto the teak floor. And there were dirty glasses and ashtrays left on the table.

I kicked aside one of the duffel bags, to follow Lexie to the helm. The desktop of the navigation station had a lip around the edge to prevent charts from slipping off when at sea. Sometimes this surface lifted like the lid of a child's desk. I yanked it open, and found a storage area. There was no laptop. Only charts of Newport Harbor and Long Island Sound and a plastic compass.

Looking out the helm window, over the bow, I could see a boat coming from the harbor toward us. It was a large red cigarette boat, increasing its speed as it distanced itself from shore. A passing boat going too fast, or too close, creates a wake, which can be like a small tsunami. I gripped the wheel for support, but the cigarette boat veered off early in the opposite direction, leaving us unscathed.

Remembering the CDs spilled on the floor, I backtracked to the salon. I was thinking that if we couldn't find the laptop, at least there might be a few disks stored with Rurik's footage of the girls.

I knelt before the entertainment center to examine the CDs, but it was all music. Joss Stone—which must have been Lexie's—Rammstein, and a lot of European techno. I opened the cabinet and rifled through the largest collection of heavy metal and rap ever. But all of it had commercially produced labels. On the bottom shelf I found two DVDs, movies, and what looked like an installation guide for digital camera software.

Below in the cabin area, I heard the slamming of drawers opening and shutting. "It is not fucking here!" Lexie shouted. Next came a string of what I guessed was cursing in Russian.

I moved to the U-shaped sofa on the other side, knowing there would be several stowage areas under the base. I removed another duffel bag, which appeared to be more dirty laundry, pulled off one of the smaller cushions, and opened the lid.

I thrust my hand between life jackets and flares, and pulled up a plastic bag. But inside was just coiled rope—extra line, probably to tie up a dinghy.

I dropped it back into the stowage compartment and carefully replaced that cushion before pulling up another. This was a long cushion and this lid was long, too, opening to a deeper stowage compartment. This area was filled with blankets. Again, no laptop. But wrapped up in the top blanket, I found another Baggie. Inside were three flash memory sticks.

My grip on the bag tightened. I remembered something that Bennett had said: *The smarter ones download it right to a flash memory stick. . . . You can get rid of it a lot easier than a laptop.*

This could be the mother lode. I grabbed the plastic bag with the memory sticks and put it in my pocket.

I was about to replace the lid of the stowage area, when at the very bottom of the compartment, I saw something that looked like metal. I stuffed my hand deeper and touched what felt like the long, thin barrel of a gun.

I pulled out an AK-47.

"Holy shit." I plunged my hand in and felt around. There were at least two handguns in the bottom of the compartment. My heart was racing. This was exactly what Matt was looking for. If more of these were stowed throughout the boat, he could finally get Pauley on weapons trafficking.

I had to take a deep breath, try to slow the pounding of my heartbeat at my temples, so that I could think clearly. I was a little sketchy on procedure, but I was pretty sure that it would be best for the prosecution to find these guns on Pauley's property, and that a tip from me would be enough for Matt to get a search warrant. I did my best to wipe off my fingerprints with the bottom edge of my T-shirt. Then I carefully returned the AK-47 deep into the compartment and covered it with blankets.

Just then, I heard the sound of an engine approaching. It was a small engine, buzzing through the water.

"Lexie?" I shouted. Was it the launch coming back for us already? I was still on my knees and peered out the glass slider into the cockpit. It wasn't the launch, but a large dinghy, with a single driver, pulling up to the stern.

A man in a hat. I could not make out the figure. He had twisted around, toward the engine, fiddling with something. The color of the hair under the hat was bright yellow. Like Rurik's.

I began crawling on my knees through the salon, slipped around the sofa, and pressed myself against the port side, desperate to reach the companionway and get below to the cabin before the man boarded the stern and could see through the glass.

Someone cut an engine.

Lexie was in the galley. "Go!" She was pointing to a stateroom opposite the galley. "That is where I sleep. There is a closet. Quick. Hide."

"Lexie!" a male voice called. "Lexie!"

"Hurry," she said, closing the door on my feet.

Centered in the cabin, a queen-sized berth, unmade, completely dominated the small space. Immediately to my left was a locker. I pulled open the door and was overwhelmed by the stench of cedar, perfume, and sweat. The locker was crammed with clothes, hanging from the top and piled high from the bottom. High-heeled shoes sat atop the clothes. No way could I squeeze myself into there.

I crawled around the foot of the bed, through a narrow passageway to a small space between the side of the bed and the paneled wall of the ship. I crouched, weight on my knees, pressing myself into the corner, with my head below the level of the berth.

I heard the glass door slide open and held my breath.

"You are back early, Rurik," Lexie said too loudly. I could hear her nervousness. "What happened to the meeting?"

Rurik didn't seem to notice. "Chuck called me. Halfway there already, he cancels." I heard a thump of something he must have dropped on the floor of the salon. "You make something to eat?"

Tell him no, I silently begged. *Make him go back to shore and pick something up. Let me get the hell out of here. Let me escape.*

I heard her steps down the companionway to the galley. A door swung open. She asked him something in Russian. I guessed it was a food choice.

Idiot. My legs were beginning to ache, and I wished to hell I'd brought that gun. Suddenly I remembered my cell phone stuck in the pocket of the jean jacket wrapped around my waist. Thank God, I'd turned it off. Then I had another thought. If Rurik stayed in the salon, and Lexie made enough of a clatter, cooking in the galley, maybe I could call Matt. And he could get the coast guard to come rescue us.

"You can hold off dinner," Rurik said. "I have work first." His voice had gotten louder. He must be at the helm, which was almost above this cabin.

How long could I hide here, undetected? And what if the launch driver came back, asking for us?

Another couple of minutes passed. I'd hoped Lexie would come into the cabin so I could tell her to make noise or distract Rurik. But she didn't. It sounded like she climbed up the steps back to the salon. And then I heard the murmur of her voice saying something to Rurik.

There was a sudden rumble of the engine below coming to life. Rurik must have started the engine to charge the onboard batteries that keep the refrigerator, lights, and electronics operating while away from shore power.

The engine was loud, reverberating through the teak flooring. It provided enough audio cover that I could call Matt. Slowly, I shifted my weight, dropped into a seated position, so I could get the cell phone out of my jacket pocket and click it on.

I waited for what seemed forever to get a signal. It was weak, only one bar. I hit Matt's number and the cell began dialing. There was a long pause, nothing happened. I checked the phone. Please God, let this call go through.

I heard footsteps thumping down the companionway into the galley and snapped the phone shut. A door swung open. The refrigerator? Then the sound of a pop top. He said something in Russian to Lexie that sounded like a question. She barked something back, sounding nervous, abrupt.

Only a thin wall and door separated us. Afraid someone might be able to see over the bed, I dropped to my rear end first, then all the way down, on my side, curling up next to discarded gum wrappers and an empty book of matches. If there were any space at all beneath the bed, I would have shoved myself into it.

I heard the sound of plates scraping each other. Washing them? Putting them away? Lying flat on the floor, I inhaled oiled teak and cigarette ash. All the portals and the skylight in the cabin were shut tight. I would have done anything for a gulp of fresh sea air.

And then suddenly, "The Hokey Pokey" began to play.

It was still in my hand. I fumbled for the END button, but it was too late. Suddenly, the door to the cabin kicked open. The cell phone slipped out of my hand, skittered across the teak flooring to the base of the bed.

"Rurik." I heard Lexie's voice. She shouted something in Russian. An order. Stay out of my room?

The melody of "The Hokey Pokey" grew louder.

I pressed myself into the floor, the rumble of the engine in my ribs. I heard the footsteps enter. The locker opened and slammed shut. Now I could see the toes of the shoes: thick, dirty sneakers.

The footsteps stopped. I heard Rurik fumble to grab the phone. The melody stopped. "What the fuck?"

The footsteps turned around the edge of the bed. I jumped back into a crouching position, ready to jump over the bed. But I never had a prayer. Looming over me was Rurik, with my cell phone in one hand and a nine-millimeter semiautomatic in the other.

He stared at me, momentarily perplexed. "Reporter girl," he said. "You are pain in my ass."

22

"Get up," he said, pointing at me with the gun.

I grabbed the edge of the bed to haul myself up. My arms were shaking.

"Go," he said, pointing me out of the cabin and leading me through the galley, and up to the companionway. Lexie was sitting on the small L-shaped sofa, directly in front of me, looking scared out of her mind.

With the gun, he pointed to the seat beside her on the sofa and ordered me to sit there. Then, he started barking at Lexie in Russian, a fury of questions. She started to say something and he cut her off. More Russian. It sounded like it came from the intestines instead of the throat. The metal stud in his lip looked about to spin off as he spit. Twice, first at the floor and then at her.

Tears welled up in Lexie's eyes. She began talking fast, a thinner flow of consonants, a wheedling tone.

He looked down at her with disgust. His cheekbones began to quiver with anger, as she went on and on. He ripped off the baseball hat he had on and threw it at the floor. She started to say something else, and he interrupted to ask her a question. Her eyes darted briefly to me. She lifted her palms and shook her head, as if she had no idea how I got on board the boat. He exploded forward and smacked her in the face.

She began to whimper, but he didn't even look at her. He turned to me. "You are after what on this boat?"

I didn't answer.

"You come here, for what? Ha! You have nothing on me if you must come across harbor for proof."

Again, I said nothing, afraid to set him off. Afraid he'd take it out on Lexie again.

"This girl, she tells lies. She does nothing she does not want to do," Rurik said.

I wasn't sure if he was talking about Lexie or Whitney or all the girls. But I leaned forward to feel the reassurance of the memory sticks digging through my pocket into my thigh. Please God, let these be proof. And let me get the hell off this boat alive so I can use it.

"These girls. They make good money. They get what they want. Customer get what he wants. It hurts nobody," he continued.

"It hurt Whitney." It came out of my mouth, despite myself.

"Spoiled, crazy girl," he said. "She does things to herself. I cannot help."

Lexie shifted in the seat next to me, but said nothing.

He glanced at her, and for a moment his fury abated and his brow dropped low over his eyes, an expression approximating concern. Then it occurred to me that no matter what kind of monster Rurik was, after all this time living with Lexie, he might actually feel some sort of responsibility toward her. And that this might be the best angle of attack.

I struck a softer tone. "And taking Lexie from her parents. You don't think that didn't hurt her at all?"

"You know nothing about her father. He was pig."

Like Rurik wasn't? But he sounded oddly sincere. As if he truly believed himself the better option.

Lexie swiveled toward the window and said something so low under her breath that I couldn't tell if it was English or Russian. He looked up at her swiftly, and I saw it again. He cared what she thought.

"She had hard life, her mother." He began explaining it to me. "Maybe she couldn't help her problem. But the father . . ." An excuse to soften his last statement?

But Lexie was not mollified. She began crying again, a loud wail.

Rurik turned, furious at her tears. The piercing in his eyebrow dipped as his scowl line deepened. He barked something else to her in Russian, an order, and began gesturing toward the bow.

She made some sort of objection, and he pointed the gun at her. She stood and slowly crossed the boat to a narrow door on the starboard side that went from the helm to the deck. She hesitated at the door, and he yelled something at her that sounded like *hurry up.*

Through the window, I watched her outside on the deck, climbing onto the bow. After a couple of minutes, something splashed in the water. The mooring? I felt a wave of alarm. Had he ordered her to drop the mooring?

"You move, I kill you," Rurik said, keeping the gun pointed

at me as he took the captain's chair at the helm. On the dash, he began fiddling with the panel of electronics, searching the many buttons on the board directly in front of the wheel. Only about half of the lights were lit, but he didn't seem to notice. He put the boat into gear.

Where the hell was that launch? If it came back while Lexie was still on the deck, she could jump into it, and come back with help. But there was no sight of it. And when she lingered on the bow, looking out at the harbor, Rurik shouted something at her. Some sort of threat that scared her because she ran back along the deck, as fast as she could, into the boat. She crossed behind Rurik at the helm, and took the same seat beside me on the port-forward sofa.

When her eyes met mine, I could see the raw fear.

We began heading through the harbor, around Goat Island until we had the Newport Bridge behind us and Jamestown on our starboard side. I didn't get the sense that Rurik was a particularly adept captain, but he knew enough to go slowly, so as not to attract the attention of the harbormaster.

Where the hell were we going? New York?

Or just far enough away to dump my body?

"Where are you taking us?" I asked.

"Shut up," Rurik replied. He pointed the gun at me. "Or I make you shut up."

The sky had turned from steel to dark gray, and a changing front had brought a wind that was churning up the harbor water. Although nothing for a boat this size to maneuver, whitecaps in protected water did not bode well for the storm conditions in open sea.

About ten minutes passed. After we rounded Fort Adams,

the state park that marked the western edge of the harbor, the boat began pitching and yawing in the growing swell.

Rurik turned his attention to the dials on the panel, probably trying to find the autopilot. But he couldn't get it to engage. It was tricky in rough weather. This was good, I realized. As long as he had to keep one hand on the wheel, it would be hard for him to keep the gun steady, to aim.

"Go slower, Rurik, I am feeling not so good," Lexie whined. There was a greenish cast growing on her pale skin.

"Tell him go slow or I will throw up," Lexie said to me.

But he had heard her. "So throw up." He sounded angry she was sick. "I don't care if you throw up."

Instead of riding with the swell of the waves, he kept trying to drive through them. They smashed over the starboard side of the boat and splashed on the helm windshield, making it hard for Rurik to see. The decks and cockpit were soaked.

One of the dirty glasses on the salon table slipped off and smashed on the floor.

Looking past Lexie, I could see a stubby conelike structure in the distance. This must be the Castle Hill Lighthouse, which meant we were still heading to open ocean. I gripped the underside of the bench, trying not to panic. After a long while, we passed Point Judith, on Rhode Island's southern edge. Soon a flat of land appeared in the distance. Block Island. But Rurik did not turn the wheel. We were not on course for the Block Island harbor.

I didn't get seasick, but my stomach was tight with growing fear. There could be only one reason Rurik was forging ahead, away from other boat traffic, out to sea in these conditions. I couldn't sit here and let him drive me to my death. I had to do something. I thought about the guns stored under the U-shaped sofa in the salon. Were there guns stowed underneath the bench where I was sitting, too? Did they keep them loaded?

I stuffed my hand under the upholstered cushion and tried to feel for the finger hole of a stowage compartment lid. I could make out the outline of the compartment edge. But what were the chances there was a loaded gun, here? And that I could get to it before Rurik shot me?

Maybe Lexie and I could make a break for the dinghy that was trailing behind the boat. Even with two hands on the gun, it would be hard for Rurik to aim accurately in these seas. We might just get to the dinghy unscathed. But would I have time to untie the line attaching the dinghy to the boat? And Rurik hadn't bothered to pull the engine out of the dinghy, or mount the dinghy to the stern to keep it dry. It was probably swamped with water.

It was nearing seven o'clock now, and the gray sky was not getting any lighter. We passed a commercial fishing boat heading toward Newport Harbor. Was it turning around because of bad weather? Another wave crashed over the starboard side and splashed water over the bridge.

With each new wave, Rurik seemed more rattled. The boat's speed drove the bow deeper into the oncoming wall of water. The boat shuddered as the engines tried to free the hull from the water's grasp.

My body lurched with the waves, and my head began to ache from all the vibration. I had been in seas before, but not with these loud, ceaseless engines.

I wondered how often Rurik had been out on the ocean, how strong his stomach, how steady his sea legs. He was fiddling with the dials again, trying to get the autopilot to engage, to stabilize the boat. The moron didn't realize that in these seas, the autopilot could make things worse.

A clunk from the galley, and then the sound of something rolling across the floor. Probably one of the dirty pots piled in the sink had fallen on the floor. Rurik didn't know enough to pull the dinghy out of the water or stow things before going to sea. If he didn't kill us, the storm would.

Then I saw it. Coming at us on our starboard side was a sportfishing boat, at least sixty feet, with a tuna tower and pronounced bow. It was returning home to harbor at top speed. Unlike us, the sportfishing boat rode with the waves instead of against them. It was hard to tell distances in the water, but it looked pretty close, maybe a hundred to two hundred feet away. If it was going fast enough, it might throw a pretty big wake.

I glanced at Lexie. She was holding her stomach and looking out the port window, probably trying to keep her eyes focused on the horizon. Scared and in a weakened state, she would be of little use in any attempt to wrestle control from Rurik.

I was on my own. Slowly, I moved to the edge of the upholstered bench. I shifted my weight to my feet, eyes on the sportfishing boat as it approached.

I waited. Finally, it roared past us, displacing the water beneath it. The wake looked benign at first, then grew quickly. A wave rose from the sea, growing larger and larger. It slapped over the starboard side of the boat, thrusting us to port, and lifting us all from our seats.

I jumped with the boat, lunging at Rurik and grabbing him by the elbow. The gun dropped out of his hand and crashed to the floor. A shot went off into the air and hit the port-side window directly behind Lexie. She screamed. I froze, stunned. The window began to crack.

"You fucking bitch!" Rurik shouted.

The gun had skidded across the floor, past me, and landed next to Lexie's feet. We all scrambled on the floor, trying to get to the gun. My knee hit someone's arm, and I felt my finger touch metal. Rurik thrust his elbow into my stomach, and I wailed and let go. Another wave crashed over the side. With no one piloting the boat, it swung wildly. Another drinking glass smashed to the floor. We all began sliding back to starboard.

Rurik just about got his hand around the gun, when suddenly, Lexie, who was crouched beside him, got her knee free and kicked it away from him. It skidded again, this time toward me. I grabbed the gun and stood up, holding the edge of the nav station for support. Rurik was still on his knees on the floor. Lexie was beside him.

I struggled to catch my breath. I sat on the captain's chair so that I could clasp the gun with two hands. I tried not to shake. Tried not to feel the boat rumbling beneath me. Or see the crack of the window growing. I pointed the gun at Rurik. "You stay where you are."

His eye traveled from the gun to my face, in assessment.

I summoned all my bravado. "I've got a gun at home, asshole, and I know how to use it," I said. Then, keeping the gun aimed at him, I took my left hand off of it, crisscrossing under my right arm to grab the wheel.

I doubted I could steer that great with my left hand, but I knew that there was no way could I shoot with it.

Lexie was still on the port side, close enough to Rurik to make me nervous about shooting. "Come over here," I said. "Stand next to me and take the wheel."

"There is rope in there," she said, pointing to the bench, where we'd been sitting. "I could tie him up."

She didn't have enough strength to subdue him, and he was smart enough to figure out that I didn't dare shoot if he started wrestling with her. I waved her toward the helm again. She quickly got to her feet. She took the captain's chair to my right and grabbed the wheel from me.

"No," I said. "I need you to steer the boat."

She looked terrified. "Just keep it going straight for now," I said, "and pull back that gear, go slow."

I needed to establish our position and call on the VHF radio to SOS for help. I was sure there was some sort of GPS system, but I wasn't about to fiddle around with it now. We were off Block Island, but visibility was terrible. I had lost sight of Point Judith behind us.

With my gun pointed at Rurik, I flicked on the radio. Nothing happened. There was no sound. No static. No lights.

"Fuck," I said.

"Problem?" Rurik asked. He'd gotten off his knees and was now sitting on the bench.

"I told you to stay where you were," I said.

"So shoot me," he said with a smile. "You got the gun."

Shit. I was maybe four feet away from him with a gun in my hand, and he wasn't afraid of me. Which meant he'd try to attack me the moment he saw an opening. Another wave and he'd pounce. And surely he knew where every other gun on this boat was stowed.

I needed to do something to contain him before I attempted to turn the boat around. "You don't want to test me," I said.

"Maybe I like to test."

"Shoot him," Lexie said. "Make him afraid."

My eyes cast around the salon, looking for somewhere to

lock him up. I squinted through the gray light. Beyond the glass slider, I scanned the cockpit. There was a fish locker out there, probably big enough to store those mega swordfish and tuna. But even if I got him to crawl into the locker at gunpoint, there wasn't any way to keep him in.

My gaze returned to Rurik. His expression was belligerent. What if I did shoot him? In the leg? Just to immobilize him. Could I be that accurate in these seas?

"Lexie, keep your eye on that compass. Don't go too far right or left, just keep us going real slow, but on course with that compass. Don't let the boat swing."

She put her hand on the wheel, but looked unsteady.

I searched for somewhere to brace my arm, to keep my hand steady, and aim. Maybe the nav station. Suddenly, another wave broke over the bridge.

The boat heaved to port. Rurik lunged at me. My hand flew upward. The gun went off and another bullet hit the ceiling above us. My fingers quivered on the metal. My whole right arm was shaking.

The boat reverberated with the gunshot. My ears felt numb. The world muted. But the gun was still in my hand. And I was upright.

Rurik had been thrown to the floor. He was on his ass, looking stunned at first. Then pissed off. He scrambled to get up.

I had to collect myself. Find my balance on the shifting floor. I had to stop him before he made another attack. He got to his feet and held on to the back of the sofa for support. I aimed at his leg, but he looked up at me. I saw his eyes, his human eyes fixed on me. My finger froze.

I heard a thud behind me. Lexie had jumped off the captain's chair. I felt her body weight pressed against my back. Her arm slipped around me. Her hand was over mine, crunching my finger into the trigger.

Another shot blasted. Clamped together, our hands stayed steady, guiding our aim. Rurik shouted and dropped to the floor, clutching his groin. Lexie pulled away, leaving the gun dangling in my hand.

"You fucking whore!" Rurik shouted. His eyes were on Lexie.

"Not anymore," she said quietly.

23

Crumpled in a fetal position on the floor, Rurik groaned. Lexie stood above him, bracing herself against the back of the captain's chair and staring at her hand, as if she couldn't believe what she had done.

With no one at the helm, the boat began to roll again.

My stomach pitched, and I clung to the edge of the nav station for support. Then I dumped the gun on the dash panel and grabbed the wheel. Dropping into the captain's chair, I forced myself to focus on the compass. I began punching toggle switches on the overhead navigation cluster, trying to turn on the GPS and the radar. None of the lights flicked on. This was why the radio hadn't worked earlier. Rurik must have turned on only half the circuit breakers on the main panel, which was somewhere below and beyond my reach.

Through the glass slider, I could still see the stern of the sportfishing boat. Hopefully, it was going to Newport. I decided to try to follow it to the harbor.

My pulse pounded in my ears, but I forced myself to be patient, waiting for what looked like a break in the swell. Slowly, I began turning the boat to port, through another ninety degrees. Two more waves hit us broadside. We dipped and swayed, but finally the boat completed its turn. Riding the swell instead of smashing into it, the boat stabilized.

"Get my cell phone out of his pocket," I told Lexie. But she just stood there, still staring at her hands, unable to move.

"You think he will die?" she asked softly.

The blood was oozing out of his wound now, a dark stain growing on the teak cabin floor. "He will, if we don't get him back to a hospital," I said.

"To hospital?" she said.

"Yeah. And fast. Please, find the phone. Maybe we can get the coast guard to help us."

Lexie looked at me a long while. Then she took a step toward Rurik, curled on the floor. She bent over him and rummaged through his pocket, as he said something in Russian. A curse of some kind. She backed up, afraid.

"Go ahead. He can't hurt you now. Just get my cell phone from him. Or his cell phone. Anything I can use to call police."

"Police?" she said.

"Call 911. They'll call the coast guard."

But Lexie didn't respond. She leaned toward Rurik, but he began writhing on the floor. She recoiled. "He can still get us," she said. "He is powerful man."

"He's got a bullet in him, for God's sake. Just get the phone."

But instead of leaning down to search him, she backed up

another foot, staring at the blood pooling beneath him. Finally she said, "Why? Why must we take him to hospital?"

"Because he's losing blood. He'll die otherwise."

She said nothing. The engines, working hard beneath us, coughed through a wave.

I was trying to keep my eye on the stern of the sportfishing boat, which was going faster than we were and disappearing in the distance. I advanced the throttle and the engines now roared. The boat sat up as our speed increased. With the bow raised, it became even more difficult to see ahead of us. I began scanning the dimming horizon, trying to look for a recognizable landmark to try to figure out my position, in case we lost the sportfishing boat.

Rurik had managed to get his cell phone out of his pocket and slid it along the floor, toward Lexie. His weak voice was barely audible above the engines. "Take it. Call."

"Lexie, get his cell phone!" I shouted.

She stood there, immobile.

"Oh, goddamn it." I left the wheel, slipped off the chair to try to reach for it myself. Lexie swooped in front of me and grabbed it.

She took the phone and turned. For a moment, she stood, arm raised, as if she were going to try to hurl it through the cracked window. Instead, she stuffed it in her skirt pocket, and stepped away from Rurik, so that she was out of reach.

"Lexie, we can't let him die!" I shouted above the engine.

She pivoted to face me. The boat was vibrating, and she gripped the edge of the nav station to steady herself. She had a crazy, scared look in her eyes.

"Hurry," Rurik moaned. I glanced down. His eyes fluttered shut. He was losing consciousness.

"Just call 911," I ordered.

She shook her head and stormed away from both of us, into the salon.

"Lexie, please!" I shouted again, but I had to turn back to the wheel. The sportfishing boat was nowhere in sight. I fought back panic and searched the terrain for anything familiar. After a couple of minutes I saw it. A flash of light to starboard. *Please God, let it be the Castle Hill Lighthouse and not someone's flare. Let it be the entrance to Newport Harbor.*

What little sun there was had dropped below the horizon. It would take maybe another half hour to get back, and it was getting hard to see. If I could just get to the harbor, there would be shore lights to guide me. I could maneuver my way into the dock. Get someone to help me tie up.

Lexie was behind me in the salon. I looked over my shoulder and saw her staring out the sliding glass door at the dinghy trailing behind the cockpit. Like she was contemplating an escape.

"It's going to be okay."

"I am never okay as long as he lives."

"You won't be free if he dies, either, believe me."

She must have been straining to hear above the engine vibration. "What?"

"You want to be charged with murder? The best thing you can do for yourself is make that 911 call. They'll enter it in your—our—defense. If you don't give a shit about him, do it for yourself. For me."

"Defense?"

"The police will be sympathetic, I think. But it all gets more complicated when someone dies."

She walked slowly back through the boat so that she was almost beside me. She gazed at Rurik a moment and started to bend down, as if to check his condition. But she pulled up again, afraid to get close.

"He is faking, maybe," she said. "He is sneaky man."

"He is dying man," I said.

She shuddered and turned away. There was no getting through to her.

The sky and sea were darkening into a solid sheet of charcoal, and it had started to rain. The visibility got even worse. I remembered something Matt had said once, about all the rocks just under the surface near Newport Cliffs. Without a depth sounder letting me know how much ocean we had below, I could easily go aground, or slash the hull. We wouldn't last long in these seas if we started to take on water.

"Lexie, forget making the call. Okay? I need you to go below for me instead. Can you find the main panel?"

"Panel?"

"It'll look like a bank of switches, with little red lights next to them. Turn all the switches to on. I need the depth sounder or we could go aground." I didn't tell her that it would also turn on the VHF radio, and I could make the call for help myself.

"Yes, I find the panel for you. Below." She sounded weird, exhausted, but miraculously compliant.

She disappeared down the companionway. Above the steady drone of engines, I still could hear the opening and shutting of drawers and cabinets below. At first I figured she was having trouble finding the panel, but it went on and on. Was she changing her outfit or what?

"Lexie?" I called.

There was no answer. But the lights on the control panel came to life. I felt an overwhelming sense of relief. I checked our depth, which was a good sixty-five feet, and flipped on the radar. In the meantime, I squinted, straining to see the flashing buoys that marked the channel in the waning twilight. If I could just make it to the harbor, we'd be okay. I glanced down at Rurik again. Could you tourniquet a groin? Should you?

I reached for the radio receiver to call for help. Just then I heard Lexie coming up the steps again.

"Put it down," she said.

I looked up.

She was standing in the companionway with a rifle in two hands. An AK-47. They must be stowed all over this freaking boat. "We go back to mooring. Not dock," she said.

"What? Why?"

She walked around Rurik to stand directly in front of me at the helm. She grabbed his handgun, the one I'd dropped on the panel, and leaned back to toss it down the companionway. It clattered against one of the steps. "We do not call police. Do not send to hospital." She gestured at Rurik. "We let him die." Her voice was cold, her eyes steely.

I took a moment to absorb this. The gun on her shoulder. The stark command. "We let him die, and we face more trouble," I argued.

"You face trouble. Not me."

"You pulled the trigger!"

"I think you make that up," Lexie said coolly. "And when police see gun, they say same thing."

She was talking about the fingerprints. Those were my fingerprints on the gun. Under hers. "You are going to lie to the cops and tell them you had nothing to do with it?"

Something flickered in her eyes. Guilt? Remorse? But then, as if by supreme will, her mouth tightened with resolution. "I will be gone by then." Her gaze traveled to my pants pocket. "Give me my money. Now."

Slowly, I pulled the envelope out of my pocket and tossed it to the floor. How far did she think she was going to get after I sent the cops after her?

She bent carefully to pick up the money, the rifle aimed at me the whole time. She looked like one of those child soldiers photographed at base camp of a third-world revolution. Her eyes had the same haunting look of misery and mission.

And suddenly, I understood that mission. Felt it like a slap of cold water from the sea. She was going to escape this horrible memory. And what if she wasn't planning on leaving me around to alert police?

Lexie stationed herself on the sofa opposite the helm and kept the AK-47 raised on her shoulder and aimed at me all the way back to the harbor.

I was praying for another wake, or rogue wave, but we were getting closer to the harbor entrance. Once we approached Fort Adams, the swell ceased. There were still a few whitecaps, but by contrast to the ocean, these protected waters seemed like a still pond. I eased off the throttles and the boat immediately sat down, the bow sinking back into the calm waters of the harbor. As the noise and vibration from the engines subsided, Lexie seemed to stand with more confidence. She began scanning the harbor, looking for something.

I wondered what her plan was. If she wanted to pick up a mooring, one of us would have to go out to the bow. This would give me plenty of opportunity to grab one of the other guns.

She walked a step closer to Rurik. The AK-47 must have given her confidence. This time she was brave enough to lean down close to him to see if he was still breathing.

"Lexie, I know you've got every right to hate him, but—"

"Shut up." She stood up, pivoting so that she could point the gun at me.

She had a heated, charged look on her face, as if she were operating only on fear and adrenaline. "This is your fault," she said. "You should have just given me my money at the market. We should have never come back here."

The money. Another thought rose frantically above the fray. Whitney had Lexie's money on her when she was found dead. She'd been planning to meet Lexie that night.

"Did you kill Whitney, too?" I asked softly.

"Whitney wants heroin. It kills her sometime anyway."

I took that to be a yes. "Why? Why would you kill your best friend?"

Her tone was cold, detached, as if she'd separated herself from the event. "She was not true friend. She wants only to tell everything to police. She does not understand what that means."

"What does it mean?"

"It means I will be sent back home to Russia." Here her voice cracked. "By police."

She meant immigration. "Don't you want to see your family again?" I asked. "Your father?"

"Fuck you," she said.

It occurred to me that maybe Rurik was telling the truth. Maybe her father had abused her worse than Rurik did.

"Why did you finally agree to meet with me, then? Why did you agree to bring me back to the boat?"

"I wanted my money," she said. Relenting, she added, "And because it had to stop. This thing to me. This thing to the young girls. I wanted you to get what you need to stop it." She glanced back at Rurik. "He deserves what he gets," she said, but now it sounded as if she were trying to convince herself.

We heard the sound of a motor. In the distance, about fifty feet away, we could see the running lights of a boat riding low in the water. It looked like it could be the launch.

I thought of the memory sticks still in my pocket. "We've got the evidence, Lexie. We can stop this from happening to other girls."

But she shook her head. "Evidence?" she said. "You are evidence that I shoot him."

"It was self-defense," I said.

But her mouth had tightened again. Her lip curled under. "Just keep your eye on the water," she said. The AK-47 was too heavy for her arm. She had to hoist it back up.

Then she stepped over Rurik to stand beside me, in front of the helm. She was scanning the control panel—searching for something.

I had a horrible thought. Was it possible that Lexie knew that the anchor was mechanized? That with one push of a button, the anchor would be lowered to the sea and neither one of us would have to go out to the bow to pick up the mooring. Once the anchor was set in a quiet part of the harbor, she might feel safe enough to shoot me. No one would hear the gunshot.

She pointed in the distance, to the shallow end of the harbor, where there were only a couple of ancient-looking sailboats bobbing on their moorings. "There. You take the boat there," she ordered.

I turned the boat. Out of the corner of my eye I saw the

launch, maybe twenty feet away. It looked as if it were on a path to cross right in front of us.

"Turn on the boat lights," Lexie said, pointing to the panel. "He does not see you."

A collision, I suddenly realized, was my best hope.

Pretending I was hunting for the running lights, I slid my hand up and over several switches and dials.

She put the barrel of the gun against my left rib. "Turn that way!" she pointed to starboard. "Now. Before you hit him!"

With my left hand, I nudged the throttle, increasing the speed slightly. Then in one motion, I elbowed the gun away from my rib and with the other arm, I swung the boat as hard to port as I could.

The boat careened. Glasses smashed against the floor as the stern swung. I had to hang on to the wheel with both hands so as not to lose my balance. Lexie stumbled backwards and tripped over Rurik, landing facedown on top of him. The AK-47 dropped from her arm and slid close enough to me that I could bend down and reach it.

Lexie began cursing, but Rurik made no sound. No movement. No indication of pain.

Panting, I picked up the gun. It was surprisingly hard to maneuver at this angle. With the gun in my right arm, I staggered back to the helm. With my other hand, I turned the wheel in the opposite direction and brought the throttle back, until we were steady again.

Lexie pulled herself off Rurik and tried to get to her feet.

"You stay right there, on the floor," I said, aiming the AK-47 at her. She looked up, blinking. Could I shoot her? My whole body was shaking. But I wasn't going to give her any more chances, either.

Up on one knee, Lexie halted. She looked down at herself. Her upper torso was covered with Rurik's blood.

For a moment she was horrified. Then, the hardness in her eyes dissolved. Her narrow shoulders collapsed. She turned back at Rurik and threw herself over his inert body. Then she began to sob, her small body heaving. A child again.

24

I could see the flashing lights of at least four police cruisers in the parking lot next to the dock, along with the ambulance and a fire truck. A throng of curious tourists watched as I clumsily maneuvered the boat into the slip usually occupied by one of the commercial party boats.

I scanned the crowd of faces now on the dock, searching for Matt. After I'd SOS'd on VHF radio, I'd called, leaving a message on his machine. Then I'd called Newport police and told them to call him, too. I hoped to hell he was on his way.

Still, seeing all those cop cars made me realize what was about to happen. With or without a warrant, there would be a search for evidence.

I'd left Lexie sobbing. At first, I was afraid this might be some sort of trick to get me to lower my guard. But the sobbing didn't stop. It had turned into a curdling pain, a bellow from somewhere deep inside her small, young body.

I threw a line to some teenaged boy on the dock who looked like he might work for the launch. Then, I ran below to the helm to cut the engine. Standing at the wheel again, I glanced at Lexie. She was quieter now, collapsed over Rurik, with a glassy, unseeing look in her eye as she murmured to him in Russian.

Maybe I should have been angry with her. But the Russian words, usually so harsh-sounding, were soft and pleading. Out of fear, she had shot him, and out of fear, she was begging him to survive.

Two uniformed cops were heading down the dock. I dug into my pocket and grabbed the plastic bag. Maybe these memory sticks were blank or contained files that were duplicated on a laptop somewhere. But if Rurik had any computer savvy at all, the only evidence of the teenage webcam ring might exist here in my palm.

I suddenly thought of what Bennett had said: *You should freelance that webcam story to your old paper, or to* The New York Times, *or something. Really piss the* Chronicle *off.* My fingers tightened around the plastic bag.

This was my jackpot, all right. The documentation that would convince a reluctant editor.

Lexie finally lifted herself off of Rurik. She looked at me strangely and I realized I was holding the plastic bag like a chalice. "Where did you find them?"

"Stowed in the sofa, with the guns," I said.

Piss the Chronicle *off.*

It was so damn tempting. But if I wrote that story, Matt would have to recuse himself from the case. Even if I just handed these memory sticks over to police now, I'd have to testify where I found them, and there would be a conflict for Matt. He'd have to let some other prosecutor lead what could be a career-making trial.

The two uniformed cops were now standing right outside on the dock, figuring out the best way to board.

I thought of what would happen to Lexie in all of this. A minor, without a guardian. An illegal immigrant to boot. She'd end up in some DCYF facility, or be sent back to her father in Russia.

With the back of her hand, she was trying to rub off a streak of Rurik's blood on her cheek where she'd touched her face. She stopped when she caught me studying her. "What?"

If I didn't do something, she'd be worse off than if I'd never found her.

"Take these," I said, handing her the memory sticks. "Hide these on you. Tell the cops you need to talk to Matt Cavanaugh. You have information, but you want to give it to him only."

She looked at me blankly.

"The files on this . . . this will prove that you were a victim in the operation."

Exhausted, confused, Lexie did not seem able to understand what I was telling her.

"This is like having money."

She shifted her gaze from me to the memory sticks and back, still confused.

"Like a bribe."

This she got. Nodding slowly, she stuffed the memory sticks under her T-shirt into her bra.

I'd brought the boat in bow first, with my port side parallel to the dock. The cops were looking over the rail, amidships, trying to peer in, assess the situation.

"In here. We need an EMT in here." I waved them toward the sliding glass door.

To Lexie, I said, "You tell Matt you know a lot about Pauley Sponik and about those men who came to the motel. You know where they kept the files. You have proof. If you agree to be a witness against Pauley, Matt can help you. Maybe get you some help, a social worker, and a place to live."

Lexie's eyes met mine. I'd gotten through.

The cops had walked across the deck to the cockpit and were just outside the door. They had guns in their hands.

"You don't need to tell them everything." I gestured to the sofa in the salon, where I'd stowed the AK-47. "We don't need to go into that."

"I would not have shot you," she said.

There was no way of knowing what she would have done. But I pretended to believe her. "You were just really scared."

I had held it together for so long. Had maintained my composure through the initial questioning, when EMTs wanted to know just how long ago Rurik had been shot, and whether I knew of any family members or next of kin. I'd held it together while I told cops that Rurik had planned to kill me and dump my body at sea.

Adrenaline had carried me through most of it. But now, upstairs at the Newport police station, sitting in the interview room with two detectives, I wanted to collapse. My throat hurt from having to yell above the engines, and my muscles felt bruised by every pitch and yaw of the last three hours.

Even though we were on dry land, my inner ear thought we were still on the ocean. Halfway into my explanation of how I'd met Lexie and why we'd gone to Pauley Sponik's boat, the interview room began to ride a major swell. A wave lifted me off my chair and dropped me again.

"Are you all right?" Detective Santos asked. She was a forty-year-old woman with an ample figure, who'd told me that she'd just gotten back from maternity leave. Her eyes, weary and circled, were keenly focused on mine.

I wasn't all right. I'd been held at gunpoint. I'd fought fear and the sea. When I closed my eyes, I kept seeing the stain of blood on Rurik's pants, and the dark red puddle growing beneath him. "I'm okay," I said.

"You sure?" I didn't know whether Detective Santos had just pulled weekend call duty, or whether the cops had called her in especially because I was Matt's girlfriend. Maybe they'd heard I was a reporter and I was getting the benefit of their media manners, because her tone had been gentle from the start.

Now, for the second time, she assured me that I was not under arrest, not in custody, and not a suspect. But this also meant they didn't have to read me my Miranda rights or offer me a lawyer.

Detective Santos gazed at me with what looked like professional compassion—sympathy she used for just these occasions—and prodded. "In your own words, just tell me what led up to the shooting?"

In my own words? I wondered vaguely. *Who else's words would I use?*

But for some reason, she was working extra hard to be nice, so I told her again that I had been trying to get Lexie out of a bad situation. That Rurik had discovered us aboard the boat and held us at gunpoint as he headed the boat out of the harbor to open sea. I explained how the wake of the sportfishing boat knocked Rurik off balance, how we all scrambled for the gun, and how Lexie had kicked it to me.

"So you shot him?"

I chose my words carefully. "I pointed the gun at him. But I couldn't do it. Lexie was scared of Rurik. She put her fingers over mine and together, we pulled the trigger."

"Together?"

"My finger was underneath," I said.

"But you couldn't do it before that?" she said.

"Right."

"Pretty good aim." This came from Detective Sergeant Gormley, who had arrived late, wearing shorts and a Hawaiian shirt, as if he'd just come from an outdoor barbecue. He was in his midfifties, and despite the outfit, appeared to be in charge. But he'd been standing against the closed door this whole time, and he hadn't said much until now.

I felt myself stiffen. Was he challenging my story?

But apparently, it was a compliment. "I'm not saying anyone deserves to die," he said, "but . . . if this guy you shot—"

"Rurik," Santos offered. She was reading from her notes.

"If this Rurik worked for Pauley Sponik, he wasn't about to cure cancer. It's not like it's a big loss for mankind," Gormley said.

"He might still make it, right?" I said.

The two detectives did not respond. Finally, Santos shrugged, as if to offer a *maybe*. Then she said, "I'm guessing this guy Rurik wouldn't have thought about you twice if he'd dumped you in the sea."

Maybe I recoiled at this. She reverted to the compassion gaze and the soft tone. "Look, you might want to talk to someone—

someone professional—in the next couple of days. You are suffering from a trauma. You need someone to help you process it."

I nodded.

She looked at her notepad again and asked, "About what time was it when you shot him?"

I had no real idea. "It was still light, I think. Maybe six thirty or seven o'clock."

"And after that, you were able to turn the boat around and come back to the harbor?"

I had a vision of Lexie standing at the companionway, aiming the AK-47 at me. I must have shuddered.

"Were there other problems?" she asked.

"The weather was rough," I said. "And we had trouble finding the main panel to turn on all the circuit breakers. That's why I didn't call for help right away. We couldn't get the radio on."

She and Gormley exchanged a look. I must have answered one of their outstanding questions.

"You were driving the boat. What was the girl doing during all of this?" Gormley asked.

"She found the circuit breaker panel, downstairs," I said.

They were listening with a keen interest in what I'd tell them about Lexie.

"She needs some kind of legal protection. She's an illegal, but Rurik kidnapped her. From Russia. Forced her into child pornography, here."

"Don't worry about that right now. Try to focus on the trip back. How long did it take you?" Santos asked.

"An hour, maybe, an hour and a half." I told her about trying to follow in the sportfishing boat that disappeared.

She wrote notes, and when I was done, stopped to reread them. Then she seemed to want to go back to the beginning.

"Can you tell me what route you and Lexie took to get to the boat?" she asked. What route I took to the boat? How could that matter?

"We walked back down Thames Street to the . . ." I was about to say the Oldport launch, but stopped, midsentence. I remembered something Matt had said about interrogation tactics. They ask you small, stupid, detail questions, to see if Lexie and I provided the same answer. I might not be under investigation, but they might be trying to trip Lexie up.

"And?"

Another thought occurred to me. "Do you know if Matt Cavanaugh ever got to the boat?"

"Assistant AG Cavanaugh will supervise the search. I'm not sure when." Gormley's use of the formal title halted me in my tracks. He was pretending he didn't know that I lived with Matt.

"Do you expect him at the station?" I asked.

Gormley answered. "He's just finishing up with the girl, right now. If he needs to talk to you, he'll do that at a later date."

The stiffer tone conveyed the intended message: Everyone would go to great lengths not to create an appearance of conflict that could compromise the investigation.

I must have shifted my gaze too quickly, because another wave hit the interrogation room and the world slipped just slightly off balance. I held the edge of the table. "I feel like I'm going to throw up," I said.

"You want us to get you something?" Detective Santos asked. "Water? A paper bag?"

I did not dare shake my head or the room would spin again. And I didn't want to hang around and trip up my own story. It was becoming clear to me that the less information that came from me, the better. If I was not a material witness, the cops would have to rely on Lexie's testimony. And Matt could be the one to prosecute the case against Pauley Sponik.

I stood up slowly. "I really don't feel well. And since I'm not under arrest, and not a suspect, and not in custody, as you say, I think I'm just going to go home."

Santos looked alarmed. "We have several more questions we'd like you to answer."

"We've been through it twice. Anything else, ask Lexie. She knows a lot more than I do." In a deliberate tone I added, "And I know she wants to do everything she can to help."

The two detectives exchanged another look. They could have threatened to arrest me if I didn't stay. But then they'd have to get me a lawyer. A moment passed. Then Santos said, "We'll get a patrolman to drive you back to your car."

She walked me out the door. It was Gormley who reached for the phone.

No patrolman met me outside the police station.

Matt was at the wheel of his Audi, waiting for me.

I got into the passenger seat and immediately collapsed into his arms. He let me cry a good ten minutes, massaging my shoulders, then finally he dried my eyes with a Kleenex. "Are you going to be all right?"

"Yeah," I said.

"You're going to get yourself killed one of these times."

"Last time. I promise."

His eyes were skeptical, but he pulled me to him again and held me. Several minutes passed before his arm relaxed, and he let me go.

This wasn't the time to talk about our fight, or our reconciliation, but he promised he would come home later that night after he was done at the station. In the meantime, he'd called Walter, who was getting one of his cabbies to drop him off at the station, so he could drive me and my car back to Providence. Walter was going to stay with me until Matt got home.

"What's going to happen to Lexie?" I asked.

"I don't know. We'll either call DCYF to take custody, or . . . I can't really talk about it, but she'll be okay."

Behind us, the headlights of the cab appeared. The cabbie parked, and Walter got out of the passenger side and headed toward us. Matt started the engine of the Audi. "Where did you park your car?"

It seemed like so long ago when I drove into Newport to meet Lexie. "It's on one of the side streets between Spring Street and Thames."

He nodded.

"What did she tell you?" I asked.

Matt's eyes sought mine. "I can't talk about this case with you," he said. "And you can't talk to me about what happened today. That's going to be hard on both of us."

"I'm sorry. I didn't mean about the shooting. I meant . . . did she tell you about the memory sticks?" I asked. "And the guns?"

He started to say something, stopped. Finally, he said, "I can't talk about that, either. I can't talk about anything with you until I put that scumbag away."

He meant Pauley Sponik. I nodded.

But then, just as Walter reached for the door handle to get in back, Matt leaned across the console and whispered in my ear. "But thanks, Hallie. We're going to nail that asshole this time."

THE PROVIDENCE CHRONICLE

Newport Celebrity Arrested on Gun and Child Pornography Charges

BY JONATHAN FRIZELL

NEWPORT—Pauley Sponik, the Newport personal trainer once featured in *People* magazine, was arrested and charged with numerous gun trafficking and child pornography violations yesterday after one of his employees, an illegal Russian immigrant, was shot aboard Sponik's 52-foot yacht.

Police responded to a 911 call from two females who brought the boat back to the dock under emergency conditions late Saturday night. Detective Sgt. James Gormley did not immediately name the females, but said that one of them, a minor, confessed to shooting the Russian in self-defense.

Rurik Kosovske suffered a gunshot to the groin and was transported first to Newport Hospital, and later to Rhode Island Hospital, where he died early this morning. Police said Kosovske may have been trying to murder one of the women and dump her body at sea.

A search of the vessel by police revealed a cache of a dozen semiautomatic handguns, and five AK-47 machine guns, which had been reported stolen by a Cumberland gun collector early last month. Evidence of a local child pornography ring of teenage girls in webcam productions was discovered on three memory sticks that had been aboard the boat.

The female minor who confessed to the shooting had been forced into these webcam productions, police believe. She said she'd been involved with "other crimes," but police would not elaborate.

Police are conducting an in-depth investigation into allegations that young teens were recruited, and recruiting each other, for live webcam shows. These shows were allegedly sold nationally through a subscription service and performed before a "live audience" at the Surfside Motel, owned by a corporation in which Sponik had a financial interest.

Assistant Attorney General Matt Cavanaugh held a press conference yesterday to warn parents to monitor their children's participation in the popular local social networking site, RI Buzz, where he said, "Pedophiles are making contact with your children."

Arms trafficking, child pornography, *continued on page* **A-9.**

"What other crimes?" I asked, pushing the newspaper across the table, back to Matt. Had Lexie told them about Whitney? Or broken down and told them about holding me at gunpoint, after all?

"Not answering," he said, holding up a hand. But he took the paper and scanned the story, trying to figure out what I was talking about. It was two days later, and we were having coffee in the morning before he went to work.

His eyes landed on the pertinent part of the story. "You don't have to worry about her. She's a smart girl."

"But if she faces murder charges with some lame public defender to represent her . . . she'll wind up in jail or deported or—"

He was shaking his head.

"What?"

"She's going to be all right."

He folded the paper in half and stood up. His briefcase was on the dining room table. I followed him there from the kitchen.

He was searching for his car keys, in a hurry to get away from this conversation. I spotted the keys under one of the files on the table and got to them first. I dangled them in front of him. "*How* is she going to be all right?"

"Off the record?"

"I'm not even working as a reporter anymore," I reminded him.

"At the moment, maybe. But once we release your name, the *Chronicle* is going to be all over you to come back and write the story."

"Which will make it all the more satisfying when I refuse."

His eyes doubted mine.

"I mean it."

"Or the *News-Tribune,* or *The New York Times* . . ."

"Whatever story I have to tell, I'll tell it *after* you get Pauley's conviction."

He thought about that a minute. "Hallie, I'm hoping we can get them to plead so this never goes to trial. And we've got enough on them, it looks good. But if it does go to trial, I can't tell you how long that will take."

Did he think I'd never covered the courts? "I don't care how long it takes. I owe you this."

"You mean that?"

I tossed him the keys. He caught them. For a moment, we just looked at each other. Then he put his arms around me. I pressed into his chest, absorbing his relief and wondering why it had taken me so long to realize that this was more important than the twenty-four hours my name was under a headline on the day's front page.

Finally, we pulled apart and he picked up his briefcase. But before he got to the door, he turned again. "You know, I personally can't tell you what's going on, but I can't stop you from talking to her yourself."

I'd had Lexie's phone number on my cell phone, which I'd never gotten back from police after they'd searched the boat. "I lost her number."

"You're not very observant for a newspaper reporter," he said.

"Former newspaper reporter."

"Either way. Check the corkboard in the kitchen," he said. Then he ducked out the door.

The Harbor View condominiums, where Lexie was staying, were in Warwick, with a view of the marina where Matt's brother kept his boat.

The afternoon was clear and sunny, and we were able to sit outside on a small balcony that overlooked a kidney-shaped pool. Beyond the pool and Amtrak railroad tracks was the sprawl of the bay, alive with early summer boating. Several outboard motorboats buzzed between the docks at the marina. In the distance, you could see the bright-colored sail of a windsurfer struggling with a fluky wind.

Lexie looked even smaller than I remembered, but older, too, with a new sadness that clouded her eyes. But she must have been swimming in the condo pool—which was only marginally larger than a hot tub—because there was a wet bathing suit over the balcony rail. For the first time, there was color in her skin.

Finally, she turned her eyes to me. "I am sorry I had the gun on you. I was so scared. So crazy, I am so sorry."

"I know," I said, accepting her apology.

"And I am grateful that you didn't want to tell police about what I did. But I had to tell. Everything. Because—," she started, but interrupted herself, shifting tones. "I had to," she said again. "I did so much bad already. It was time for me to do the right thing."

I nodded.

"The social worker, she says this is the right thing for me," Lexie continued. "That I must tell the truth so that I can heal inside."

Below, two teenage girls, wearing lifejackets over their bathing suits, were boarding a catboat. Lexie watched as they wrestled with the rigging of the boat, fascinated in their efforts to raise the sail.

"And about Whitney?"

"I tell everything. That she calls me, and I give it to her, the heroin. I should not have given it to her. I said no at first, but she wanted it so badly. I did not know. I did not know that it would kill her. I left her in the bathroom, for maybe ten minutes, and when I came back, she was dead. I didn't know what to do. I ran away."

"Did Rurik know what you were giving her?"

"I don't know for sure, but he was not surprised when she was dead. He said it was good thing for both of us that she was gone. That she had big mouth. And was stupid girl. I hate him for that. That I think is when I started. When I want to make him pay."

The sail flapped like mad as the two girls struggled to get the sailboat steady, with the wind at their beam.

"What did the cops tell you?"

"Mr. Cavanaugh, he says they will protect me as witness. To give evidence," she said. "They rent this place for me, is nice, with view." She gestured to the bay. "And he was the one who sent to me the social worker this morning. She says maybe I can go to school here."

It was summer. Regular school was out of session. "Not the training school?" This was where the state Division of Children, Youth and Families put juvenile offenders.

"No. Mr. Cavanaugh says I can stay here. I will be eighteen in August. They say if I tell truth, maybe they help me get my green card and I can stay. Get job. There is some new law in Rhode Island that protects girls like me."

I'd have to get on Matt's laptop and see if I could still access the *Chronicle*'s database—see if my password still worked. I'd heard there was a new statute on human trafficking. "How old were you when Rurik took you away from your parents?"

"My father . . ." She looked away, unable to finish. "He was a terrible man. Rurik took me away when I was thirteen.

"We were in Moldavia first, and then we came to New Jersey, then Connecticut. We came here two and a half years ago."

"And when did the webcam shows start?"

"Last year. Rurik needs money, but he did not do anything to me, himself. And he tried to protect me, sometimes, from the other men. He . . . sometimes, he was good man."

It seemed important to her that I believe this about Rurik.

So I nodded, even though my opinion of him had not changed. "And Pauley Sponik? Did he . . . when did he get involved?"

"He meets Rurik two months ago, through man at the Buzz, and he wants to bring this to Newport. To his motel. And he has people who can take the credit cards on the Internet and make it big."

"And you told Matt all this?"

She nodded.

"But Pauley never went himself? To the shows?"

"No. He never touches the young girls. But he was asking Rurik all the time to get new ones. To make more money. Mr. Cavanaugh says he will punish Pauley and all the men who work for him. Who wanted to make it big business with the men who pay to watch from their homes."

She looked off across the harbor, following the girls on the sailboat. On a beam reach, the boat was disappearing around a small peninsula to our south.

"Is it lonely here?" I asked.

She nodded. "It has been lonely since Whitney died."

We shared a moment of silent mourning for Whitney. I wondered if Lexie could ever recover from that kind of guilt. Maybe it was nothing compared to recovering from all the other trauma in her young life.

Before I left, I promised that I'd come back to visit again. "Maybe we could go to a movie next time?" I said. Then, pointing to the now distant sailboat, "Or maybe I can take you out on Matt's brother's sailboat."

"Movie, yes," she said. And then I saw the first glimmer of a smile. "But never the ocean, again. Not for me."

25

I'd come home to two phone messages beeping on our answering machine. The first was from Dorothy, who must have put two and two together after Matt's press conference about the webcam ring. Her tone offered no apology, just a breezy hello and a request to call her back as soon as I got home.

I deleted it instantly.

The second message was harder to ignore. It was from Bennett, who said there was a rumor going round that Ian Clew was getting axed. "Call us," he said, without referencing recent events. "We miss you."

Although I knew enough about investigative reporting to know Bennett might say anything to get me to call him back, I still felt conflicted about not returning his call. On the one hand, I owed it to Matt to keep my mouth shut, on the other hand, Bennett had been my friend.

So I sought solace in the garden. At four o'clock in the afternoon, the high heat of the sun was dissipating, and the attack of the mosquitoes had not yet been launched. I'd stopped at the landscaper's on my way back from Lexie's condo in Warwick and picked up three new hosta plants with variegated leaves. Come fall, they would shoot tall, spindly purple flowers up against the back fence.

It was a shady spot, under one of the massive red oaks, and the soil was cool and comforting. I decided that there was just no point in calling Bennett when I'd have to stonewall all his questions. Maybe what I should do was wait until I knew he had left the newsroom for the day, and leave him a message that for personal reasons I could not comment on recent news events.

I was working at this speech, midway into digging the first of three foot-long trenches, when I heard a car pull into the driveway. I didn't pay much attention. Now that I was home all the time, I'd learned that our neighbors on the second floor got home amazingly early from work.

What kind of job could you get, I wondered, that would let you start the day early and come home before the mosquitoes came out?

It wasn't the neighbors, after all, but Walter. He'd been dropping by between fares since the Newport fiasco and had learned that he could find me in the backyard this time of day. From the driveway, he walked along the side of the house to the backyard, nearly tripping over the garden hose on his way to the fence. He had a package of bulbs for me and the day's newspaper in his hand.

I thanked him for the bulbs, which were pink cyclamen and would bloom in the shade come fall. But I waved away the newspaper. "I've already read it," I told him.

"*The Wall Street Journal?*"

I dropped the bulbs on the ground and peeled off my muddy gloves.

"You'll be happy to hear that the deal's off," he said, handing me the paper. It was already folded over to an inside page.

Media Conglomerate Cancels
Online Acquisition

The Ink and Mirror Media Group, the newspaper and cable television conglomerate, which had announced a strategy to expand its digital presence through acquisitions, yesterday backed away from a plan to buy regional social networking sites.

The Sacramento-based Ink and Mirror, which owns two dozen metropolitan newspapers and several smaller chains nationwide, earlier said it wanted to acquire up-and-coming sites as a means of quickly increasing page views and online advertising revenue.

Lowell Harcourt, chief executive officer of the company, did not give a reason for the sudden change in plans, but one of the target acquisitions, RI Buzz, a social marketing site in Rhode Island, is believed to be under investigation by the state attorney general's office there.

Sources close to the company have said that Buzz founder Jason Keriotis is also under investigation.

RI Asst. Attorney General Matthew Cavanaugh refused to confirm or deny these reports.

But at a press conference yesterday he warned parents to monitor children's Internet use in the wake of a recent arrest in connection with a child pornography scandal. He promised there would be more arrests shortly and said federal investigators were also looking into the case.

Harcourt refused to comment on the Rhode Island scandal.

"So maybe Ian really is going to get the ax," I said, mostly to myself.

Walter looked puzzled, so I explained to him about Bennett's phone message and the scuttlebutt that the publisher had been the one to put together the acquisition deal.

"Oh, that reminds me—" Walter dug into his pants pocket and pulled out a pile of business cards. He sorted through them and handed one to me. "Geralyn wants you to call her when you're ready. She's got two jobs to fill on her news staff and wants to talk to you about coming back to the *News-Tribune*."

Could I go back to work at the *News-Tribune*? Maybe. Geralyn would be a good editor and the hour commute to Boston would be offset by the fact there would be no conflict with Matt's career. Already, his boss had mentioned the possibility of his promotion and transfer back to Providence.

Walter was studying my face carefully. "I thought you'd be more excited about this."

"I am excited. This is great. . . ."

"But?"

How did he know there was an objection coming? I hadn't known myself, but there it was, a knot of resistance in my stomach. A tightness in my shoulder blades.

I wasn't sure if I had been too discouraged about the way the *Chronicle* had killed my story to ever go back to journalism, or if I was just temporarily burnt out. But suddenly, I knew I needed a break from this dark world I'd inhabited these last few years, the constant search to find the worst that people did to each other.

Maybe I could go back if I could be like other reporters, operating professionally instead of always jumping into the deep end of the pool. Maybe if I learned the limits that were supposed to go along with the job.

But I'd never been very good at limits. That was the problem.

I glanced down at the trench I'd dug along the fence, and the hosta plants lined up in their plastic containers waiting for a transplant. The only time I really felt at peace was when I was in this yard, digging up the earth and patting it back down again.

"I was thinking maybe I'd like to get a job where I got to work outdoors," I finally said.

"Like a landscaper?" Walter made a face. "What you going to do in the winter? Plow people's driveways?"

How many times had Walter told me that my newspaper job had become an addiction? How many lectures that I was too singularly focused on trying to make the front page? And now he was incredulous?

"It's not such a bad job," I said. "No one ever tries to kill a landscaper."

Walter considered this a moment; then he smiled wickedly. "Not yet."